Peace in an Age
of
Metal and Men

Anthony W. Eichenlaub

To: Isaac and Gabe,

who lead me in a new adventure every day

Chapter 1

There's a moment between the time something breaks and the time it goes bad. It's a moment of tension, like standing on the edge of a canyon when the other side is a gray wash of fog. It's like touching the sky. There are a lot of words for that time before things really go wrong.

I call it peace.

Four years had passed since I was sheriff of the town of Dead Oak. I'd given up on trying to set right every wrong in Texas, and the peace that followed formed something like happiness for me. Four years I walked the desert with the Hopi in the South Chihuahuan Desert. Life was dry and hot and tough, but we scraped our living out of that hard-packed land. The tech of the world, with its neural enhancements, human cybernetics, and genetic modifications, passed them right by. They didn't need it.

My left arm was Texas Army–issued black metal—a long, three-fingered clamp designed to crush heads and heft heavy weapons. Most others could get away from tech, but not me. It was too much a part of me.

My skidder's antigrav hummed smoothly fifty meters above the flatlands. Topaz flames that had once decorated the sides of the skidder were now faded, scraped away by dust and wind. The skidder wasn't in as good a shape as it was back when I bought it off impound, but neither was I. Skidders were flying motorcycles named for their propensity to fail at high speeds, leaving their rider skidding across the ground in a spectacular demise. This one was more and more a risk each day, which is why I was scouring the desert looking for an upgrade.

The horses thundered across the plain in some hurry to get from nowhere to nowhere. Their faint shapes were barely visible in the dust cloud. Reds and browns dominated the herd. One lone black ran in front of the rest. The black turned hard and the whole team followed.

I turned too.

Twisting the accelerator, I braced myself for a burst of speed. It didn't come. I twisted again.

Nothing.

The horses galloped, headed straight for a canyon. Perfect. I'd corner them and catch the black, lead it back to the village. Maybe the rest would even follow.

I twisted again. Kicked at the rockets with the heel of my boot.

With a crack of thunder, the skidder burst forward. My cowboy hat flew off my head. Metal fingers gripped tight while every other part of me flailed helplessly in the wind. Muscles strained against the pressure.

Hooves thundered. Dust choked my lungs. The horses below me split from the group, peeling off left or right. The fastest headed straight for the canyon. Slowing and dropping, I fell in behind them.

A lasso hung from my hip. Carefully, keeping my metal left hand clamped hard to the handlebars, I loosened the lasso and readied it. It looped easily onto a hook on my skidder and I gave myself a bit of slack.

With another crack of blue flame, my skidder burst forward. I cursed, dropping the lasso as my body flew from the seat. Again, my metal hand held tight where my muscles failed. The rope dropped loose, loop dragging useless across the ground.

More horses broke from the team. Half of them were gone. Then more. As I pulled myself back up to position, only the black remained in front of me. The rocky soil blurred by, only a couple meters below my boots. I gritted my teeth and hunkered down. The black was almost close enough to touch.

The original plan was to herd them into the canyon, trap them in a dead end, but as the canyon grew closer the black veered right. The idea of jumping off the skidder and mounting the horse crossed my mind, but since I wasn't stupid or suicidal I put the idea on a back burner. The lasso was my best bet.

The lasso still dragged across the ground.

It caught on a rock the size of a longhorn. Slack snapped out of it in a second. The skidder twisted hard and stopped. I didn't.

I hit dirt and skidded hard along a flat stretch of ground, catching cactus and scrub grass to slow down. At that speed, it would have been nothing to bash a head open or snap a neck. Nothing ever seemed to go so easy for me. Rocky earth scraped through my duster, my shirt, and then the skin of my back.

Then there was pain. Hours seemed to pass. I'd failed. What was the point in moving? Defeat wasn't going anywhere. Me and failure were just fine there on the ground. Alone.

My hat flew through the air and landed on my chest.

"Howdy," someone said. A man.

The sun was too damn hot and my body hurt too damn much for me to remember that there was such a thing as polite. I didn't respond.

"Zane Edwards," the man said. He offered his hand, though it was hard to tell if it was intended as a lift-up or just a shake. I didn't take it.

"J.D.," I said, still prone. The sun was making a towering silhouette of him, so I lifted the hat from my chest and used it to shield my eyes. "You just passing through?"

Zane removed his black hat and held it to his chest. "No, sir. As a matter of fact, I was hoping to meet you out here." He was wearing a prim suit of black and gray with a tight shoestring necktie. His beard was closely cropped, a few days of shadow trimmed and styled with immaculate precision. The glint in his eye was part amusement and part tech.

"Don't see many city boys out these parts." I sat up, wincing. My whole back was rubbed raw and the hot wind set the whole thing afire.

He nodded. I wondered how he had found me. With little tech in my possession, there weren't a lot of good ways to track me. He might have learned my approximate location from my tribe, but that implies earning their trust. That's not something a city boy could easily earn. He might have tracked my skidder, but to my knowledge the device had been stripped of any location-sensitive equipment years ago. I might've asked how he found me, but asking implies not knowing, so I stayed silent.

I wrenched myself up off the ground. Zane stood a bit shorter than myself, and not much younger if the gray in his beard were any measure. He had the kind of smile that made a person think there was an inside joke that nobody else was getting. His eyes twinkled with amusement as they tracked up and down my disheveled form. For an instant, I felt conscious of my dust-covered coat and ruined clothes, but really it still wasn't far off from the best I could show him. Judging by the draft on my backside, he might be seeing more than he bargained for.

After a minute, I offered my hand and he shook it. It was a firm grip, but not overly so.

"You been looking long?" I said.

"No, sir." Zane smiled and nodded to my skidder, which still hovered a couple meters up. "Didn't have any trouble spotting you once I knew how to look."

I grunted and started limping over to the skidder. Zane followed.

"My employer has need of someone with your talents, Mr. Crow."

"There it is, then."

"Yes, sir. There it is." Zane straightened his tie. "There are few out here who can help us, and Chester Goodwin himself gave us your name."

"Goodwin? That son of a bitch?" I had met the man once, but didn't think I had made much of a good impression. Or, rather, the impression had been fist-shaped and not likely to win any employment opportunities.

"He didn't have so many good words for you either." Zane looked like he was picking his words carefully. "But he seemed to think you were the kind of man who could be persuaded to help."

"You don't know how stubborn I am."

"You don't know how persuasive I can be." That smile again. Damn if he wasn't a good-looking fella.

My skidder hung crooked in the air like a boat taking on water. The rope was pulled taut by the continued pressure from the antigrav, but the rockets were powered off completely. The sad wreck of a skidder just limped there, seeming to bemoan the fact that it may never be fast again. Straining against the stiffness in my back, I reached up and cut power. The whole thing dropped like a granite balloon.

Zane caught it.

He gently lowered the machine to the red earth, hardly showing any effort.

I nodded my appreciation and put my hat back on. Zane was a modder, then. Tech was even more prevalent in the city, so it was no surprise that he'd be more machine than flesh. It was impressive that I couldn't see it. Except for a slight sheen on his skin, there wasn't any indication of it.

"I rely on technology," Zane said.

"Sure."

"Most people do. That's why I'm here."

I nodded. "I'll leave them to it."

"Not you, though. You can see what's really there."

My rope was still looped around a rock, so I untied it and started coiling it up. Zane watched in silence. Once the rope was ready, I hooked it to my belt and climbed aboard the skidder. Antigrav hummed as it powered back up and soon I was nearly a meter up.

"People need your help, J.D." Zane walked a short distance and a vehicle appeared in front of him, seemingly from nowhere. It was a beauty of a ride, hot-rod red with a fender that flared up in the front. Its open top revealed plush leather seats and chrome trim. "Innocent people. They're being used. Maybe killed. We need a man who can handle a gun and doesn't have modded sight or hearing."

"Plenty of people like that." As soon as I said it, I doubted if it was true. Modified eyes and ears were very common. Most folks who had taken up a career that involved weapons already had some mods. If not, they'd get them fast or they'd be dead. Competition among armed groups is a fierce motivator for improvement.

I urged my ride forward at full speed. The rocky Texas landscape rolled behind me.

Slowly.

Without functioning rockets, the skidder couldn't do more than five or ten kilometers an hour. It was going to be a long ride back to the tribe. I'd planned for a long trip, but the hope had been to return with horses, not a broken ride and a bruised ass. Still, it was better than walking. I laced my fingers behind my head, leaned back, and kicked my feet up to rest on the handlebars.

"You know you can't outrun me." Pulling up beside me, Zane flashed his crooked smile in my direction.

"My world's a lot smaller these days," I said. "When someone in the tribe needs a ditch cleared, I clear it. When they need a longhorn tracked, I track it. I do plenty good for my people."

"I'm sure you do."

"The rest of the world's on its own. Your world and me are square. Maybe it goes to the crapper. Maybe it pulls through. My business is to make sure my own people survive. We do that by not messing with your people. That's just how it needs to be."

The time passed in silence for a while. Kilometers rolled by.

Finally, Zane spoke. "I understand."

That made me blink. Did he really understand? Could he possibly know what it was like to struggle for twenty years, trying to bring justice to a land that just wasn't going to have it? Could he understand what it meant to see suffering and be powerless to stop it? He couldn't. It must have been a new ploy to convince me to do whatever it is he wanted.

Zane tossed something my way and I caught it. It was a metal circle, like a coin. One side had a thin, shiny tendril snaking out of it.

"If you change your mind," Zane said, "just stick that in your ear."

"Not likely I'll do that."

"No, it's not."

Zane pulled forward and fell in line in front of my skidder. He climbed out onto the trunk in the back and looped a towline around the front of my bike. Without saying another word, he returned to his vehicle and slowly accelerated.

"Tucker Hale," I shouted over the rush of wind.

"Pardon?"

"Tucker Hale. You're looking for a man who ain't modded and can handle a gun. Look for a guy named Tucker Hale. He's an old army buddy. He'll take your money. Might not thank you for it."

Zane smiled and tipped his hat. "Much appreciated, Mr. Crow."

Chapter 2

The little town called Overpass was a cluster of several dozen stone buildings. These limestone houses were rammed up into the shadow of the great structure that had once been a crumbled section of road and bridge. The ruins of the overpass cast sharp shadows over the little town that bore its name. In the center of town, tall grass surrounded the Kiva, a mostly underground rectangular structure used for ceremonies and meetings. The vegetation around this little pit of a town was dry and angry; bones of trees clawed at the sky, as if trying to slow it down. Smaller shrubs still grasped at green in a painful attempt to stay alive in this last refuge against the punishing sun. East of town, small fields held the community's agriculture, which consisted mainly of millet, potatoes, and piñon. This was not so much a safe place as a secluded corner in a vast, untamed wild.

Zane had dropped me a few kilometers from town. He'd laughed at the idea that I didn't want to be seen with him, but he respected my need for privacy.

By the time I drifted back into town, night had fallen and the waxing moon had risen with an army of stars at its back. Cool night air tickled the raw skin on my back, the flesh already tightening in places where it was damaged. The nanomachines in my bloodstream were doing their best to fix the damage, but the nannies did nothing to help the pain. The night was quiet and had an empty feel, like there was nobody from one horizon to the next.

But I wasn't alone.

"Hey," said a voice not far off. "What're you doing here?"

Squinting at the dark, I was able to make out the woman's shape as her eyes flashed with lavender light. I powered down my skidder and hopped off. The machine would do just as fine here as anywhere. Nobody would take it, and if they did they sure weren't going very far very fast.

"Mina," I said, recognizing her voice. "You walking rounds?"

"Just started." Mina Honanie came closer and I could see her in the moonlight. Dark hair fell in piles on her shoulders, unkempt and wild as the woman's soul. Deeply tanned skin showed the creases of smiles at the corners of her eyes. Mina always had laughter in her eyes, but when she thought you weren't looking there was sadness too. To a man interested in women, she'd be quite the catch, but that's not my deal. She was probably the closest thing I had to a friend. "Wanna join?" she asked.

We made our way to the edge of town, following a path that someone from our tribe walked every day and every night. The desert was a dangerous place. There were animals that'd rip you apart and people who were worse. We Hopi followed the old ways as best we could and kept things low-tech, but we weren't stupid. We were well armed and well prepared. Mina's rifle was slung across her shoulders with a loose strap.

"No horses?" Mina asked.

"Next time."

She nodded. "Never met a horse stubborner than you, J.D."

"You ever met a horse?"

"Once. When I was little." She smiled. "And there's Vincent."

"The donkey? That's not the same thing."

We worked our way up a steep slope, picking our way over the broken stone of an old wall. Moonlight cast sharp shadows under the clear sky. A million stars stretched across the night sky in a great, broad brushstroke.

"People still kept horses back when I was little," Mina said.

"Some still do."

"There wasn't a use for them back then. Not really. Still, my papa knew a woman who had a few. She said she loved them like her own kids. She said they were the sweetest things she'd ever known." Mina grinned. "One of them bit me."

"Maybe it thought you were an apple."

Mina barked a quick laugh and quickly tried to stifle it. Her face flushed and her laugh lines dug deep. I tried to scowl to quiet her down. It wouldn't do to draw attention ourselves while we were walking rounds. Soon her laugh was tugging at the corners of my own mouth. Next thing I knew, we were both howling with laughter. It felt good, like a huge weight coming off of my chest.

We moved on along the path, silent for a while. The air grew cooler, gently tickling me where my clothes were ripped.

The wind changed direction and brought a heavy musk, warm and thick.

Mina must have sensed my tension because she stopped.

Long moments stretched on. We were up on a rise, overlooking Overpass. From this angle, the town was nearly invisible. Scrub bushes and dead grass made for plenty of cover for critters up there. A layer of dirt and dust had covered and reclaimed the asphalt of the ancient highway. My ears strained against the constant whisper of the wind.

Nothing moved for several minutes. I motioned Mina to follow and saw that she'd already pulled out her rifle. Good. There wasn't likely going to be any trouble, but it was better to be ready for it.

Crouching low, I sniffed the air. The musk hung on the wind like a piss-soaked blanket, moving heavily in from the north. Slowly, I crept closer to one of the thicker patches of grass. Something had rested there; something big had trampled the area. Starting there, I crept in a circle, looking for more signs of disturbance. Some grasses were crushed. In another place, there was a branch chewed down to bare wood. I took it and stuck it in my duster pocket. The teeth marks might be interesting, but in the moonlight there was no way to properly look at it.

One fat, well-formed print sat perfectly formed in a section of soft soil several meters away from the trampled grass. It had four small pads and marks of long, wicked claws.

"Coyote," I said.

Mina moved up behind me and peered at the print.

"Big coyote. Probably more than one." I bit my lip. "They bedded down over there for a bit. At some point one of them pissed right here and another one stepped in it. That's how we got that print."

"It's not a wolf?"

I shook my head. "Not quite right for wolf. Size is right, but the claws are wrong. It's coyote, but probably bio-engineered. Maybe escaped or something."

"We walk this path all the time, though. We'd have noticed giant coyotes this close."

Coyotes coming this close meant there was something odd about them. A coyote was likely to see just about anything as food, but they were smart enough to fear humans. Maybe whoever was walking the path hadn't noticed them, but those coyotes had been there a while. The grasses might have concealed them, or maybe the creatures had moved away when they heard people coming. It was like a coyote to be cowardly.

"Folks ought to walk in twos for a while," I said. "Might be safer."

Mina nodded. "You think they'll come back?"

"All that noise we made might have scared them off. If they like it here, they'll come back."

"You can tell Broadfeather what you saw when you go see him tomorrow."

"Pardon?" I said.

"Elder Broadfeather said that you should speak with him when you get back. It's very important."

"Thanks for the message."

She slung her rifle back over her shoulder. Her expression got deadly serious. Mina put her hand on my shoulder and looked me straight in the eyes.

"J.D.," she said. "There's just one thing I'm gonna ask you about today and I want a straight answer."

"Sure."

"Can you please tell me the reason that your ass crack is showing out the back of your ripped-up pants?"

Chapter 3

My back creaked in protest at the mere thought of movement. Bruises lined my legs and arms, tying the muscles into rock-hard knots. My very bones ached, like maybe coyotes had chewed them on. It was luck that kept those bones from getting broken in my fall off the skidder, but I sure as hell didn't feel lucky.

One advantage of a metal arm is that it doesn't have the same vulnerabilities as the rest of my body. It could drop from the sky into an active volcano and not show so much as a scratch while the rest of me lit up like a bonfire. I had some tactile feeling in the hand, but it never hurt, no matter how hard it got hit.

That morning, the arm throbbed with dull pain. It had a low battery, which was not surprising, given that I hadn't charged it in a month. The low-battery warning presented as a dull, irritating ache in my elbow.

It was still dark. Why was I awake so early? Sure, pain made it hard to get a decent night's sleep, but why was I sitting up looking around at my dark room?

A gentle rap at the door gave me the answer. A visitor. How long had they been there? Who was it? My heart raced. Where was my gun?

The gentle tap came again, slightly more insistent.

Light. I needed light.

A sweep of my human arm knocked my glow cube from its position on the little table by my worn-down cot. I swore out loud.

There was another gentle tap at the door. In my experience, death didn't knock. I forced myself to calm down. Deep breaths.

"Just a minute," I said, though it might have come out as a rhythmic cadence of grunts. I rolled off the cot and landed on my knees on the earthen floor. The cube had to be close. Crawling, I carefully swept the area for the device, finding it after only a few seconds.

My thumb found the indentation on the top of the device, and a blue glow filled the room. A red light indicated some kind of message, though I couldn't figure who it might be from. There wasn't time for it. I stood up and opened the thatch door. Only once it was open did I remember that I was wearing only an old pair of long underwear, one of the few remaining intact items of clothing in my possession.

Isi Broadfeather was the tribe's chief by the simple authority given a brilliant, charismatic man of advanced age. Like many folks of his years, he was not of a mind to sleep much more than a few hours a night. Maybe his body didn't require it, or perhaps he felt the looming end of his long life pressuring him to make the most of those final days. Even my sleep-addled brain should have figured it was him at the door.

"Morning," I said. "C'mon in."

Elder Broadfeather's eyes twinkled with amusement when he saw me. His gnarled wooden cane tapped the earthen floor as he waddled past me. There was only one chair in the place, and he settled comfortably into it and folded both hands on the end of his cane. The old man wore tanned leather and a modest assortment of feathers. His gray hair was pulled back and tied neatly away.

I sat on the cot across from him, and there we stayed for several minutes. My neck and arms benefited from a good stretch, and soon felt like they could move as reliably as a person could expect.

Broadfeather spoke first. "Good to see you walk back to town last night."

I nodded, wondering if he saw me come into town or if Mina had told him.

"Didn't want to come back on horse?"

"Not badly enough."

"Maybe they would rather be free."

"Wouldn't we all?"

Broadfeather smiled at that. He had always supported my attempt at taming the horses, but I couldn't help but feel like he'd been betting against my success. Yet, every time I came back he'd lay out a new ploy to try to catch them.

"It almost worked," I said. "Had them running right for the canyon, but the skidder failed and they got away. That black's a smart one, I think. She had an eye out for me."

"I once heard a story of a man who wanted horses, but all he had were apples. The man would walk out into the field with apples each day, leaving them for the wild horses that roamed the area. Soon the horses started visiting that location each day, and each day the man would get closer to them. One day he fed an apple directly to a beautiful mare."

"He made friends with it?"

"No, of course not. He tricked her and broke her until she would do his bidding."

"Seems a broken horse wouldn't be as good."

Broadfeather shook his head. "Nonsense. A horse must be broken to be ridden. That is how it's done. The horse is no good if it's too free. It won't obey orders or let its rider ride. If it can't be broken, then the horse is no good to its owner."

I grunted.

Long minutes passed in silence. The sky eased from the gray of predawn to a stunning mix of reds and yellows. There was movement outside and somewhere a rooster crowed. The tribe was waking up and my head was starting to clear. The ache of fatigue and injury faded into the background of a life lived hard.

"The tribe needs you, son," said Broadfeather quietly.

I raised an eyebrow.

"We do our best to follow the Hopi Way, from before the land was ruined." The twinkle was gone from his eyes, replaced by a grim expression. "It guides us in how we live and how we care for the earth. How the earth cares for us. Few of us remember anything. Stories of the Hopi have passed the generations by, and most of what we know is from the books. Word of mouth is much better, but there isn't much left."

"Agreed."

"No doubt, you know of the Navajo."

The Navajo and Hopi traditionally were rivals, but little of that rivalry had survived the ages. When America fell, the Navajo Nation asserted its own independence.

They rejected the technology that changed Texas and since they lived so close to the Yellowstone caldera, Texas left them alone. Even the desert-dwelling Texans considered land too close to the Yellowstone supervolcano to be uninhabitable. Not the Navajo. When the supervolcano brought America to its knees, the Navajo survived. Then they thrived. The Navajo Nation was notoriously independent, even hostile to outsiders. Their people were spread thin along the Rocky Mountains, loosely organized but very powerful due to a fierce loyalty. With all its technology and power, Texas had never been able to stretch its borders too far to the northwest. Not that there was much will to do so.

"We need you to be our ambassador," Broadfeather said.

I blinked.

"They will visit with a spiritual man in two days. They are bound by the word of this two-spirit and they would like us to send our spiritual leader."

My jaw opened like I had something to say, but nothing became readily apparent that needed saying. The Navajo never visited Texas. They stayed to themselves and expected Texans to do the same.

"You'll negotiate an alliance. We don't need trouble."

My head was starting to hurt again. A dull throbbing pounded on the backs of my eyeballs. Broadfeather's walking stick tapped out an even rhythm as he made his way out the door. The laughter had come back to his eyes. Was this a joke?

"Spiritual leader?" I asked dully as the old man stepped outside.

He turned around and winked at me before hobbling on his way. It took me nearly an hour before I stood up. I dressed in some old jeans and a button-down shirt. My duster was ruined. Huge sections had been worn clean through, and a tear ran down its length. Tossing it onto the chair, I grabbed my glow cube and tried my best to find room for it in the pocket of my jeans. Eventually, I gave up and tossed the thing on the table. It was still blinking red, but that could wait.

My Smith & Wesson Model 500 hung on the wall. Heavily modified, but without an ounce of tech, it had always been my go-to problem solver. It was a big gun—a revolver with significant heft and enough stopping power to give pause even to armored foes. I kept it well maintained, but it had been a while since I'd shot anything other than coyotes or the occasional armadillo. The services I provided my tribe were nonviolent and I liked to keep it that way.

The gun's heft felt good in my hand. Its balance, perfect. I'd been a lot of things with this gun at my side: a Texas Ranger, a lawman, a hunter. It seemed like the gun had been my partner my whole life. It had helped me be whatever the world needed me to be.

But a spiritual leader?

I hung the gun back up on the wall.

Chapter 4

The day passed in relative quiet. In the concrete shadow of the broken bridge, I spent my whole morning watching the spot on the hill where there had been coyote tracks. The spot remained empty, except for periodic patrols of tribespeople. They walked in pairs now, which they probably always should have done.

I turned the coyote's stick over in my hand, looking at it in the bright daylight. It was mesquite by the smell, but I couldn't recall any thickets of mesquite anywhere nearby. That meant the coyotes either traveled long distances with their stick or there was a grove somewhere close that I didn't know about. If my skidder had been functional, it wouldn't have been hard to scout around. I tossed the stick to the ground and went to look at that skidder. Maybe it would be an easy fix.

The skidder wasn't in good shape. It still floated when I powered it up, and I could get it to propel slowly if I leaned forward and nudged it just so. The boosters were worthless, though, and I had no clue how to fix them. They needed expert attention if the skidder was ever going to be anything more than a fancy wheelbarrow.

I wasn't sure I wanted it working again. The laid-back life suited me fine.

After the sun set, I was sitting a good ways from the small fire someone had set up for cooking. The hunters were back with rabbits and an armadillo. Most of the tribe gathered nearby, chatting up about the day's events.

"He hit the thing from fifty meters," said Edgar Buck. He lined up the day's kills next to him and started sharpening his knife. "Hell of a throw."

"Mmm," said Mina. She stripped apart wheat and filled a large stone bowl with the grain while the chaff went into a pile at her feet.

"Boy's turning into a fine hunter, just wish there was more out there to hit."

"You think we'll need to move?"

"No." Ed pulled the skin off of a rabbit. "Water's clean here. Long as the well doesn't go dry we can manage."

"Water's good, but we need food."

"Bah. We can trade for food. Grow it."

"Trade what?" Mina started grinding the wheat with a stone.

The conversation continued, but I stopped paying attention. It was the same conversation every day—comfortable in its consistency, but not very informative.

A wisp of dust lazily circled in the wind. It was a gentle breeze. A quiet breeze. Hardly a breeze at all. It was, in fact, not nearly strong enough to pick up that little bit of dust on its own. That dust must have had help. Something was there, stalking me from just beyond the light of the fire. The hunter was so absolutely silent that I could hardly hear it coming even after I knew it was there.

But I could smell it.

Sweat. Dirt. Piss. Only one creature had this particular combination of scents. Only one kind of monster fed off grown adults right in the middle of a settlement. I was being stalked by the most frightening creature around: a kid.

Maybe more than one.

A scrape. I dropped forward, evading a lunge. The kid stumbled and fell with a grunt. Another hit me from the side, stepping right on my metal arm and launching herself at my head. I caught a flash of blonde hair as she laughed and slammed a black sack over my head, then rolled away.

I roared in mock fury and crouched into a defensive stance.

The sack smelled of earth and rice. A footstep. I lunged.

Nothing there.

Someone yanked hard on a rope, cinching the sack tighter around my neck. I gagged and breathing got hard. I grabbed the rope, pulled so I could breathe again. At the same time, I shifted my weight and pulled away from the rope holder.

My shoulder slammed into something soft and solid. It was one of the bigger kids, then. That meant whoever was on the string wasn't their biggest muscle. I tucked and rolled forward, still blind.

Feet under me again, I yanked hard on the rope and shoulder-blocked in that direction. I made fleeting contact before that kid skittered away. The rope was loose. I started to pull the sack from my neck.

There wasn't any time to get it off. A quick footstep from my left warned me of incoming, and I dropped straight down. The kid's center of mass hit above me and I lifted and tossed. The satisfying thud put a smile on my face.

It didn't stick.

The rest of them hit me all at once. Two low and one high. My back hit the dirt hard. I was pinned.

Then, I laughed like I hadn't laughed in a long time. Laughter made my whole body hurt, but it felt so, so good. The kids mercifully pulled the sack from my head and let me sit up.

Marcus, the twelve-year-old I'd tossed, handed me my hat. He had a goofy grin on his face. "Didn't think you'd put up such a fight."

I nodded and brushed the dust off of my shirt. "Not a bad play, there," I said. "Distract me, then blind me."

"Yeah, but you heard it coming," said Gertie, the smallest of the group. She stood next to her brother, Dustin.

"I didn't hear it at all. Was that you that snuck up on me?"

"It was me," said Haley. "Mama made me some sneaking shoes." She had a big grin on her face and soft leather shoes on her feet. She was a few centimeters taller than Gertie, but not much younger than Marcus.

"Well, that's good news. We ought to get you out hunting."

"I've been practicing my shooting," Haley said.

"I killed a rabbit today," said Marcus.

"Boomerang?" I said.

"Yeah." Marcus grinned. "From a hundred meters, at least."

"Heard it was a hell of a throw," I said.

Marcus glowed at the compliment.

"Shooting's good," I said, turning back to Haley. "But it seems like you ought to learn to use a bow or a boomerang. Maybe a knife." I stood and tipped my hat to the other adults, who had been watching. They knew my arrangement with the kids. I taught survival skills. Then those skills got tested on me.

Her grin spread wider, and her eyes twinkled.

Marcus didn't look so amused. "With just a little tech we'd a been able to see you better in the dark. Made ourselves invisible and silent. Hell, a decent gun might have taken you out at a thousand meters."

"Eyes adjust to moonlight if you don't look at the fire. Doesn't matter if you've got a sack on your head." My expression turned dead serious. "And there's only one good way to defend against a bullet from a thousand meters."

"What's that?"

I walked over to the fire, grabbed a bowl of stew, and started back for my home. The mood of the evening had darkened for me, soured by memories of war and fights that I'd fought and lost. The world was full of fights I'd never win and enemies I'd never defeat. There was injustice everywhere and I'd done what I could, but that wasn't much and I knew it.

"What is it, J.D.?" Marcus asked. "How do we defend against a sniper's bullet?"

I looked him right in the eyes. "Don't make enemies."

Chapter 5

Ben Brown's image appeared in flickering holographic imagery above my glow cube. Ben had grown since I'd last seen him. He wasn't much taller but he'd filled out with muscle. Working on the ranch would do that. Ben was a good man, still a boy at sixteen, really: strong and stubborn in a way that fit him perfectly to a hard life in the outlands of Texas.

When his parents died, he and his brother had taken responsibility for the ranch, including various power generators, livestock, and their siblings. It wasn't an easy choice for the boy. He'd been headed for more than one kind of trouble before life hit him. Now he was mired down in running the ranch. The modern ranch involved a wide range of technology and production; it wasn't uncommon to host both solar and wind generators along with longhorns or sheep. It was a tough life and not one that young Ben had envisioned for himself.

"J.D.," he said in the image. "You gotta help me. Stop by the ranch sometime today and I'll tell you. It's—It's about Francis." There was desperation in the boy's voice that I'd never heard before.

It was too late in the day to do anything about it. His words gnawed at me as I fell into a fitful sleep, dreaming of nothing at all and everything at once. My body still ached and it was keeping me from any kind of proper rest. My dreams wandered to war.

Dreams of war were few and far between for me, though, and they didn't stick. My dreams turned to Zane, the handsome man from the city. He looked at me with that amused expression. He smiled and showed his too-white teeth. His voice...

His voice was speaking to me. "J.D.," he said. "J.D., you gotta pick up the earpiece." Seemed an odd thing for a person to say, even in a dream.

"Just put the damn thing in your ear, J.D."

I blinked and shook the grogginess from my head. The voice wasn't in my dream. It came from my duster, which was still hung on my chair. My muscles protested, but I sat up and rifled through the pockets until I found the earpiece.

"J.D., are you hearing this?"

I nodded. The earpiece was loud enough that I could hear it just fine, even though it wasn't in my ear.

"J.D., come in. You sleeping or what?"

"Not anymore."

He seemed to hear me. "It's worse than I thought. Put the earpiece in and you'll see."

"What about Tucker?"

"I'll tell you about Hale when we meet up." His voice took on a sharp edge. He was getting upset.

"Alright."

There was a long pause. "Did you put it in?"

"What? No."

"I thought you were going to put it in."

"Never said that."

"Just put it in, Crow."

"I don't trust you and I can hear you just fine."

"There's more to that tech than talking." He sighed. "It lets you see and hear what I need you to see and hear. Plus, if you want it out you can always just grab and pull."

"That easy?"

"Well, it hurts and can cause minor brain damage if you yank it too hard."

"Oh, well, in that case I'm sold."

"Really?"

I bit my lip. This was clearly important to him, but I didn't know the guy. For all I knew, it was some kind of trick, though I couldn't imagine why he'd be trying to trick me. It was a simple matter of trust and I didn't have any for the city slicker, even if he was brave enough to come all the way out into the desert to talk to me.

Sometimes bravery means trusting folks who haven't earned it yet. Sometimes being smart means not trusting anyone ever.

A minute passed.

"You do it?" Zane asked.

"No."

Zane's voice came through tense. "You need to see something."

"Send it to my cube."

Zane muttered something that I couldn't quite hear. It didn't sound like pleasantries. Soon, my glow cube lit up and I tapped the top to project the incoming image. While it loaded, I stuck a cigarette in my mouth and lit it. Puffs of smoke drifted through the image, sharpening the picture but causing it to waver and distort.

A man was sharpening blades on a spinning grindstone. Behind him, shimmering translucently at the edge of view, was a long table and a hook hanging from an unseen ceiling. Next to the table was a stocky steel machine with a flared opening in the top. The man had a scruff of a beard and overalls unbuttoned to allow the straps to hang loosely at his sides. His hands were covered with black gloves, and white-hot sparks from the grindstone showered his chest and arms but didn't seem to affect him.

"What's this all about then?" I asked.

Zane was silent.

The man in the video continued his work. When he had finished one blade, he moved out of view for a moment and returned with another knife. When that was finished, he returned again with a third knife, this one barely longer than his thumb. Once he had ground all three knives, he used a whetstone to carefully work each blade until it was razor sharp. He tested each on a strip of leather, showing that each knife could slice through with little resistance. The ash lengthened on my cigarette as the man toiled.

"A man's sharpening knives, city boy." I tapped ashes onto the dirt floor next to my bed. "Implication is that he's planning a murder, right? Sounds like something the law ought to handle."

"I told you," Zane said, his voice shaking with uncertainty. Or was it fear? "We have a strong interest in not involving the sheriff. In fact, the less we can involve anyone, the better."

"The law handles stuff like this. Even out here."

"It's not that I don't have faith in their well-meaning," Zane said.

In the hologram the man set down all three knives and left the field of view. Long moments passed. Just as I was about to break the connection and go back to sleep, he returned. The man dragged something behind him, but the object wasn't visible in the hologram. It struggled. I leaned in close so I could see, and the smoke from my exhale briefly obscured the view.

I waved to clear the air, but managed to trigger the controls on the cube at the same time. The image disappeared, instead switching back to the main console. Cussing, I quickly gave the gesture to move back to the video, but the signal got misinterpreted and instead brought up some still images of the surrounding area.

Zane gasped, his voice clear through the earpiece.

"What is it?" I asked. "I lost the feed."

"It's..."

My gestures started working. Flipping madly through control screens, I managed to bring up the video, but it was stuck for a painfully long time. The image was distorted, but the image of the man was clear and behind him—

The picture cleared and resumed motion. The man had moved again and was much closer to the camera. He was testing a knife's sharpness on his arm. Then he moved and I winced because deep down I knew he'd have a man on that hook.

I was wrong.

It was a boy, not more than ten years of age. His legs were bound tightly with rope, and tears streamed from his eyes. The boy wore ragged clothes, like a he'd been dragged off the street. There was no sound, but I could almost hear the wails as the boy screamed and pleaded. The man didn't seem to hear anything. He smiled, pursing his lips like he was whistling the whole time.

He slit the boy's throat and slashed his wrists in three fluid motions.

It took the boy no more than a few seconds to die. A quick death is a mercy sometimes. It can be a kindness.

What I saw there sure as hell was no kindness. Rage boiled up in my belly. This needed justice. Someone needed to get in there and make that man face what he'd done. Someone needed to stop this from happening again.

The cigarette dropped from my lips.

"Call the sheriff," I said, my voice barely more than a whisper.

"We can't," Zane said.

"Why not?"

"Take the job, J.D." Zane's voice shook. "Take the job that Goodwin's offering. Make this right and earn some money at the same time."

"Where did this happen?"

"You won't bring Sheriff Chin into it?" Zane said.

Sheriff Trisha Chin was in charge of justice for a hundred-kilometer radius around Dead Oak. She had been my partner for a time before I stepped down. She cared as much about justice as I had, and so when she took over as sheriff people had been happy. They got someone who was both tougher and nicer than me. Prettier too.

"Something's gone wrong in the town of Swallow Hill," said Zane. "Something bad and you might be the only one who can fix it."

I didn't answer for a long time. Peace. I'd known peace. Could I really put that aside for this?

The image of the boy still flickered above my cube and in its light my guns seemed to dance on the wall. I'd seen boys like him before. Poor, hungry, tired. Abandoned. I'd neglected them before, too. Were they ever really better when I tried to help?

The moment was broken by the acrid smell of burning fabric. I quickly patted out the fire on my shirt where my dropped cigarette had landed. My jaw was set so hard that saying the words was difficult.

"I'm in."

Chapter 6

Bad things happened in the desert. Corporations made profits on the backs of men. Bandits killed for upgrades. Most who'd be called innocent weren't even close. A religion of pain grew like a cancer in the darkest corners of the wasteland. Injustice thrived everywhere from city to town.

None of that put to rest my outrage at what I'd seen. Something had to be done. That man, that horrible man who had murdered a kid, he had to be stopped. Killed.

What did I need? I grabbed my gun and clipped the holster on. Plain, simple justice. That's all this was going to take. The glow cube might be helpful. I stuffed it into an ammo pouch, which I hung from my belt. The ruined duster wouldn't do me any good in the desert, so it needed to stay behind. A man can't leave the house without his hat or a good knife. Knife, gun, hat. Yes, that's all I needed.

But I hesitated. The gun felt so heavy at my side. So awkward. How long had it been since I'd carried it on a regular basis? How long since I'd dispensed justice? How long since I'd killed someone? That wasn't me anymore. A good sheriff could do that. Not me.

I drew the gun and looked at it. My hand shook and no matter how hard I tried, it wouldn't stop. The butcher wasn't a bandit. He wasn't a gunslinger. He was just a man. He could be stopped without a bullet. This was a test. Years ago I'd sworn off guns. Killing never did me any good back then and it wouldn't now.

Would it?

Ben and Francis Brown could answer that. Were their lives better with their mama dead? Was that the justice they needed for her killing their pa? If I'd let it go from the start, they'd still be together. She'd have guilt eating at her, but guilty is a hell of a lot better than dead. The gun went back on its peg.

My skidder was still a ruined mess, and getting around the desert on foot was a slow suicide of heat stroke and dehydration. Nobody deserved that, not even me.

The aches in my body were easy enough to shake off, but the one in my metal arm still throbbed. It needed a half a day at a charging station, but since that wasn't an option I opted for the next best thing: ignoring the problem. It wasn't a great solution, but it was the best I had. The thing would last days on low battery. Experience had taught me that much. It took time for my eyes to adjust to the black of the moonless night. The scattered mess of the Milky Way stretched across the night sky.

My skidder's antigrav still worked, but propelling it would be a problem. I had no rockets handy, so my best idea involved pushing myself along with an old steel bar I'd picked up from a scrap pile. I got my bearings with the stars, pointed my skidder in the right direction, and pushed. It was just like poling a boat.

Movement was slow at first, so I pushed again. Then again. Soon I was moving at a reasonable clip and the kilometers vanished behind me. Cool, dry air tugged at my hat and chilled my bones. It would take an hour or two to reach Dead Oak, but it was better than walking.

The glow of that small town graced the horizon right around the same time that the eastern sky lightened with the impending morn. Dead Oak was a town of modernized hogans. They were lumps on the surface of the desert. Along the outskirts of town were some of the old structures: buildings constructed before the megastorms started scouring the land on a regular basis. Most of them were crumbled into ruin, but a few still stood, monuments to a time when Texas was a far friendlier place.

A few stabs with the steel bar adjusted my direction. On the near side of town, over a short rise, was the junkyard. That's where I needed to go. My skidder slid forward silently, taking a slightly sideways angle toward its destination. It slid effortlessly over the rise, cresting with a gentle leap off the top of a hill.

The junkyard was closer than I remembered. Too close. A couple hundred meters away, there loomed a junk pile outside of the metal wall, mangled into sculpture of expressive anger. It was a heap of hurt with jagged metal and slender spikes of glass sticking up everywhere.

I grabbed the steel bar in both hands, braced myself, and jammed it hard into the ground in front of the skidder. It hit a rock, jerked back, flew out of my hands sliding straight through my giant metal fist.

The force of the impact slowed me a little, but now the skidder was spinning. I gripped the handlebars.

Nearly a hundred meters away now, the junk pile gleamed in the first rays of morning. Steel and stone jutted from the heap like jagged teeth getting ready to chew a meaty breakfast. Fifty meters.

I yanked the bars right, trying to compensate for a hard counterclockwise spin. It wasn't enough. My head whipped around as I tried to track the incoming heap.

Twenty meters. I leaned hard. The skidder was sliding fast, but if I could get hold of some scrub on the ground maybe I could—

Ten meters. It wasn't working. I was going to hit and there wasn't anything—

I cranked the antigrav as hard as I could. My stomach dropped and the skidder launched straight up, catching the top spire of the heap as it passed. The skidder spun faster, up, up, over the wall and into the junkyard proper.

With a twist, I cut power. The skidder plunged down, hit the red dirt with an ear-splitting crash, and sent me flying into a dingy shack. My back hit the door, tumbling through with enough noise and violence to wake anybody a hundred meters around.

It didn't need to. The two women were sitting at a tiny table holding cards and smoking cigars. When I crashed through the door, neither one of them so much as flinched.

The older of the two women placed her cards down on the table, took a swig from a bottle of amber liquid, stubbed out her cigar, and smiled at me. "Evening, J.D.," she said.

The younger woman smiled. "It's morning, Auntie."

The older woman frowned at that. After a moment, she smiled. "Morning, J.D."

I stood up, realized I was still terribly dizzy, and fell flat on my ass.

Chapter 7

Josephine Jefferson had a laugh like a hyena—a hyena that had just spent a hard day drinking and a hard life smoking. She laughed so hard that tears welled up in her eyes and rolled down the smooth, dark skin of her cheeks. She clutched her belly as if to keep it from shaking right off. Jo was a big woman with the grimy fingernails of someone who worked and the nimble fingers of someone who knew how to operate tech. She wore overalls and her bare arms were covered with scars. When she laughed, her age showed in the tiny wrinkles at the corners of her eyes. She had lived in Dead Oak all the while that I was the sheriff, but I'd had little to do with her other than to have her work on the cruisers from time to time.

The young woman across from Jo was probably in her late teens and pretty as they get. She was just as dark as Jo, but where Jo's skin bore the lines of a life well fought, this girl had the smooth shine of tech-enhanced skin. Her hair was a long, dark mess of unkempt dreadlocks. She was nearly drowning in a pair of Jo's old overalls, and her feet were bare. She looked at me with wide eyes that glittered with tech and struggled to focus, as if a night of drinking whiskey had taken its toll.

The younger woman's eyes showed just as much laughter as Jo's, but she had significantly more tact. That's not to say she kept from laughing entirely. Rather, she covered her mouth politely and snickered like a pot of humor was nearly ready to boil over. The restraint was appreciated, but a man's pride can only take so much humiliation.

My head steadied itself so I stood up, tipped my hat, which was somehow still on, and said, "Howdy," to the young girl. "Name's J.D."

"I gathered."

The shack was little more than a machine shed with workbenches along three of the four thin, metal walls. The fourth wall sported a lofted bed and a hammock. Shelves covered every surface that might support a shelf and some that looked like they didn't. Elaborate overhead storage dominated the center of the room. To my left was a collection of brutal, heavy tools like saws, vices, and hammers. Moving clockwise, the tools got progressively higher-tech. Wrenches gave way to spanners, arc-circuits, and nano-gel. Directly to my right, an array of rockets was prominently displayed above a row of parts from old combustion engines that would do any museum proud. The whole place was filled with cigar smoke.

"Bit of a time crunch," I said.

Josephine gasped a noisy breath of air, then coughed up another peel of laughter.

The younger girl spoke. "Auntie was just telling me how much we needed a man around here."

"That so?" I said.

Josephine clutched the edge of the table and, with apparently great effort, kept her laugh down to a low chuckle.

"It's true," continued the girl. "Why, we were just having a nice, pleasant drink and a game of hold-em this evening." She peered at the door behind me. "Morning," she corrected. She indicated a nearly empty whiskey bottle, reached behind her to produce a second empty bottle, and then pointed across the room to where the remnants of a third bottle were shattered next to a garbage can. "Well, the topic of men did come up once or twice, though I must say it wasn't the main topic."

Josephine shook her head.

"Well, it was not five minutes ago we decided just exactly how much a representative of the male community was needed around here."

There was a long moment of silence.

"Not very much," said the girl.

The high, hyena laughter burst out of Josephine like TNT out of a coal mine. I endured it for what seemed like an age. It finally settled, and the two women looked at me expectantly.

"Ms. Jefferson," I said, "remember that skidder I stopped by with a while ago?"

"That death trap?" Josephine stood up and brushed past me on her way out the door. The girl and I followed. "Well, look at that. The rockets finally crapped out?"

"That they did."

"Antigrav?"

"Still not bad."

"Well, that's not a surprise. These puppies ought to last a good long while. It's the regulators and rockets that'll probably kill you."

I nodded like I had some idea what she was saying.

"'Suppose you need this fixed up?"

"Right quick too," I said. "Got some business to attend to."

Josephine clicked her tongue, circling my broken skidder. The sad-looking thing was upside-down and dented in at least five new places. The blue flames painted along the sides were worn down to metal so badly that the faded paint was hardly recognizable. The sharp chemical smell of solid fuel tickled my nose. The girl must have smelled it too, because she took a step back and stubbed out her cigar.

"Abi," Jo said to the younger woman, "why don't you head down and get my arms for me?"

Abi stared, wide-eyed, at the skidder. She didn't look like she was going to move at first, but then she dashed away behind the shack. Josephine continued to prod at the upended skidder.

"Yep," she said. "Leak's right here. Looks like you cracked it open on your landing." Her eyes twinkled with amusement. "Why you in such a hurry, J.D.?"

I turned and squinted at the sunrise. Why was I in such a hurry? Anger tasted like acid in the back of my throat. The boy's death had affected me. Zane must have known how I'd react. Even knowing that he was manipulating me didn't affect the feeling of urgency.

"There's a need," I said.

Jo must have read the anger in my face. "Thought you didn't do this kind of thing anymore, Sheriff."

I nodded.

"The new sheriff's not bad, you know. She does a fine job."

"True."

"So what is it that's happening that she can't take care of? You into something illegal?"

"I aim to stay on the right side of the law."

Abi returned, struggling to drag a backpack made of dull metal and scuffed plastic. She dumped the thing at Josephine's feet, panting from the effort. Josephine looked at it with one eyebrow raised. She tapped her foot.

"Well," said Josephine. "You going to put it on or what?"

"Me?" Abi's eyes got wide.

"Yes, you. You think I trust J.D. with any kind of tech? That boy breaks every damn thing he touches."

Abi squatted down and fit her arms into the straps of the backpack. The pack whirred, clicked, and fastened itself to her, effectively pinning her to the ground. A collar emerged from the top of the pack, clamping around her neck. Her eyes flashed an unnatural green, and a wisp of a smile crossed her face. She stood up, lifting the pack with ease.

A dozen slender, articulated arms supported the pack and nearly lifted the girl off the ground. Her toes barely scraped the dust. Larger arms emerged from the top of the pack, thick as a cigar and long enough to reach around the skidder twice. She slid a few steps forward. With three of her articulated arms, she grasped the skidder and gently righted it. She held it aloft with seemingly no effort.

Josephine peered at the skidder, prodding at damaged parts and fiddling with the controls. She frowned as she did so, her brow furrowing in concentration. She located the crack in a fuel cell, gently extracted the cylinder, and replaced it with one that appeared to be in much, much worse shape. The new one didn't stink, though, so appearances might not be everything.

After half an hour, she stood back and shook her head. "Rockets are busted. Regulator's two spits from shot. Fuel cells are all good now, but without rockets you're not going anywhere quick."

I swore and kicked at the dirt.

Abi set down the skidder. "Needs a paint job too," she said, and then flinched at my scowl. "It does."

"Talk to Trish," Josephine said. "She'll help. She still talks about you sometimes, you know. She respects you."

I shook my head. "There's no reason to involve her."

"She's sheriff. That's reason enough."

"No."

Josephine made a disgusted noise and went back into her shack. Abi followed.

I followed. "It's the corporations, Jo," I said. "Goodwin sent a man to talk to me. There's something bad happening out around a town called Swallow Hill." Zane had given me the location, but almost no other details.

Abi seemed to shrink back into herself.

Jo's expression got dark. "You stay away from Swallow Hill."

"People are dying."

She shook her head. "Just stay away." My expression must have been enough, because her shoulders sagged. "There's more about that place than you need to know."

"I expect there is."

We looked at each other for a long moment, neither of us backing down.

Abi had backed all the way against the wall and knocked a cascading series of saw blades off their hooks. She winced at each one that fell, but Jo didn't flinch.

"I'll bring the sheriff in when I know the story," I said. "Until then, I don't want her involved. She might cover something up."

Josephine locked eyes with me. "You don't trust her."

"I don't trust anyone."

She nodded. She bit a lip and peered at the sun, now sitting fat in the sky. "That's a good policy if you're headed to Swallow Hill. What about that man from Goodwin? Are you trusting him more than you trust Trish?"

I shook my head. "I trust what I see with my own eyes."

Josephine sighed. "Fine."

"Fine?"

"You remember back when you were sheriff and a big fella rolled into town and started hitting ladies and robbing stores?"

"Sure." She'd just described about a dozen instances from my time as sheriff.

"This was maybe ten years ago. Fella was tall, really big. Really ugly. Had a tattoo of a snake across his face."

This was starting to ring bells. The man wouldn't leave town and he wouldn't settle down. Every time I locked him up he'd promise to never cause trouble. One day I'd had enough.

"I shot the man," I said. "Right in the eye."

"That's right. He was mean, but he was slow on the draw."

"What's that have to do with this?"

"He was my husband."

She peered at me for a minute, her face all kinds of serious. I didn't give an inch. There was no doubt at the time that shooting that man was the right thing and there was no point in saying otherwise.

Was there? It seemed that maybe the conviction of my younger days was too strict. The man might have lived if things had been handled differently. He might have been turned around or even sent off to prison. Was a bullet the right answer for that man, or was a bullet just the simplest answer?

The grin crept back onto Jo's face. "Sheriff," she said, "you did me a favor back then, so I'm doing you a favor now. I'll let you ride my Bessie there and back." She whistled and somewhere in the junkyard the subsonic hum of power started up. "If you so much as scuff the fender, though..."

A crack like thunder rolled through the yard. A mass of metal and plastic floated over to where we stood, hovering with a rumbling roar that I could feel in my chest. The mass didn't even look like a vehicle, with jagged shreds of metal sticking out in all directions. Rockets flared in sequence, helping to stabilize what was presumably a mess of antigrav.

Josephine spoke in barely a whisper, but I could hear it clearly over the rumbling roar. "If you so much as scuff her, you'll be paying for it from your hide."

I believed her. "How do I drive it?"

She looked at me like I was stupid.

"I suppose you think you're coming with?"

Josephine's eyes widened for a flicker of a second, but she shook her head. "Abi will take you where you need to go."

"No."

"She'll be taking you where you need to go or you ain't going there."

"But—"

"But nothing. I've been teaching Abi everything I know and she's been learning it. She'll get you there. If you're not dead, she'll get you back." Josephine turned on her heel and disappeared into the shack.

Abi disengaged her articulated arms, rubbing her neck where it must have attached directly to her spine. She gave me a sheepish grin and gestured for me to step into the vehicle.

I took a closer look at it. The thing was actually mostly shaped like a car, but plates of armor jutted at odd angles from the sides and bottom. A dozen rockets flared in various places on the bottom and sides. Some even seemed to be pointed upward. The thing made little sense, but it was clear that there was room for several people right in the center of it all. One thing was not clear.

"How in the hell do I get up there?"

She whistled—long, slow, and low. Two slabs of armor slid to the side and a slip-thin ladder lowered itself to the ground. Abi, with a flourish, gestured again for me to step inside.

I climbed into the car, shuffling sideways on one of two utilitarian benches. It wasn't comfortable, but it sure as hell felt safe. Armored panels jutted up, nearly closing off above our heads. Abi climbed in, belching out a whiskey-scented cloud as she sat down. Panels slid closed and a series of screens flickered to life around us. Abi put a hand on the center console and with a jolt sent us spinning into the air. Within minutes, we were cruising in relative comfort over the baked desert.

"You always drive people around for Jo?" I asked.

Abi squinted at me. "You always a nosey gossip?" She hiccupped. Smiled sheepishly.

"Not certain I've ever been described as such."

She seemed to consider me for a while. "Aunt Jo keeps me safe." There was a bitter taste of resentment in her voice.

Abi reeked of whiskey. It wasn't that she was drunk so much. Her body clearly had enough tech in it to handle the alcohol; Nanomachines would process toxins without much trouble. Still, that alcohol had to go somewhere, and by the smell of it she was either belching it out in a gaseous form or sweating it out. There was a slick look to her skin. Truth was, she was hard to place in my head. She seemed like a kid to my old eyes, but really, she was a grown adult. Maybe it was her oversized overalls that made me think she was younger.

"I appreciate the ride," I said.

She looked like she had something else to say but chose not to say it. Instead, she silently ignored me and concentrated on the many screens around us. On them, the desert slid by. We weren't going fast, but that was all right with me. We didn't have a huge distance to go, in the relative-to-Texas sense. A couple dozen kilometers weren't much in the grand scheme of the Republic of Texas.

"You're buzzing," Abi said after a long stretch of silence.

"What now?"

She pointed at my pants. "Buzzing. In there."

I felt the ammo pouch and realized that she was right. My glow cube was humming pleasantly. When I brought it out, it stopped buzzing and flickered to life. A distorted hologram appeared above it, but I couldn't make out the image.

"Hello?" I said.

The answer was a distorted string of noise. Abi shook her head and grabbed the cube from me. She opened the center console, revealing a square hole.

"The shielding interferes with it, but it's all Quintech," she said. "It's all compatible. It's what they used to be known for, Auntie says." Before I could protest, she jammed the cube into the slot.

Francis William Brown appeared as a sharp, bright hologram above the center console. He stood there blinking at me for a long minute. His white hair had grown long and unkempt. It was hard to remember that the boy was only twelve. His set jaw and emotionless eyes made him look so much older. Francis was the kind of kid who always had a hard time with life but whom nobody ever felt sorry for. The boy wore the same thin white shirt he always wore and his eyes flickered with a purple light.

"Sheriff," he said by way of a greeting, "where are you?"

"I'm where I need to be, son," I said. "Where are you? Your brother's looking for you last I heard."

"It's just..." He licked his cracked lips. "I'd like you to see something."

There was a long silence. Seeing the boy always brought up painful memories, but it sounded like he was showing interest in something. That was a rarity for Francis and it would be terrible to fail to encourage that. "Sure," I said. "I'll stop by the ranch soon as I can."

His mouth opened as if to say something, but then he seemed to reconsider. A smile tweaked the corners of his mouth but didn't touch his eyes. His image flickered and disappeared.

Abi said, "What was that all about?" She popped the cube out of the console again and tossed it to me.

"Francis Brown," I said. "I killed the boy's mama a few years back, and now he has an odd view of our relationship."

"Is he dangerous?"

"Is anyone not?"

She nodded. The ride passed in silence. Abi, after a while, turned to me and said, "You really live out in the wild?"

"Something like."

"What's it like out there?"

"Hard." The image on the monitor slid by like it was nothing but a model landscape in an old museum. "Every day's a struggle. We scrape for food and water. We fend off predators, both human and otherwise. Worst is getting noticed. When you're the littlest guy around it pays to keep quiet."

"But you like it."

"It's better than the alternative."

Abi chewed on her lip. "Auntie Jo thinks you're crazy for living out there."

"Fair enough. I think she's crazy enough for living in that junkyard."

"She doesn't leave it. Hasn't since she took me in." Abi's eyes met mine and I could see a shadow of a painful past lingering there. "She's afraid someone's going to take it from her. She's afraid of men from the city coming to take everything. She won't let so much as a field mouse sneak into her junkyard."

"I got in."

"And you're lucky she likes you so much. I've seen how she deals with strangers."

There wasn't much to say about that. Josephine's paranoia might have been justified. Maybe someone *would* take the junkyard from her. Could be that they'd take it even if she stayed. The rule of law held a lot of folks in check, but not everyone followed the same rules. Jo's floating tank started to make a little more sense.

Abi maneuvered Bessie around to land on a dusty outcropping of rock. "We're here," she said.

The vehicle unfolded to let us out onto the rocky soil. Abi had landed us in the middle of the remains of an old building. Wooden parts had long since decayed to nothing, but meter-tall stone walls still stood partially buried in fine dust. Clusters of cacti stretched tall from the surrounding landscape, providing a relatively secluded feeling. Not far from the building, the remains of an old road still clung to the idea of existing. The asphalt had long since crumbled, but the soil beneath was packed hard enough that nothing of any significance grew there.

"There's a zone just over there that's giving weird signals." She pointed down the road, where a crooked WRONG WAY sign stuck out of the dry earth. The paint on the sign was still legible, despite having been worn down by years and bullets. "That's where your friend was telling you to go."

"We can't fly any closer?"

"No, sir. It's a few more kilometers at least, but if we get any closer our guidance systems will fail and we'll drop like a rock."

"I'll walk, then."

"Yes, you will." She chewed on her lip for a moment. "Can I come with?"

"Nope," I said. "Too dangerous."

She blew out a whiskey-scented sigh. "Danger's fine by me."

I shook my head.

"Do you know how boring life is, living in a junkyard?" She gave me a moment to answer, but I didn't. "Pretty damn boring. I want to *go* somewhere. Do something."

It would be nice to have someone by my side again. The extra eyes would help me spot trouble. Her experience with tech would no doubt be valuable. I liked her. Something about her earnestness was charming. It would be safer to have her with. It would be better.

"No," I said.

I walked.

Chapter 8

Swallow Hill wasn't hardly big enough to spit at.

The town was Main Street and a few outlying structures nestled comfortably into the cleavage of two rounded hills. The hills protected this little town, making it a beaten-down version of what might have passed for quaint a hundred years prior. Brick façades faced the main thoroughfare. A tavern, a bank, and a general store all lined up nicely across from a clock tower attached to what must have long ago been a church. Farther up the street sat squat residential buildings—some apartments and some single-family dwellings. Beyond that were more hills: cracked, broken mounds that made jagged edges of an otherwise pleasant horizon.

The sun had climbed up the sky, baked the life out of the land, and now, having ravaged another perfectly good day, was lazily drifting back down. Stark, gray towers, about a kilometer out of town, hadn't bothered me one bit. Cracked earth and punctured armor told of a battle long ago, but still these towers stood, sentinels against the sky.

A man stood at the edge of town. His white hair fell in wisps down his back, and his filthy overalls looked like they barely held together. He had a rifle, clutched in his knobby hands. His eyes seemed to stare off into space.

"Howdy," I said by way of greeting.

He didn't respond. I waved a hand in front of his face and touched him on the shoulder. Nothing. He was alive and breathing. His eyes flashed a bright blue—light visible even in the sun. Still, he didn't move to acknowledge me.

What was I doing there unarmed and unprepared? The question nagged me as I passed the man and strolled into town. What was going on had to stop, and a clever man could solve problems without violence. Words were his bullets and truth was his fist. There was a man killing children in Swallow Hill. All I needed to do was figure out who that murderer was and it would be easy enough to hand the evidence over to the town's law.

Zane had somehow known about the murder, but how much did he know about the town? Closer up, the buildings looked broken. Old. Some even seemed structurally unsafe. The tavern leaned right up against the polished stone bank. Dry earth had blown up against that side of the street, causing the place to have an abandoned look. Other buildings were in much worse shape: even the old church at the head of the square seemed ready to topple. Tables had been set up outside to form an open market, and the theme seemed to continue tentatively into the building. All of the town was worn down: drab and ragged cloth decorating time-scoured wood and stone.

There were people, but they didn't look much better than the town in which they lived. A sad couple passed me in threadbare clothes. The man's skin had yellow, unhealthy patches and his fingernails were broken and cracked. The woman at his side was pretty in her way, but sallow cheeks and thinning hair told of a hard life. Her eyes

54

flashed blue as I met them, revealing the tech hidden behind them. I tipped my hat and wondered what they thought of a stranger wandering into their secluded town. Their expressions were filled with worry as they pulled each other close and hurried away. How might they have acted if I'd moseyed into town fully armed? Would their worried caution be replaced with open hostility?

There were others, all of them looking my way as I strolled casually through the center of town. An ancient woman scowled at me from under a flowered hat. Two teenage boys watched me from the shadows of an alley. Across the street, a man in a light-tan duster and a star saw me and approached.

"Long way from home, mister," he said.

"Sure."

The man looked me up and down. His fingers touched the pistol at his side.

I didn't give any ground. "I'm not looking for trouble, Deputy…"

"Sheriff Flores."

"J.D. Crow," I said, sticking my hand out for a shake. He didn't take it. "I'm not here for trouble, son. All I want is a few answers."

His eyes narrowed. "Folks here don't see many outsiders, stranger."

"No, I don't suppose they do."

"If you're looking for trouble—"

"I'm not." Thought that had been established.

"If you are, there's plenty to find." He glanced down at his sidearm. "More than you might like."

"How many people live here?"

"Last fella come through here looked a whole lot like you. We ran him out of town real quick."

"What do you folks do out here? Ranching? Manufacturing? Not much trade or you'd have more visitors."

Flores grabbed my arm. "Listen here, fella." His eyes flashed brightly enough that their internal glow was visible even in the sun. "This here's a quiet town. We ain't rich, but we got our place and all these nice buildings and fancy clothes don't mean we got anything worth stealing. You so much as look funny at any my people, you'll find yourself on the wrong side of dead."

I pulled my arm free. Sheriff Flores wasn't going to give me anything, so there didn't seem to be a point in pressing matters.

Nothing was going to happen outside of talking, so I went where talking was best. The tavern was a crooked, smoke-filled mess of oak and steel. Blue lights hung from the ceiling, piercing the cigar haze with razor-sharp rays. A more diffuse glow came from somewhere above, reflecting from the smoke and doing more to obscure than illuminate. Paint on the inside walls was caked on in layers, chipped down to the wood in places. The bar was solid mahogany with tarnished metal stools. There were only two tables in the entire place; one was circled by four men playing poker.

The bartender, a white-haired man with big belly and a finely articulated artificial right hand, frowned at me as I moseyed slowly up to the bar.

I held up two fingers. "Whiskeys."

He nodded, filled two shot glasses with a golden liquid. The aroma calmed me and brought me back. There was a time when I'd have had trouble with the alcohol. Drinking one whiskey would lead to another, then another, then another. That was years ago. I hadn't had a drink in so long.

"I'll have another," I said. My first two shots were down. "Make it two."

The barkeep's frown deepened. "Eight stars," he said. "Coin. No credit."

I fished the coins out of a pocket and dropped them on the bar. The barkeep nodded and poured two more glasses. Then he turned around to a stove where he was frying up something that smelled like fat and spices. Thick sausages rolled around in the pan. He looked back at me questioningly.

Bile bubbled up in the back of my throat. The image of the slaughtered boy flashed in front of me. Sausages. He had been next to a sausage-making machine. There was no way to know if that boy had made it into the sausage machine, but I sure as hell wasn't going to take the risk. The two shots of whiskey looked up at me like the yellow eyes of death. There was peace in them. An answer. Get lost. Let it all go. Be at peace.

Be dead.

It was good whiskey. The best. Those first two shots still lingered in the back of my throat, calling out to their friends. The alcohol had little effect. The nannies in my blood burned it off almost as fast as I could drink, but alcohol slowly killed the bastards. All that tech inside of me would die if I drank hard enough. Eventually, I'd overload the nannies and they'd stop repairing my body from the damage done by my metal arm.

They'd recover, though. They always did. It always hurt.

Behind me, one of the poker players won a hand, hauling in hundreds of stars in a single bet. I glanced sideways at him. Of all the men there, he was the only one who looked like he made some money. He was a man in his thirties, smooth-skinned and bright-eyed. He grinned at winning, but he didn't look down at his money. Instead, his gaze flickered from one opponent to the next, as if sizing them up. As if expecting trouble.

"Mighty nice town you have here," I said to the barkeep.

The barkeep turned to me, bent down so our eyes were level, and said, "Mister, we plan to keep it that way."

Our scowls locked, his face twisted into a mask of disgust that didn't seem to fit his rosy cheeks and soft jowls. The poker players stopped, filling the room with a heavy silence. The barkeep's hand moved slowly under the bar out of sight, but he kept his eyes right on me. Muscles in his neck tensed, like he was some great bear ready to rear up and maul someone for waking him up. His eyes flashed with an inner light.

I spoke through gritted teeth. "Barkeep, best take your hand off of that weapon." For a second, I didn't know if he would back down. A man protecting his place of business could be a fierce thing. "I'm unarmed."

His scowl turned to a mirthful grin and he stood back from the bar. He laughed from his belly. "Just giving you a hard time."

I grunted.

The poker players anted up.

"Why are you in town?" The barkeep pulled out a rag and started wiping down the already clean bar. "Swallow Hill ain't on the way to anywhere, and it ain't on the way from anywhere."

"Well," I said. "Heard the whiskey was good and the people friendly." I downed another shot.

"You're half right."

"That's good whiskey."

He polished the bar with a scrap of filthy cloth. "We're not so bad. Just don't like rough-looking strangers walking into town, especially after all that's been going on."

"Trouble?"

He bit his lip and leaned closer. "Don't think it's a bad town, but we have our issues."

I met the man's gaze and gave him a questioning look.

"Kids gone missing. Three of them now. Just gone."

"Seems like a lot of folks have gone missing. It's mighty sparse out there considering the size of the town."

His face was hard to read. "Lots of folks working long hours."

I nodded. "The way of the world."

He was peering at me and I could see the lights flashing in his corneas. "When we find the fella responsible for them kids, it ain't gonna be pretty."

"No." My voice was barely a whisper. "I don't imagine."

"Another whiskey?"

"Nope." The taste of bile still hung in the back of my throat. No amount of whiskey was going to chase it away. "Tell me, though, is there a pig farm nearby?"

Chapter 9

A man named Keith Woeberg ran a pig farm about a kilometer north of town. Hard to miss. It didn't take me long to find it. There were pens and the stink of pigs. There was even a sign declaring the place as Woeberg's Farm on the walkway. Seemed like the right place. Only, something was very wrong with that pig farm.

There were no pigs.

I pulled a piece of grass and stuck it in my teeth to help me think. The farm was huge and mechanized. A tall, metal barn loomed to the right of the path, with soil around it so grease-stained nothing grew. The other side of the barn was a series of fenced-off pens—some outdoors, some partially shaded. The nearest ones were empty. Buzzards circled lazily above.

The farm made up for its lack of pigs with an excess of stink.

If this was where the video came from, then a quick scan of the room with my glow cube would be evidence enough. There was no need to find the scruffy farmer. Once the evidence was in hand, Sheriff Flores would handle the problem. Probably. Flores would handle this locally, not bothering to bring in Trish. Zane wouldn't have a problem with that, would he? It made me wonder why Zane thought my particular set of skills was needed.

There was nobody in sight, so I left the path and circled around the barn. The close end was a concrete loading dock, its metal doors wide open to the world. The scorching wind of the late Texas afternoon gently swayed the doors, rhythmically serenading the putrid homestead with a wailing metal-on-metal screech. The dry grass between my teeth tasted like dust.

The shadow behind the barn was deep and cool. It wasn't cold in any real sense of the word, but it was certainly cooler than the blazing heat of the sun.

That's when I heard the farmer.

"Here, piggy, piggy."

The land outside of the barn was a flat stretch of dead earth. Running was an option, but talking might get me the information I needed. It just had to be done without confrontation or violence, since I was still unarmed. "Howdy," I hollered. "Reckon you and I have some business."

"Here, piggy, piggy," called the farmer. "You done volunteered to be next."

"Howdy!" There was no way he couldn't hear me. He was calling to the pig at half my volume, so unless the man was completely deaf, he'd heard me just fine.

But he didn't react to my voice.

The farmer, Keith, rounded the corner. His plain white shirt was crusted with black, dried blood. His untrimmed beard stuck out at angles from his chin. In one hand he held a wicked knife; in the other he held something that appeared to be a bolt gun. When he saw me, his eyes flashed bright and his face twisted into a mask of rage.

"You!" he snarled.

He swung his heavy bolt gun up.

Too slow. I took two long steps forward and backhanded the gun aside. A shot rang out, a slug of metal launched high into the air. The farmer twisted backwards and ducked down. He held hard onto the gun. With a tinny thunk he reloaded and brought his weapon straight back up.

But I wasn't there.

Bolt guns are short-range weapons. Heavy equipment used to slaughter pigs, longhorns, or any animal that proved itself more useful dead than alive. Bolts will easily scramble a brain from two meters, and at five they could crack a skull. Any farther and it'd leave a person with a bruise and a good story to tell.

I ran hard. Who the hell did he think I was? I sure as hell didn't know him. My muscles—my whole body was sore, but it felt good to stretch my legs. By the time Keith was back up and around the corner I was halfway down the length of the barn, where I skidded to a halt. There was a painted metal door, pockmarked with rust. I grabbed the doorknob with my three metal fingers and pulled, ripping the door from its hinges.

A wave of rotten stench rolled out of the gaping door. Bile welled up in my belly again, but I bit it back and plunged into the darkness. The buzz of flies welcomed me, enveloping everything in white noise. They landed, crawled across my face and arm. It was all I could do to ignore them.

Light trickled in from a window set high in the far wall, one that likely looked out over the slaughterhouse. A polished steel table dominated the center of the room. Behind it was another door. All of the corners of the room were inky blackness, made more so by the harsh light at my back.

I leapt up and slid across the table, meaning to head straight for the door. Soon as I hit the surface, though, I understood my mistake.

The table was slippery as snot on a glass doorknob. My butt slid fast, throwing off my balance and landing me hard on my back.

Keith was at the door. "You think you can come back here?" There was an edge of pain in the farmer's voice. "You took my Suzie and now you think you can take my pigs?"

"Do I know you?" I didn't. Who did he think I was? I spun, kicked the table hard, and made for the door. The table tipped and I heard a grunt from the farmer. My shoulder hit the door, and I was through before he was able to fire another shot.

My eyes hadn't adjusted to the gloom of the building any more than my nose had adjusted to the stench. Fat flies crawled over my skin and I had to shake them free before moving again.

The floor was a metal grate, slick with blood and filth. The door to my left opened easily, so I took it. This door had a solid feel, so I slammed it behind me and braced myself against it. The flies were thicker there, buzzing so loud it sounded like a band saw cutting oak.

Nobody ever wants to see the inside of a slaughterhouse. They think of a pig farm as a magical place where cute piggies go in and ham steaks come out. Hooks, knives, pliers, hammers, bone saws, and bolt guns hung on pegs. Chains—filthy chains—dangled from a dark ceiling. The whole place reeked of death and pig shit. There was blood everywhere: dried blood, fresh blood, slick blood, and hardened blood all across the table, all over the floor.

Even the metal grate of the floor was caked with ichor. Like before, I had to force back the urge to vomit. Unlike before, I failed.

I turned and emptied my gut onto the ichor-covered floor. The sharp burn of whiskey and stomach acid coated my mouth and overwhelmed my nose.

"Shouldn't a come back here, Tom," called the farmer. "You know what I got for you." There was a click and a low hum, presumably the bolt gun powering up.

The farmer thought I was someone else, an enemy of his. Why? He was going to shoot me on sight, which put a kink in my plans to talk things out. Could he even hear me? I pressed my palm to my forehead. There had to be a better plan.

Of course, there was. Violence.

No. It was a matter of principle. I'd die right there if it meant proving that I could go without violence. I'd meet a horrible, violent end just to prove it to myself. Shit. That didn't prove anything, did it?

"C'mon out. Get what's coming, Tom," said the farmer on the other side of the door. His heavy footsteps started again, clomping past my door and farther down the hall. He must not have known where I was. He was trying to draw me out.

Then I saw the hook. It hung from the ceiling right where I'd seen it in the video. Dirty, black, and wicked, it had held the body of a boy less than a day ago. The sausage machine was there too, jammed up in the corner. This was where I needed to scan. A sample from the floor and a scan of the area was all I needed.

My cube lit the room with a flickering green glow. The scan started, lights taking everything in. With a scrap of cloth from my shirt, I sopped up some of the muddy blood on the floor as the cube worked through its array of scans.

A few more moments were all I needed. Then I could run.

The footsteps stopped.

Where was he? He'd been clomping down the hall, past the room I'd gone into. How far had he gotten? I held my breath and pressed an ear up against the steel door. It was cold against my face. Cold and silent.

Thoomp! Something hit me hard in the ribs, sending waves of fire through my left side. I dropped to my knees and spun to see Keith at the opposite end of the room. His boots were off and his face was a mix of triumph and rage.

"When you ran off with Suzie, I thought of coming after you, you know." The bolt gun clicked and hummed as another bolt locked into place.

I gasped for air, but each breath was a fresh kick of pain in my ribs.

He stepped closer, leveling the bolt gun at my head. Behind him, the glow cube flickered through the cloud of flies, finishing its scan.

"A farmer can't leave his pigs, can he? Not when he's got no kids and no wife. Never had kids, but you"—he kicked me hard right where the bolt had tenderized my ribs—"took my damn wife!"

The floor hit my face. I felt bad for the guy. He'd had a tough life. He was a victim of this as much as anyone, maybe even as much as those kids he killed. It's hard to hate a guy who's had it so tough.

But I managed it, anyway.

The farmer shook his head. "Tom," he said, leveling the bolt gun at my head. "You got no idea how good this is gonna make me feel."

I sucked in breath through my teeth, reached up with my metal hand, and gripped the business end of the bolt gun so that it was aimed straight at my metal palm. He'd have to be a damn fool to fire with the barrel blocked like that.

An explosion of light and noise ripped the two of us apart. My arm thrown backwards, twisting me and sending a fresh batch of pain through my ribs. Everything went silent, replaced by the ring of damaged eardrums.

Keith got it worse. The impact of the bolt with my indestructible hand sent shockwaves back down the barrel of the gun. The whole thing shattered under the pressure and shards of it peppered the surrounding area, including the poor farmer's chest and arm. He staggered back.

It was my chance. I struggled to my feet, staggered forward, and pegged him to the wall with my metal forearm.

"Listen up." I met his gaze, scowl for scowl. "You're done. I don't want to do nothing to you and you're disarmed, so—"

He wasn't disarmed.

His knife plunged into my belly and he spat in my face.

I took half a step back, punched the man in the gut, then lifted him high in the air by the ribcage. I sent him up, above me, thankful that my metal arm was long enough that he wasn't able to stab me again.

Slamming him down hard on the table, I pulled out the needle-nose pliers I'd taken from the wall. I jammed it into his ear, nabbed a little tag of metal, and yanked. Blood and wire pulled free, more than I thought possible. His screams pierced the haze of my ringing ears. Wires just kept coming. His blade dropped to the floor.

Once the tech was out of that ear, I flipped him and pulled out the one on the other side.

"You need to listen," I said. "And these aren't helping you do it."

His eyes regarded me with pain and fear. His body was so tense he seemed frozen to the spot.

I leaned down close to him and said in the clearest, calmest voice I could muster, "I'm not Tom. There's no more pigs on this farm. You'd best go after Suzie, because there's nothing good that's going to happen here when these townsfolk figure out what you've been feeding them."

He stared at me slack-jawed. Blood covered the sides of his face.

Clutching my bleeding belly, I staggered out of the room. After looking back a few times to make sure he wasn't following, I did a quick check of the wound.

It was ugly. A deep, gaping hole oozed a river of blood. Pressure. It needed pressure. And stitches. The farmer's house wasn't far away. Maybe I'd find a kit there and I could stitch up. Maybe there was a place in the barn where the man worked on pigs. He would have some basic veterinary supplies.

Sunlight pierced right into my skull when I stepped outside. Then the dizziness hit.

Right about there was where I collapsed.

Chapter 10

The thick odor of fine barbecue tickled my senses as deep sleep grudgingly gave me up. I didn't open my eyes at first; I just soaked in that smell. There wasn't any pain. Everything was calm. Finally, peace was all I could sense. There really isn't any better peace than that of a good barbecue. I pulled in a long, slow breath. Beef brisket, I thought. Someone who knew what they were doing was cooking because there wasn't too much spice, but a perfect amount of char.

There was something else, though. It was just behind the beautiful scent of charred meat. The sour sting of rot hung in the air.

Gears started turning. Where were my aches? The painful reminders of my scrapes and bruises were completely gone. There wasn't even any pain where I'd been stabbed in the gut.

My eyes snapped open.

A too-bright light shone down on me, eclipsed by a man's shaggy silhouette. He leaned over me with a razor-sharp scalpel in one hand and a red-hot poker in the other.

"Mornin'," said the farmer, his scruffy beard sticking out around a grimy surgical mask. He fumbled with his tools, getting them both in his left hand so he could offer his right for a shake. "Name's Keith. Keith Woeberg."

"Crow," I said. "J.D." My right arm wouldn't move.

"Oh, right." Keith reached down at something I couldn't see, something on my chest. With a tug he removed it.

All of my pain hit like a longhorn running. I choked back a scream. Nearly blacked out.

Keith took a step back. The red-hot rod gave him an ominous cast. "I'm done. Got her all cauterized for you."

I felt my belly with my fingers. Sure enough, where the cut had been there was a jagged series of bumps. My fingers still came away wet, but it wasn't a gusher. Gingerly, I pushed myself up on my elbows.

Then crashed back down.

"You lost a bit of blood." He nodded to a couple of empty plastic bags. "It'll take some time for the synth to replace it for you."

I lifted myself again, then swung my feet around so I could sit up. Keith had fixed me in just about the filthiest operating room there'd ever been. There were flies everywhere, and the steel table was a slick mixture of old blood and new. I only hoped that I had enough blood nannies left to fight off the dozen infections that Keith had probably given me.

"'Preciate it," I said, eyeing him suspiciously.

"Well, seemed like patching the hole was the right thing to do after stickin' you." He peered at me, squinting. "You care to explain for me why you looked like Tom?"

"Can't say that I understand it myself." My hat was on the table next to me so I picked it up, cleaned it as best I could, and put it on.

He blinked a few times and shook his head as if to clear it. "You messed up my headgear something serious, then everything went to shit. Once I saw you weren't Tom, I figured I'd better fix you up."

Keith offered me an arm. I ignored his help and hopped down to the floor on my own. The dizziness nearly dropped me, but a hand on the table was all I needed to keep my balance. After a minute, I was walking again.

"Well, Mr. Crow." Keith's voice was flat. "What business you got here?"

Did he know? It seemed odd, but this polite farmer in front of me didn't give me the feeling of someone who would kill children. "Maybe Zane forged the video." That didn't make sense either. Why did Zane want me to be here so badly?

"Come again?"

The glow cube was still on the table, so I snatched it up and shoved it in my ammo pouch. The information it gathered might be useful, but I wasn't quite ready to hand it over to the town's sheriff.

The first step lit my ribs on fire. The second was worse. It took a minute to regain my composure. "Keith," I said. "You notice anything funny going on in town? Anything that doesn't belong?"

Keith seemed to think about that for a minute. "Swallow Hill's nothing but simple. Small town, we keep to ourselves. Some small trade for goods, but no real outside contact. Folks like it that way." He touched the table, where sticky blood coated everything. "Mr. Crow, what's happening here?"

"Haven't figured it yet."

"But where are my pigs?" His voice was getting high. Panicked. "I looked. All my pigs are gone. Where are they?"

I braced myself against the pain and pushed my way out of the room into the big slaughterhouse. From there, I made my way outside, squinting at the setting sun.

"Thought you said it was morning," I said.

"Figure of speech. It's still afternoon."

"That bank still open? How long was I out?"

He blinked at me. "Most places close during the hot part of the day and open around evening and stay open past sunset. Why do you need a bank?"

"Why does anyone?"

"Well, changing money, I suppose." He scratched at his scruffy beard and sent a dozen flies into the air. "Long-distance transactions. Savings. I don't know. All my loans are community backed, so I've never much had a use for a bank."

"Exactly."

He fell in step next to me. The pain in my ribs felt like a fresh stab wound every time I took a breath, but the actual stab wound felt numb. More than once I stumbled and Keith had to get an arm under me to keep me from falling. More than once I shoved him away and stood on my own.

When we reached the main street, I found a nice bench and had myself a sit. Keith plopped down next to me. There were more people out this time of day. Every one of them gave me the stink-eye as they passed, though now I didn't blame them. I was just about as bad as Keith; blood drenched my torn shirt.

I didn't know what I was looking for. Part of me wanted to get an idea of who went into the bank. Instinct told me that if that was a base of operations, it probably was best if I did some survey before going in. Zane must have sent me here for something and if that was the case then I wanted to know everything that was happening in town. Another part of me thought it might be nice to sit awhile. A long while.

Nobody went into the bank. Nobody came out.

"Well, I don't remember the last time I ever went to a bank," said Keith. "Been years since I used cash for anything. Got it all up here now." He tapped a finger on his forehead. "Headchecks. You switched yet?"

I grunted something that I thought might be interpreted as an answer.

"Well, it sure is nice. Stars being mostly credits in the system now. Cash is for outsiders. This way, I just think my money to someone and they got it."

"Never heard of it."

"It's been common around here awhile now."

The man who had been winning poker left the tavern. He looked around, then marched straight to the bank. Apparently, his winning streak had held, because he carried a pack heavy with coins.

"He uses coins," I said.

Keith squinted. "Can't play poker with headchecks."

"Is he a local?"

"You don't just think it, though. It's all up in the neuro-tech. You think images to unlock the transaction. Usually you pick images that you wouldn't usually think of—aw, dammit I just thought of mine."

I stood up. A wave of dizziness hit me. I sat back down.

"Hold on," said Keith. He closed his eyes, pensive thought on his face. "There. Got it locked up again. Now as long as I don't think—dammit. Hold on."

Standing up slowly this time, I made my way across the street to the bank. Keith didn't follow. I pulled the heavy steel door open and slipped inside. Harsh white lights stung my eyes. Straight ahead sat a single teller's desk: polished steel with a gold inlay. A steel railing separated the teller's desk from what was presumably the customer section of the bank. Behind the teller's desk was a wall of steel and black metal. Set inside that reinforced wall was an outline of a door with no hint of doorknob. The poker player was nowhere to be seen.

The hum of power vibrated in the floor and the teller's desk lit up. Behind it, the projected image of a perky, young blonde appeared. Her image seemed to tap her fingernails on the desk as she silently regarded me. Her smile was wide and almost made it up to her eyes.

"Can I help you?"

I quit my rubbernecking and stepped up to the desk. Hat held close to my chest, I bowed my head slightly and cleared my throat. "Looking to put something in safety deposit, ma'am."

Her eyebrows shot up. She acted just like a person, but it was hard to know if she was a projected image of a real worker or just a clever machine. Maybe this was a testament to how good machines have gotten. Or maybe it reflected poorly on the state of humanity.

"I'm sorry, sir," she said. "There are no safety-deposit boxes in this location."

"You sure?" I leaned close to her flickering, projected face. She was semi-transparent and close up it was easy to see the door behind her. "'Cause, I can see the door to the vault right there and it makes not one bit of sense for a bank to have a vault but not rent out space in it."

She blinked. "Come again?"

"What's that vault for?" I leaned even closer, gripping the steel railing with both hands.

"This location does not contain a safety-deposit box. There is no vault for storing customer goods. The vault is for the sole purpose of holding cash reserves."

I leaned back, pulled with my metal hand, and snapped a steel bar off the railing. "Whoops," I said. With a quick twist, I bent the bar into a cane and leaned on it heavily as I walked out of the bank.

Sheriff Flores stood at the entrance, a scowl on his face. His pistol was out, but not pointed at me. He didn't say anything, but his eyes were flashing with artificial light.

Hands raised, I said, "Just doing a little banking." He didn't respond, so I edged my way past him and crossed the street.

Once I was back on the bench with Keith, I lay the cane across my lap.

"Y'all are insane in this town, you know that, right?"

Keith blinked hard at me. "That you, J.D.?"

"Yup."

"You've had a long day. Sun's coming down. Should we head back to the ranch and I'll let you bunk up at my place?"

"Nope."

He looked at me.

"Too much work to do," I said. "And too much walking."

With that, I stood up and walked into the falling dusk, using the cane to keep me from stumbling. A clever man might be able to figure out this problem without violence. Maybe clever wasn't my thing, but with enough time to ponder I was sure to come up with something.

To my surprise, Keith fell in step beside me.

"Go home, Keith."

He didn't answer. The sun ducked behind the horizon and soon the moon was out. As the air cooled, exhaustion crept in. Between blood loss and a poor night's sleep, I was fading fast. It wasn't long before the mere act of walking was making me breathe fast and my heart race.

"Nice town you have there," I said.

"Swallow Hill wasn't always like that." Keith looked a mess. He spoke a little louder than was strictly necessary—probably a side effect of his ears getting messed up so badly. It was a little surprising that he could hear at all, really.

"Sorry about your ears."

"The war messed up the town something fierce," he continued. "It was bad before that, though. I wasn't big enough to understand what the war was about, but I knew lots a folk who didn't come back. Nobody visited Swallow Hill after the war. Nobody."

A stray hunk of asphalt tripped me up and Keith kept me from falling. It was getting harder to focus. The road ahead doubled in my vision for a moment, but I aimed for the middle and kept walking. Abi wasn't far. I'd make it. I had to.

"Folks fell to subsistence farming. My family's pigs made me popular. A man has a lot of friends when he's the only source of bacon in town. Life was good for a time. Comfortable." A pained expression crossed his face. "Hardly anyone ever left for a while. The few goods we needed from outside were delivered by automated systems."

"Sounds nice."

"It was peaceful. That's all we wanted after the war."

That's all anyone wanted after the war. Any war, really. After all that sacrifice, aren't we owed a little peace? "You pay for peace," I said. "You pay hard for it."

A time passed with the only sound being the tap-tap of my makeshift cane on the broken road. The story of Swallow Hill saddened me. The thought of a small, peaceful town existing after the war sounded like a dream come true. Most towns had been forced into servitude to one degree or another. We in the outlands provided resources that the city consumed. Here was a town that didn't do any of that. Here was a town that was left alone. But what did they sacrifice to gain that independence?

I stopped walking and turned to Keith. "You killed kids, Keith."

"I know." His lower lip trembled. "I figured it out once you wrecked my headgear."

"You didn't know what you were doing."

"I should have." His voice was barely a whisper. "Everything looked so perfect through the tech. Sounded perfect too. I should have known something was wrong. I just didn't think..." His voice choked off in a sob.

A hundred questions swam around in my head, but I couldn't make much sense of them in my current state. "You're following because you want to make up for it?"

He nodded.

"Good." I pointed to the spot not far away where Abi was silhouetted against the glow of the night sky. "That girl's going to take us to a place in Dead Oak. Trust her. Do anything she says." Dizziness was nearly too much for me. Bracing against my cane, I was barely able to keep myself up. My chest felt tight and breath was hard to come by.

"Sure," Keith said. "What are you going to do?"

I gasped a few breaths. "Nothing," I said. Without trying, I dropped to one knee. "Nothing at all."

The last thing I felt was Keith catching me as I collapsed the rest of the way to the ground.

Chapter 11

"Honey," Josephine said, "you look like you let a butcher operate on you."

Keith was doing his best to shrink into the corner. I lay on the steel table in the center of Josephine's shack. Jo prodded me with tools that I didn't even try to identify.

"Might've," I said.

"Well, you know that was dumb, right? Nobody knows a body like a mechanic. Butcher'll just cut you up into pieces."

I tried to say something clever, but it came out as a pained grunt as Josephine dug a three-pronged device into my sore ribs.

"Not broken, you wuss." She put the tool down and looked me right in the eyes. "And no, you don't need no doctor. You're half metal anyway, boy. What's a doctor gonna do for you? A mechanic is what you need."

"I'm getting tired of waking up on people's tables," I said.

"Always thought you were too soft, anyway. Little more tech will toughen you right up."

Keith stepped up and helped me into a sitting position. I looked down at my chest. It was cleaner, but the left side where the bolt had hit had a dark purple welt the size of a fist. The welt now had three faint holes around it where Jo's tool had burrowed in.

Josephine started cleaning her tools and putting them away. "I reinforced the ribs for you, in case there was a crack I couldn't see. They'll be tough as hell from now on. The tissue around them was badly bruised, but all I could do was numb the area. Your nannies ought to get things functional soon enough." She eyed Keith. "Long as you don't let a butcher get you, you should be fine."

A fresh wave of nausea hit as I stood up. "I need help, Jo." My voice was quiet.

She raised an eyebrow.

"Someone's messing with tech around that town, Jo. And I suspect there's something going on in the bank."

Her expression darkened.

"What I mean to say is, we need to get into that bank and figure out what's happening there. I know you're good with tech. Get into their computers and find the info I need. It's all I ask."

Josephine's jaw looked so hard I wondered if she might start breaking brick walls with it.

"I've got a plan, a start of one, anyway. I—"

"You used to be a decent sheriff, J.D." Josephine's voice was low. "Little bit of a technophobe and a little delusional at times, but we got to an understanding with you. You meant well." She put a finger on my chest. "What you're telling me now is delusion. We usually let you do your thing, but this is enough. I'm not going to get involved in anything having to do with that town."

"Everything I'm saying is true. Just ask Keith."

Keith's eyes got wide.

Josephine shook her head. "If what you say is true, then call Trish in. It's her business now, not yours."

"Can't." My voice didn't have much conviction.

"The hell you can't."

She was right. Zane wanted me to keep the law out of it. He backed it up with some vague threats. One call to Trish would set things in motion. She'd help deal with the problem, whatever it was. It made me wonder why Zane had wanted to keep her out of it.

"What if I get Zane, the guy from Goodwin, to explain why we can't call her?" I shrugged into a clean shirt Josephine had given me, only wincing a little.

"That city boy ain't welcome anywhere around here and you know it."

I opened my mouth to speak, then shook my head when I couldn't think of anything. I picked up my hat, put it on, and left the shack. Night had fallen. Abi sat on my skidder with a grin on her face. Intense flood lamps lit the scrap yard, shutting the night out into an inky backdrop. The air had lost the intense heat of the day and was edging its way toward cool.

Abi grinned at me. "She busted her ass for you, you know. Worked the whole time you were gone. I think she likes you."

"Doesn't seem like it."

She gave me a sidelong glance. "Sometimes people are like that." She slid off the skidder, walked over to me, and hip-checked me.

"I don't know anyone like that."

She checked me again, pushing me toward the skidder. "It's working now. Functional, anyway." Check. "I've never seen her turn around anything this fast. Not for a man, anyway."

She checked me again and then I was next to the skidder.

It had fancy rockets. Four articulated, slender tubes ended with flared nozzles. The new parts were bright orange, except for the back left one, which was hot pink. She'd replaced the entire control panel with a slick new interface. Instead of an array of dials and switches, the panel was a black-iron slab with no apparent controls at all.

"I can't use that."

"Sure you can."

"I was just getting the hang of the old controls."

"No you weren't." She mimed me fumbling around with the controls. It was a somewhat accurate imitation, though I don't remember her ever seeing me drive.

"It's too complicated."

Abi's grin widened. "Just the opposite, actually." She cupped my metal hand in her tiny palms. I felt cowed, like a monster being led by an innocent girl. She tugged gently on my huge, industrial claw and placed it in the shaped iron of the control panel. It fit perfectly.

"It was made for it—gah!" A pulse of tingling pain rippled through my arm, down my spine, and up through my skull. My thoughts echoed in my head, like my skull had grown eight times its size but the ideas were still little. I flexed my jaw, shrugged my shoulders, felt deep down into the length of my limbs. The throbbing pain of my artificial arm had stopped, but there was still feedback. I could feel the length of my arm, my elbow, my fingers. Sensations came from beyond my fingers. The four thrusters were extensions of my own body. The antigrav flexed like a muscle. My skidder was part of me, like it was designed to be part of me.

"Josephine has a good bit of army surplus sitting around." Abi slapped the seat of the skidder, which I felt as a dull thump way down in my fingertips. "Old stuff, like Civil War era. Really old, like you."

I swung my leg over and sat on the skidder. The control panel shifted and fit comfortably while I was seated. "They always wanted me to pick up more slack after they did this." I indicated my metal arm. "I never did it, though. Then the war ended."

"Yeah, I bet that didn't make them too happy. What you have is an interface for a whole pile of fancy army stuff. This tech was new at the end of the war and the folks who used it nearly turned the tide."

"Lot of them died."

"Most of them died."

"Tech doesn't win battles. Tech doesn't fix what's broken. It just gives you a cocky attitude and a means to show it off."

Abi was using her hand like a puppet, mimicking me talking. When she saw that I had noticed she put her hands behind her back. "Quit lecturing and give it a shot."

Flexing the antigrav, I rose a few meters, then set the thrusters to spinning me. Faster and faster, I spun, till I was nearly out of control. Then with a burst of power I stopped. It was incredible, far better precision than I'd ever had before. Then, I felt closely at the new sensations coming in. There was more.

"Shields?" I asked.

"Yeah. Environmental, mostly. But they'll stop small arms ammu..."

Silence. I'd flexed the shield and a bubble of warm, still air surrounded me. The lights shimmered, like heat rising from a hard-baked earth. Another flex and the bubble became opaque. Still another and the sound of an acoustic guitar started playing from unseen speakers.

I set the skidder down, dropping the shields. I winced as my hand detached from the console. My world snapped back in around me. The ache returned to my arm in full force.

A few minutes later, Josephine and Keith came out of the shack to find Abi and me smoking cigarettes. Abi was telling me all the latest news from Dead Oak and, well, I was listening.

Josephine looked me up and down. "I'm not helping you, J.D. You'll go in there guns blazing and you'll get nothing but dead."

When I spoke, my voice was a deep rumble. "That's not who I am anymore," I said. "All I need is a way to see what's happening there."

Josephine's mouth hardened into a thin line. Her eyes darted quickly around, looking from me to Abi, then to Keith. She breathed a deep breath through her nose. "Then what? Once you know what's happening. How do you fix it?"

"It's bad, Jo." I thought about it a moment.

"I'm not going anywhere," Josephine said.

"Nobody's asking you to."

Her eyes were wide. Something had her scared more than it should. What was she hiding? What was she so afraid to talk about? "No," she said. "I won't do it."

"Then I won't make you." I spat my cigarette onto the ground, stepped it out, and mounted the skidder. Without another word, I jammed my metal hand into the control panel, launched straight into the air, and blasted off into the night.

Without her help, the job got a lot harder. There wasn't time to visit Ben Brown at his ranch. A pang of guilt hit me at the thought of making him wait, but it was short lived. Ben could handle another day's delay.

That wasn't all of it, though. If I was being truthful with myself, I'd admit that I didn't want to have anything to do with Ben Brown or his brother Francis. There was nothing but pain there for me. My influence on their lives had brought nothing but pain. Sure, the situation in Swallow Hill was more urgent than a visit to the Brown ranch, but I was afraid. I was afraid of how he'd look at me and the feelings he'd dredge up.

No, Ben could wait.

It was time to seek help from a less reputable source.

Chapter 12

With gritted teeth, I fought against the pain all over my body, from the metallic aching rhythm of my artificial arm to the more organic discomfort in my ribs. The pain in my ribs had subsided some, but whatever Josephine had done hadn't truly healed the wound. Pressing at it with my fingers, I was able to locate an area of numbness, surrounded by the pulsing ache and deep bruising.

If there's something that gets a man past pain, it's anger.

I held onto my anger, letting it simmer my blood. Outrage still bubbled: the slow, justified anger of the righteous man. Anger at the world was set deep inside my bones. It had settled down there since the war twenty-some years earlier. There is a certain kind of rage a man feels when he sees a loss of control coming. It was the city folk. It had to be. Who else would want to control the masses so badly? There must have been some new mind-altering tech and Swallow Hill was the trial. Austin lived in fear of an uprising, so experimenting with something that would subdue the population made sense in a twisted way. Maybe it was the folks at Goodwin Dairy, but there were half a dozen other giant faceless corporations it could be.

There, on a ridge overlooking a ghost town, I looked down on the stronghold of a group that hated me just about as much as I hated them. Cinco Armas wasn't an ally by any stretch. Might be they wouldn't shoot me on sight, but what could I really hope to accomplish by talking to them.

Anger at Zane was rolling around in my gut too. He'd shown me that murder. Maybe his intentions were benign, but the more I thought of that kid hanging on the hook, the more I thought Zane must be manipulating me. Maybe he was doing it because it was the only way to get the right thing done. Somehow I doubted that. Either way, he was playing me. He'd made me leave my people. The Hopi were my whole existence for four years. I was comfortable there.

The knuckles of my fist cracked.

One good sucker punch hardly counted as violence. It'd feel good. All of that aggression and fierce rage that boiled in my blood demanded satisfaction. It demanded that I pound that city boy in the jaw when he showed up.

My shoulders slumped. No, I wouldn't do it. With incredible effort, I took my rage and swallowed it. It burned in my belly, refusing to be digested, but it was under control. A few breaths of cool night air settled me, and I was able to manage a tip of my hat as Zane flew over in his sleek, shining car.

He parked a short distance away, near where I'd left my skidder. In the moonlight, I could see him with perfect clarity. He was wearing a crisp, clean suit and his hair was swept to one side. In his hand was a walking stick, flashes of light playing off of its jeweled surface as he strolled up the slope to where I stood on the ridge. When I saw him, all of that rage in my belly melted, and I relaxed.

He hit me hard with a sucker punch to the jaw.

"Tucker Hale?" he said as I tumbled to the ground. "Tucker fucking Hale?"

The stars of the spectacular Texan sky spun helplessly above me. My jaw stung and I flexed it to try to figure if it was broken. It didn't seem to be.

Zane stood above me. "You thought you'd play a joke on me, J.D.? Or were you actually trying to get me—"

I kicked Zane hard in the gut. He staggered backward, and by the time he regained his balance, I had my shoulder in his chest, and I was pumping hard and driving him backward away from the ledge.

Zane slammed against his car, shoving it back several meters. My right hook connected awkwardly with the side of his neck, hurting my fist more than anything. Zane punched me hard in the gut as the two of us toppled into the dust. My breath was violently forced from my lungs and Zane pinned my non-metal arm. His face was centimeters from mine and we both breathed clouds of mist into the cool night air.

And we stayed that way.

Long moments passed with neither of us willing to move.

"Tucker gave you some trouble then?" I said, giving Zane what I hoped would be interpreted as an apologetic look.

Zane's whole body relaxed. He stood up and offered a hand, which I took. He heaved me to my feet. "The man was barely civilized."

I nodded.

"He stuck me in a gravity well and refused to let me leave until I'd admitted that the ranchers and farmers were better than city folk in every way."

"Did you?"

"Well, I didn't mean it."

I grunted.

"And he wouldn't help." There was a tone in his voice that I couldn't quite place.

"He'll change his mind."

Zane looked at me quizzically.

"Yes, we still need his help. What we're looking for is in the bank. Like I told you before, Tucker's got the skills you need, even if he lacks the stability."

"Right." Zane picked his cane up from the ground, where he'd dropped it. "But as I said, he's not going to help."

"He'll help, and he'll like it." I rubbed my jaw. "Did you really need to—"

"Yes."

I nodded. "Well, first we'll need to sweeten the deal. Tucker was a munitions expert and bomb maker. If we get the right combination of toys, he'll come help just so he can play."

"So we're taking the violent path?"

"It's under consideration."

Zane cocked his head, like he was trying to figure something out. He must not have figured it, though, because he didn't say anything.

"Down there," I said, pointing over the ridge, where a steep drop overlooked a seemingly empty ghost town. "Group I've had dealings with makes its home there."

"Friendly dealings?"

"Nope."

Court and her gang Cinco Armas had a healthy respect for the law, due to an impressive display of force by Sheriff Trish several years prior. Trish had proven the fastest draw and she'd shown that she wasn't going to back down. She also sported some of the fanciest mods outside of the city. The gang respected her, which meant they respected law.

Respect is not obedience.

The gang had sought a façade of legitimacy in the years since I'd left the sheriff's office. Legitimacy brought profit and presence in the more reputable areas of the wasteland. Where previously their dealings had been with petty robbery, senseless violence, and occasional bounty hunting, now they pursued far more profitable ventures. They'd begun dealing with the legal machine trade, including weapons, explosives, and vehicles. They moved livestock and people for a price. Of course, there was always more profit in smuggling. There was always better money in more dangerous weapons. There weren't many laws regulating the trade of weapons or explosives, but they did exist. There always was a line to cross, and crossing it was always such tempting profit. Respect for the law had made Cinco Armas a significantly more dangerous organization.

"What do you need me for? Backup?" Zane's fingers brushed the handle of his silver-handled pistol.

"Nope."

"What then?"

"Watch. I'm going to walk down there. If they shoot me, you go tell my people what happened. It's not polite to disappear without letting anyone know."

"That's it?"

"And don't get yourself killed."

Zane shook his head. "I can help, you know. Something like this is what I'm good at. This group you're going down to see is just another corporation like Goodwin. They move toward profit and away from pain." He straightened his bolo tie. "Groups like that are easy to motivate."

"I'm sure they are." My voice was harder than I intended.

"But you want to do this yourself…"

"That I do."

Shaking his head, Zane strolled down to his car. He turned, tipped his hat to me, and slid into the vehicle. "At least use the earpiece," he said.

It took me a moment to figure out what he was talking about. I still had the coin-shaped piece in my pocket.

"It'll give you an advantage," he said. "Plus I'll be able to communicate with you."

"You mean you'll be able to listen in on me."

"It doesn't work that way. There's encryption. It uses your own neural link to generate heavy encryption and the device can only be activated with your own brainwaves. Standard protocol, J.D. It's proven tech almost as old as you."

Not knowing how to take that, I left without another word. I mounted my skidder and drifted down to the edge of the shale cliff.

The town loomed in the moonlight like the ruins of a long-dead civilization. Domed hogans, like those in Dead Oak, sat seemingly empty; many of them were cracked open and filled with sand. Traditional buildings hadn't fared much better, with whole walls toppled into the main street. The asphalt of the street was pocked with dozens of manhole covers as if the entire town were built with underground access in mind. Concrete and asphalt was all that was left of this doomed little down, but one building stood tall: the church.

It wasn't a modern building, but it had been fitted with modernity. The red brick of the outer walls was laced with a dull black metal, similar to the metal that made up my left arm. The bell tower, far in the back, had fallen long ago, but was now replaced with a tower and turret. Similar armaments were nestled into the corners of the building, flickering spikes of unbridled aggression.

Two figures lingered in front of the reinforced double doors. A woman sat on the steps, flipping a coin with her slender metal fingers. She had long hair that glimmered in the moonlight and moved gently in the breeze. She had a young face, but her eyes seemed old, tired. She cradled a thick-stocked rifle in her arms.

Beside her was a man of medium height and deeply tanned skin. He wore shredded pants and no shirt, showing his full limb replacements of all four limbs. His knees bent backwards, and he leaned casually against one door smoking a cigar. He had a couple of pistols on his belt and a rifle across his back. I recognized him immediately as one of the thugs I'd chased long ago.

"Howdy, Legs," I said.

The man with the fancy legs started laughing when he saw me, prompting a dirty look from the woman. He didn't seem to care. He just kept laughing.

I didn't remember his real name, only the nickname that people had called him ever since he modified himself with the fanciest legs money could buy. "You got yourself an upgrade."

"Sure did," he said. "Looks like all you got was older."

I kept walking, not stopping till I was at the base of the steps.

The woman narrowed her eyes at me. "You know him?"

"Rosa," Legs said. "I know everyone. I'm a social butterfly, don't you know?"

She didn't seem convinced.

Legs came down to meet me, standing chest to chest. He was a full head taller than me. His breath smelled like oil and mint. "This man here is called Crow. He was the sheriff long time ago and now he's just a guy."

Rosa stroked her rifle. "Should we take him down?"

The modder seemed to consider this carefully. "No, I don't think so. He's probably just here to borrow a cup of sugar or something."

"I'm here to see Court," I said.

His smile widened. "Seems you came to the wrong place." He waved a hand to show me the glory of the rundown town. "This here's an empty ghost town, Sheriff. There's nothing to see here but tumbleweeds and dust devils."

"I didn't come to stand out here and chat."

"Of course not." He stepped past me into the broken street. "You're a man of action. You've come here for some sport. Fancy a game, old man?" His fingers wiggled near the grips of his pistols. "Maybe some shootin'?"

Rosa rolled her eyes.

"I've got no need no need for shooting, Legs. I'm here to talk." I spread my arms wide so he could get a good look at me. "I didn't even bring a weapon."

He raised an eyebrow at me. "Person could argue the wisdom of that, old man. This here's a dangerous neighborhood, don't you think?" He drew one of his weapons, flipped it so the grip was facing me. "Here, you can have one of mine."

When a person offers you a weapon it can mean one of a few things. It might mean that he intends to fight you honorably, or at least in a way that looks honorable. It could also be a sign of trust. He's trusting that you won't turn around and use that weapon to stop whatever device he happens to use to pump blood through his veins.

I glanced left and right at the turrets on the corners of the church.

It could also mean that he knows he has an overwhelming advantage in a fight and you'd be batshit insane to try anything.

The pistol felt good. Its grip nestled comfortably in my palm, with both a sleek design and the heft of good craftsmanship. The octagonal barrel ended in a snub nose, narrow enough that it must have either fired an energy payload or small-caliber ammunition. The piece wasn't as heavy as the metal that I was used to carrying.

"You like her?"

"It'll do."

"Well, what you say we make a little bet, eh, *pendejo*?"

Shaking my head, I flipped the gun around and held it out to him.

He didn't take it. "If you win, you keep the gun."

It was tempting. "What if I don't win?"

He clapped me on the back. "Friend," he said, "we're on the same side. It's a cooperative game."

"A what?"

"If we lose, I shoot you in the leg and have our surgeons give you some new equipment." He smiled. "See, you win either way."

I looked at his four artificial limbs. "You don't win too many of these wagers, do you?"

"I'm much better than I used to be."

Rosa let out a sharp laugh.

"When do I talk to Court?"

Legs's voice got serious. "When I say so."

"You have yourself a bet."

Chapter 13

Drones drifted up into the night sky, illuminating the broken asphalt with spotlights. The effect was worse than nothing at all, since my eyes would have adjusted to the light of the nearly full moon. With the spotlights, the light fluctuated wildly, maintaining a constant state of disorientation.

"See that ball down there on the fountain?" Legs asked, indicating an orb resting precariously at the top of a dry fountain about a hundred meters away.

"Yup."

"That's what we want. We just grab it and put it in this here bucket." He waved his pistol casually around, his finger on the trigger and the safety off. "You see anything move, you shoot it. It's worth points. The bots'll try to get in the way and slow us down. Tricky part is, once we get the ball all the bots kick it up a notch. Just get me the ball, since I'm the quick one. You hold them off while I run for it. Any questions?"

I didn't want to sound dumb, but there was one question that bugged me. "When's the part where I shoot you?"

He grinned and looked at Rosa. "You don't, I hope. It's a cooperative game, Sheriff. Nobody gets killed. If we win, we both win."

"That's the dumbest thing I ever heard."

"One more thing. Don't give the bots too long. They're slow and they're using small-caliber rounds, but they aim for your face, so it'll still sting like hell if you get shot, even with the best modded skin."

"I don't have modded ski—"

A buzzer nearly blasted out my eardrums.

Legs took two long steps to the right, then jumped four meters up onto the crumbling wall of the building, drawing his rifle as he went. He landed in a crouch, sighted through the scope, and shot something near the fountain that I couldn't even see.

Spotlights shifted from above and I saw the first bot. It was a slender thing, human shaped with long, gangly arms. On its head was a cowboy hat and on its breast was a deputy's star. It had entered the street around halfway down and hadn't yet turned the piercing lights of its eyes my way.

I held my metal arm in front of me like a cross brace, resting my pistol on it for stability. The shot lined up perfectly through the pistol's crosshair scope. I aimed right for the bot's star.

It turned my way.

I fired.

The pistol kicked like a mule, and a puff of rock and dust flew off the fountain far behind the bot. I'd missed.

The bot reacted to my shot. Its movements became quick and jerky. Glowing eyes spun to face me and it raised its pistol.

I fired again, sending another shot wide to the right. My hand shook.

The bot's pistol was pointed right at me. Its eyes seemed to meet mine.

A shot rang out.

The bot's pistol spun off into the night in an explosion of sparks. It turned its piercing gaze up to the rooftops, but Legs was already gone. When it turned back to me, so was I.

I ran hard, gasping through the pain of my injured ribs. I needed cover, a good line of sight, and maybe a couple months to practice. I settled for cover.

My back slammed hard against the brick of the nearest building. I hazarded a look around the corner, crouching down so I'd be somewhat less conspicuous. There were two bots in the street now. Where were they coming from? One was still twenty meters away, but the newest one was just across the street, well within pistol range.

The pistol's sights must have been wrong. I took a deep breath. They'd need to be sighted in later. I needed to shoot from the hip. The gun was too high-tech for me. The firing mechanism didn't make any sense, and there didn't seem to be any way to know if there was a bullet chambered or any ammo left. My breaths came in big gulps even though the run had been short. Blood loss was still affecting me or I was out of shape. Probably both.

Fighting was a matter of faith. Faith in the weapon you hold, faith in your partner, and faith that you aren't going to get a bullet to the brain when it's all over.

What I needed was faith in myself.

Stepping out of cover, I squeezed off a few rounds at the closest bot. The first missed by a mile, the second was closer, but the third knocked its damn head off.

Another bot emerged from the side of the street, its piercing eyes scanning the space around it. Ignoring it, I ran straight for the first bot, ducking into the darkness between spotlights. It turned my way.

I dropped into a slide. I fired into its chest, melting its core with several solid shots. It fell, and I caught its red-hot body with my metal hand.

The third bot fired. Flecks of hot metal stung my cheek. I returned fire, blind from pain and fear. My shots hit something metal. Something dropped. Far ahead, Legs fired several quick shots from his rifle.

"Get the ball," Legs shouted.

I heaved myself up and staggered to the buildings on the right side of the road, heart pounding. The domed buildings offered terrible cover, but it was a wall and I needed something. My vision returned, and I crouched low against the side of the hogan.

There were still thirty meters to go.

"You say it gets tougher?" I shouted up to Legs.

Legs laughed like a maniac.

"Glad someone's having fun," I muttered.

The plan of walking down the middle of the street wasn't going to work. My pistol had an effective range of around five meters, but wide-open spaces in the middle of the field guaranteed nothing would be approaching from less than ten. It'd be hard to close that distance each time. Better to stick to the tight corners and obstructed sight lines along the side alleys between buildings.

Crouching low, I dragged the bot along with, for use as a shield. I made no attempt to be silent. Silence was never really my strong suit. I was about as stealthy as a rockslide on a firecracker factory.

The hogans didn't offer great cover, but many of them were cracked and broken. With a quick hop, I ducked into one from the side, creeping through it to exit out the back. There was a bot there, its sharp, glowing eyes tracking back to where I'd entered. A quick double tap with the pistol took the back of his head and the center of his chest. It clattered to the ground in a heap.

The next hogan was intact, so I skirted around the outside of it. Most of the spotlights from above shone into the main street, so the darkness fell like a cloak around me. Once, I saw Legs jump from one hogan to the next—a flash of silver in the moonlight.

The crack of a rifle sounded up ahead, followed by the clatter of falling bots. The fountain was just a few meters away, and I could see the gleam of the metal ball shining in a dedicated spotlight.

Two bots stood on either side of the ball, scanning the surrounding area. These bots seemed faster, their movements harder to predict. I was hunkered down behind the remains of a brick wall, peeking over it with my hat off. Legs was up a short distance away, trying desperately to wave me forward. He didn't have a good line of sight to the fountain, or I expect he'd have already dispatched the bots. Once he popped up from hiding behind the rise of a dome, he'd be a sitting duck for anything we didn't drop immediately.

Putting my hat back on, I signed to Legs that there were two enemies and that he should take care of the farthest one.

Legs gave me a confused look.

I held up two fingers.

He nodded.

I motioned that on the count of three he was to jump up and take down the farthest bot with his rifle.

He gave me another confused look.

I shook my head. Using the still-glowing eyes of the bot that I carried, I checked on the pistol. There still wasn't any good indication of ammo count. Everything seemed to be in order, so I met Legs's eyes and mouthed, "One, two, three," then jumped over the wall.

The closest bot shot me before I even hit the ground. My metal arm jerked back, ringing out a clear note and throwing me slightly off balance.

I whipped the bot that I was holding up in front of me and let out a slow breath to steady my aim.

Another shot rang off of my left arm.

I fired. My target's head exploded into a shower of sparks. The bot behind it took a few plugs from Legs's rifle and ate dirt.

"Just grab it and toss it to me," Legs hollered from the roof. I could hear movement of more bots. There must have been dozens of them nearby, moving in on us. It sounded like we were surrounded. "I'll run it in while you hold them off!"

I looked down at the ball. It was a shining, silver thing with two dull eyes sunken into a painted face. I licked my lips, grabbed the thing, and pulled back to throw it.

A bullet whizzed past my ear. I ducked on reflex, almost dropping the ball. Instead of throwing it, I tucked it under my arm.

That's when the bots moved in.

First a few, then ten, then more than I cared to count. They sprang from the ground, emerging from the dozens of manhole covers that dotted the street. A wall of them formed between the bucket and myself. More swarmed from among the buildings. Rows of pulsar eyes pierced the dark blotches of night.

I dove behind the fountain, just as the first volley of bullets washed through the square. Dust and concrete kicked up around me.

There was no space, no room to maneuver in order to throw the ball to Legs.

But the buildings behind the fountain were clear.

Another wave of bullets scoured the square. The wall of bots was marching forward.

I ran for the nearest building, crashing through its ancient wooden door into a plaster room covered in dust. It was empty except—

I panic-fired three shots before I realized I'd come face to face with a mirror. Shards flew everywhere from the impact of the energized bullets.

The room only had one other doorway, so I took it. I worked my way back through the building—some kind of retail front from long ago—and exited into an alley.

My breath rasped as my lungs ached for oxygen. My poor heart pounded in my chest and I fought off a wave of dizziness. The bots scraped and clomped closer, circling around the building and moving through. There wasn't anywhere else to go.

I looked down at the ball.

It looked back up at me.

An idea worked its way into my thick skull. There wasn't any time to decide if it was a good idea, so I went with it. I stuffed the ball under my shirt. The bots were targeting eyes and that thing had a pair. I dropped the bot that I had been carrying as a shield and used my metal hand to rip the sleeve off of my shirt to make a makeshift blindfold. Once I was blind, I picked up the bot again, rubbed its face in the dirt as best I could, and then held it as far away from my body as I could.

I rounded the corner of the building by sticking the bot out first. The twang of bullets tugged at it a few dozen times. Good. They would target the makeshift decoy. Hopefully they would ignore me if they couldn't properly see my face.

The bots were close, and I pushed past the first wave of them. They'd shoot again soon, and I needed to move.

Another round of shots hit the bot, some missing and ricocheting off of my black metal arm. Others must have slammed into the bots behind me, because I could hear several of them start to flail and malfunction.

Fear kept me moving. It was impossible to know what their programming would make them do. Running might trigger more bullets. Maybe they got smarter as I got closer. Talking might trigger an attack.

"Hey, Sheriff," shouted Legs from the rooftops. "Toss it up here!"

Dozens of gunshots rang out and Legs screamed and dropped somewhere into the darkness.

I walked, ears guiding me. All of the bots were behind me now, so I turned and walked backwards so that I could hold the bot up where everything could get a good look at its pretty eyes. They were good eyes. Good for seeing; good for shooting.

Then they got shot.

I felt the bullet thunk into my bot's head, then there was the whump of an explosion.

My ears rang and my big metal hand was empty. The wide expanse of the street no longer felt all that comforting.

I turned, tore off the blindfold, and ran. Ten meters to go, I knew my timing was bad. They'd shoot before I made it.

I pulled the ball out from under my shirt, cupped it in my hand, and tossed it.

It lobbed through the air in a lazy arc.

The bots raised their pistols.

My left leg caught behind my right, and I went down in a great cowboy heap.

Shots rang out, whizzing above me.

The ball hit the bucket and went in.

Silence.

Pistols dropped.

I rolled over onto my back and didn't move until a somewhat pained-looking Legs stood over me.

"Good game," he said. He had a grin that damn near split his head in half. "You sure aren't much of a team player, are you?"

Rosa said to me, "He's been looking for a sucker to play that with him since he got Jared killed. I don't think he's ever won."

Legs offered a hand, and I took it. He hauled me up to my feet.

"Mind if I talk to Court now?" I asked.

"She's inside." Legs slapped me on the back. "Play another time, eh, *pendejo*?"

"No," I said. "No, I don't think so."

Chapter 14

Stepping into the church was like stepping into the blinding light of day after an eternity in darkness. Stained-glass windows shone with a light like sunlight, but brighter. Light from those windows all shone directly on the door, blinding me and forcing me to bow my head so my hat would shield my eyes. My vision slowly returned.

The church looked more like the writhing maw of an elder god than the proper place of worship it used to be. The floor was covered with black cords of all sizes. Like thick snakes, they crossed the walls and dangled from the ceiling. A mesh steel platform ran the circumference of the room and widened at the far side, where an altar had once been. Fourteen flat displays lined the walls, each showing a view of a town's main street or a building in the desert. They might have been live displays, because the images were all enhanced with nightvision. Holographic projectors in the center of the room displayed a map of Texas, from the Yellowstone crater all the way down to Old Mexico.

Across the room, a shape detached from the wall. Wisps of copper-red wire took the form of hair, accented with tiny motes of light that shone bright enough to be seen even in the triple daylight glow from the windows. The tall figure of an impossibly slender woman separated from its place amongst the mass of wiring that made up the far wall. The loose black of her clothing draped over her four long, slender arms in a way that was both casual and provocative. Shining steel nails tipped each of her long fingers.

I tipped my hat. "Court," I said.

"J.D." Her voice seemed to harmonize with itself when she spoke. She gestured with a hand. "Welcome."

"Sure."

Holographic projectors between us flickered, rendering the image of the street where Legs and I had just played his game. Legs was a hazy image directing drones as they cleaned up broken bots.

"I was thinking," Court said, "as you played games with the boy outside. We're not friends. We're not allies. You don't like me, and I don't like you." She leaned down and peered at me with pure yellow eyes. "So, why would you come to visit me in the middle of the night?"

She was right. Court and I were not anything like friends. Her recent respect for the law was more a matter of her respect for the new sheriff, not fear of the old one. Truth was, any other night I'd probably have run the other direction if Court came calling. She wasn't friendly, and she sure as hell wasn't my friend.

I strolled along one wall, my boots clanging against the steel walkway. The blinding lights were focused on the entrance, and once I left the spotlight I was able to take in a little more of my surroundings. There wasn't a damn bit of it that I understood. Tech laced the walls, floor, and ceiling. Conduits ran everywhere and the air smelled of a dry, electric heat.

"Stop," Court said.

I raised an eyebrow at that, but I stopped.

"You're getting too close to the Umbilical," she explained. "We can't risk you shutting down our operation, can we?"

"Umbilical?" Looking around, I spotted the cord she was talking about. It was gold with a silver stripe and ran from a central console to a junction where hundreds of other cables originated.

Her eyes narrowed. "They're hard to replace, as I'm sure you understand."

"You're afraid that I'll break it and break all of your toys?"

"No." She leaned in close and peered at me with her golden, glowing eyes. "We have a spare. I just don't want to have to kill you for such a terrible faux pas."

I cleared my throat. "Word is," I said, "that you're who people turn to for help."

Court tracked my movement with her unblinking eyes.

"Boy needs the tech to be a football star, he comes to you. Man needs to escape some debt, he comes to you. Woman needs to disappear, she comes to you." I pulled off my hat and held it against my chest. "So, here I am. I'm asking for help."

Court smiled, giving the impression of a coyote finding a day-old kill.

"See, there's some bad business going on. It's not something I can bring to the law and it's not something I can handle myself. I need weapons, explosives, and some way to get into..." I bit my lip. Court wasn't someone who would help without knowing details, but giving her details meant giving her power. "I need to crack open a vault."

Her laugh was an eerie, echoing chuckle. "Well, lawman, I was expecting you to guiltily skirt the edges of the law, but this is interesting. Are you raiding a private estate, then?"

"A bank."

"I hadn't pegged you as the bank-robbing type."

I spoke through clenched teeth. "Not my choice. It's something that's gotta be done, and I think you'll agree when you have the details."

She motioned for me to continue.

I stepped away from the Umbilical and slipped past an array of screens that appeared to be showing live feeds of several nearby towns. Dead Oak was recognizable in one of them, Josephine's junkyard visible at the outermost edge. Outside of her wall, I could see a pack of three canines sniffing around, scenting the air and moving back and forth.

"Swallow Hill," I said.

Court's expression darkened.

"Mess of trouble happening in that town."

"Tell me."

I took another step toward the Umbilical. Its weave shone in the glaring lights like the scales of a silver snake basking in the hot summer sun.

Court moved to follow me, but hesitated. "Tell me," she said again, her voice more insistent. Her exquisitely sculpted face was less than a breath away from mine.

"I need into that bank, and I need to do it without killing anyone and without getting caught. Thought you might be able to help with a job like that."

"I'm not sending my people anywhere near that town," she said. "I've lost too many already."

"I don't want your people."

"You'll owe me."

"How much?"

Court smiled again. "A favor."

I scowled. "What kind of favor."

"Oh, something simple, I'm sure."

I looked back at the screen, where the pack was circling around the junkyard's barrier. They were coyotes. It was hard to tell from the image on the screen; they might have been wolves. No, I thought, they were coyotes. Giant ones. Ugly.

"You have a deal, Court. Just get me the goods by sundown tomorrow."

She glided silently back to her seat near the altar. Her red hair flashed and flailed for a moment, attaching to the tech around it. "They're doing something forbidden, you know," she said in a soft voice.

"Forbidden doesn't bother me, ma'am," I said. "What they're doing is wrong."

"You don't understand. The sub-quantum net has only one field generator. That field is like a still pond centered around the tower and we're just little insects making waves in it." She cocked her head to one side. "That generator is in Austin; it's run by Goodwin."

I put my hat back on and strolled to the door.

"When a second transmitter comes online the two resonate. It causes disturbance in both fields, and if the power is just right, the two will collapse in a most catastrophic fashion." Her jaw relaxed and I got the impression that I was seeing her let her guard down. "Texas is in danger if that field drops, Crow."

I pulled the door open and squinted back through the blinding light at Court. "All of Texas isn't my problem," I said. "I'm just looking to save a few people in a small town from something that's doing them wrong."

Chapter 15

By the time I flew up on top of the ridge, I was so exhausted that I flopped onto the ground and didn't move until Zane nudged me with his boot.

An irritated grunt escaped my lips.

"Fine," he said. "Rest. You deserve it."

When I woke a few hours later, it was to the smell of frying meat and wood smoke. I shot up in a panic, heart racing as I felt at my chest, belly, ribs. The ribs did not appreciate me sitting up so fast. The pain in my metal arm had grown worse, and my head was pounding with a new headache. I wasn't on fire, though. Nobody was cauterizing wounds this time.

Zane watched all of this with a mildly amused expression on his face. The sky glowed red over the eastern ridge, but the sun wasn't yet up. The handsome city man had started a small fire, and on it he was cooking bacon and eggs in a thin metal pan.

"Mornin' sunshine," he said. He slid the breakfast foods into a bowl and set them down on a stone next to the fire. "Care for a bit o' grub?"

I rose, stretched, and cast off a thin blanket that I didn't remember having. The stone next to Zane was passably comfortable and the eggs and bacon were absolutely heavenly.

"The man can cook," I said.

"Among other things."

"Fine food's the way to a man's heart, Zane. Bacon's the way to his soul." Could this be the same guy I thought of as a manipulative sleaze? I crunched the last piece of bacon and licked my fingers. "Got anything to drink?"

"Just water and whiskey."

"Make it water," I said. "Save the whiskey for later."

He handed me a flask and I took a long drink. The water was warm and tasted like the sterile chlorine of city water, but any water is good after a long night in the desert. I closed my eyes and breathed the cool, dry morning air. A wind was picking up, sending the dusty scent of the wasted land up into the sky.

"Are you surprised that I can cook?" asked Zane.

"I'm surprised every time I meet a city boy who can do anything."

"You don't like us much, do you?"

I sighed. "It's not that."

"You just have this idea of what we are in your head and we're all the same to you. I know the look you keep giving me. It's distrust. You expect me to stab you in the back, either figuratively or literally."

"Will you?"

He gave me a dirty look.

"During the war your people killed mine. After the war, your people crushed our way of life. You didn't care what life was like out here, only that you had power and food."

"Life in the city isn't easy, you know." Zane was cleaning up his dishes and thrust the still-hot pan into its carrying case. "Up above it's all glitz and glamor, but down below things get pretty rough. Some of it would make life out here look like luxury."

"That's what it's all about, isn't it? Gotta be better at everything than us, even being bad?" I jammed my finger at his chest. "You just show up and demand that we jump and you expect us to jump. Goodwin's got something that needs doing, so he sends the right reasons to make me do his dirty work."

Zane pushed my finger away without breaking our locked gaze. "Your people killed mine too. *You* killed them."

We would do it again too. We might do it again. Maybe. "I don't like this," I said. "You know that."

"You backing out of this, Crow?" That quirky smile again. Was he taunting me?

"You damn well know I'm not." My fist clenched. "But you better know I'm not happy about it, and Goodwin better know that if he pushes us too hard we're not going to take it."

"You wouldn't fight."

"What did you just say?"

"You wouldn't fight. By 'not going to take it,' you mean you'll grumble and be upset, but you damn well know there's not going to be another Civil War."

My shoulders slumped. He was right. The people of Dead Oak didn't have another Civil War in them. Neither did the city folk. Corporations like Goodwin kept gaining power in the city. Nobody liked the way of the world, but nobody wanted change badly enough to risk their own life. Even my Hopi tribe's only solution was to withdraw from the world as it slowly crumbled. It was the peaceful solution, but really not a solution at all.

"I imagine you don't want to be around when I visit Tucker," I said. My metal hand slotted into the console of my skidder and the feel of power surged through me. "And Josephine won't let you near her junkyard. Looks like you're sidelined while the rest of us do the work."

Zane nodded.

"Make yourself useful." I scratched my head under my hat. "Head to the city and figure out Swallow Hill's history. Tech like I saw in that bank didn't come from the desert. We don't go for that kind of thing. It's got the smell of a corporation on it, but we're not going to know which one until you do some digging."

"Don't you think I've tried that? The data's been wiped." Zane kicked a rock off the ridge. "Obfuscated, anyway."

"Try harder."

His fists balled into tight knots. "Maybe *you* need to try harder."

"I've been."

"No, you've been sitting comfortable and playing safe." He tapped his ear with one finger. "That earpiece will help, J.D. It'll let you see what's happening, but you're too scared to take a risk. Too safe to trust one damn person."

I pulled the earpiece out of my pocket and looked at it. The slender tendril writhed in the morning sun. My lip twisted up in an involuntary expression of disgust. I flicked the piece at Zane and he caught it.

"You get that info and stick that in your own damn ear." I swung onto my skidder and hovered a couple meters up. "Did you see me play down in the town last night? Did you see how hard I had to work to get in that door to talk to Court?"

"Yeah."

"Try that hard. I'll worry about who I trust."

I launched myself up and away from the ghost town. The air was a cool breeze against my face. As I rose, the yellow sun broke the horizon, starting on its long mosey across the sky.

Chapter 16

Tucker Hale was a son of a bitch.

In fact, Tucker Hale was the son of a bitch that other sons of bitches looked to when they wanted to feel like charitable gentlemen.

In the war, he'd been one of my closest buddies. We were both naturals back then, capitalizing on our poverty and heritage to slip between the cracks in the enemy lines. Before I got my metal arm, I was one of the best. Tuck was better. He didn't hate tech the way I did. Once we slipped past the scanners he'd improvise weapons and wreak more havoc than a full frontal assault could possibly muster. He was handsome too and would often use his charm to woo his way into the secrets of those city-dwelling bastards.

He didn't look so handsome older and upside-down. I was the one upside-down, actually, but the effect was the same. His long, stringy gray hair and bulbous beer belly didn't do his square jaw many favors. His grin was missing a few of its teeth and all of its warmth.

There was plenty of time to contemplate how good Tucker had always been with traps as I spent the better half of the afternoon hanging upside-down from one of the half-dead trees on his estate outside of Dead Oak.

Tucker took a swig from a bottle of bourbon. "You dropped your hat."

I scowled at him, knowing full well that scowls have a funny way of not working upside-down.

"Wasn't sure if that'd hold you," he said. "Made it for them coyotes that've been skulking around lately."

It was a good trap. Thin metal cables held my feet while my metal arm was pinned to my body by another set of razor-sharp cables. My metal arm was strong enough to break the lines binding me, but if I tried I'd likely cut myself in half.

Tucker picked up my hat and put it on. "Well, J.D.," he said, "it was nice talking, but I'm going to be seeing you. You're not the sheriff anymore, so I'm going to assume you're just trespassing." He paused. "In fact, I've been getting a lot of trespassers lately. You know anything about that?"

"I ain't here to give you any trouble. Just talk."

He raised an eyebrow and took another swig. "Talk? Really?"

I nodded.

"I had no idea." His voice dripped with sarcasm. "Was that what you were here to do last time when you rolled in, guns blazing, and ran me and my buddies up to Iowa?"

Iowa was a prison plantation near the Canadian border. I had sent Tucker and his crew up there for a spell. "That was twenty years ago, Tucker." My head pounded from the rush of blood. "And you had it coming. You were robbing banks."

He chuckled. "We sure were. Them banks needed robbing, and you know as well as I did that it was nothing but city money we were taking. We were doing good."

"You were breaking the law."

He nodded, took a swig, and then turned to walk back to his house. "I was breaking *their* laws, J.D. Not any laws I recognized." The big, metal door closed behind him, leaving me to hang from an old oak.

An hour later, he came out, looked at me with feigned surprise, then returned to his house. I tried to call out to him, but my voice was nothing but a rasping whisper. The sun pounded down on me like it was trying to have me cooked in time for supper.

It seemed like hours after that when Tucker came out of his house again. He walked up to me, reached up, and loosened the ties around my feet, dropping me in a heap to the ground. Using a metal hook, Tucker snagged the wire wrapped around my feet and dragged me into the house. Razor wire dug deep into my arm, soaking my shirt with blood. Once we were inside, he cut the wire and let me loose.

Tuck's place closely resembled my own. He had a single chair, a single bed, and a single table. Light from circles on the walls suffused the room with a bluish glow. My place was mud and his was concrete, but otherwise we lived similar lives.

Tucker reached into a cooling unit under the bed and pulled out a couple of brown bottles with resealable caps. He popped one open and handed it to me, then popped the other and took a swig.

I sipped cautiously, feeling the cool fizz on my cracked lips. The brew was smooth, with a touch of bitter at the end. It smelled like honey and wheat, like fresh-baked bread.

"Good beer," I said.

"My own brew." He took another swig. "Gotta keep myself busy when I'm not robbing banks or holding up rich folks for their pocket change."

I smiled. "You always give folks such a warm reception?"

"You always send your war buddies to prison?" Tucker eyed my metal arm like he thought it was going to fly off and attack him.

I took another swig and rolled it around in my mouth. My side still stung where the wire had cut into my skin, but I was careful not to show any pain to Tucker. It would be a shame to give the cruel bastard that kind of satisfaction.

After a time, I broke the silence. "They say it's getting hotter next few days."

"I wouldn't know."

"Sure."

"Unless it's got something to do with brewing beer, I steer clear of the tech and trouble." He tipped his bottle at my arm. "Unless it comes looking for me."

"Can't help what I am, Tuck."

"Only what you do."

We sat in silence for a time, sipping beer and hiding from the heat in Tucker's little home. A few times I wanted to say something. An apology sat at the tip of my tongue for minutes, but never quite formed. What was I going to apologize for? Arresting him when he broke the law? Leaving him to fight the war after my arm had been severed?

"What are you here for, Crow?" He leaned forward in his chair. "You just here to reminisce?"

"Nope."

"Then what?"

"Need your help."

He raised an eyebrow and leaned forward some more. "Maybe you misunderstand the nature of our relationship."

I shook my head. "Believe me, Tuck. If I could leave you out of this, I would."

"Well, you're going to walk away disappointed, then." He stood up and stretched. "You're looking at my life here. I don't help people just for asking."

"Sure, but I have something you might be interested in doing."

"Spit it out."

"I want your help robbing a bank."

By the time he stopped laughing, I'd finished my beer and got halfway through a second. I told him everything that had happened in the past few days, from Zane's first visit to my little talk with Court. When I told him about the coyotes that I'd seen, his face got real serious.

"They ain't right," he said. "Them things are dangerous."

I thought back to the coyotes that looked like they were trying to get into Josephine's junkyard. "How dangerous?"

"They're smart. Big too." He bit his lip with crooked teeth. "Smart enough not to get into any traps I've put out, but I've seen them around. They've been close."

I nodded. "I saw tell near Overpass too. Bunch of them were up on a bridge over the town. More genetic modifications, I figure. Somebody let a population get out and we deal with the fallout."

Tucker grunted, took a big gulp of beer, and belched.

"So," I said after another minute. "Are you in?"

"What'd you get from the gang?"

I dug out my glow cube and pulled up the list of supplies. The image quivered in the air and it took me a minute to figure out that it was my hand shaking, not the cube. Tucker stared at the image for a minute, a grin spreading as he did.

"You have yourself a deal, Sheriff."

"I'm not a sheriff anymore, Tuck."

"No," he said. "No, you sure as shit are not."

Chapter 17

The sun's heat ravaged the ground below, but above, where the sky stretched forever, the air was cool. The world was at peace. With the skidder's new bubble activated, the sharp chill couldn't penetrate. I was alone without loneliness. It was serenity with none of the restlessness that comes with life. Nobody depended on me for justice or peace.

Loneliness had always been a part of me down below. It was only in the sky, truly alone, that I understood how that loneliness pressed on me. Shaped me. Even as a sheriff, when I was the heartbeat of a living, thriving community, lonesomeness ruled over me. I never had a real connection with another person. Maybe the war made me unable to connect with people. Maybe my mutilation made me too ashamed to try to connect with anyone who would care for me.

What would it feel like, not being alone?

Men of violence are always alone. Texas wasn't ever peaceful, far as I could tell. A gun or a fist were always worth more than a word and a pen. After the war, when I was a lawman, it was my gun that held the peace. My gun was the one that brought justice to hundreds of criminals and gangsters. But was it right? Was holding the people to some rules by force really doing anyone any good? Life used to seem so simple. Shoot the criminals; save the victims.

Except, nowadays everyone was a criminal. Everyone was a victim.

I'd left my gun at home because there just wasn't any way I could justify shooting anyone. I'd shot a mother in front of her kid. Sure, she was mixed up in some bad stuff. Sure, she was going to kill someone if I didn't act.

She didn't deserve death any more than anybody else. But she got it.

The gun at my hip weighed on me. I'd given up shooting, but here I was carrying a gun again. I could have dropped it from the sky. Something made me hold onto it. Maybe it was fear or an old habit, but the gun felt right at my side, even if I didn't plan on using it. Maybe it made me feel less alone.

According to Ben Brown, his brother Francis had gone missing. Francis had contacted me, and even if I didn't know where he was, I might be able to help. The Brown ranch was below, just as I remembered it. A stout farmhouse jutted out of the dry earth, and a short distance away the enormous cattle barn sat in the red earth like a black, cancerous lump. The place was surrounded by squat black windmills, collecting power from the sharp wind and searing sun of the Texas climate—two resources that were in ample supply.

I drifted down, making for a spot near the barn where I could see a dark form working amongst the dry grass. As I got closer I could see that it was Ben, no longer the kid I knew, but bigger. Harder. He was tall, nearly as tall as myself. Ben was independence and rebellion shoehorned by circumstance into the drab routine of life. His mohawk was spiked and metallic. The black poncho that he wore seemed to shift with a will of its own. His left hand was a finely crafted steel limb, which he used to direct several humming drones. His jaw was set as he worked, as if he were pushing himself forward through sheer force of will.

"J.D.," he said without turning to face me. "Thought you'd forgotten about me."

My skidder lit gently on the dry ground, thrusters igniting the dry grass. I hopped off and used my metal hand to smother the fire before it could become dangerous.

Ben waved his hand to send a couple drones south across the sea of windmills. "Go home, old man," he said.

I patted my pockets looking for a cigarette, but didn't find one. Instead, I plucked a piece of grass and stuck it in my mouth.

He turned to look at me. "Well?"

"Seems to me you still need help."

"Not from you." He waved his hand again and a couple more drones zipped away. "I called you days ago. Days."

I grunted. "Came as soon as I could."

"Great." He stepped up and put a finger on my chest. "Leave as soon as you can too, then we'll be even."

Shaking my head, I leaned back on my skidder. "Wanna tell me what's happening first?"

"No." He bit his lip. "Well, kinda." Waving a hand, he sent the last two drones to the east. "Hell, I've got nobody else. Francis is gone and I don't know what to do about it."

"What about your big brother? What about the rest of your family?" When I'd last seen the Brown family there were more siblings than I cared to count.

"Gone." His shoulders slumped. "Jason took the rest of them away to live in Austin. Said it wasn't safe to have them way the hell out here."

I nodded.

"Not with Francis around, anyway."

That got my interest. "What makes you say that?"

"Francis hasn't ever been right in the head, but since Ma died he's been..."

"Worse."

"Yeah. Not a lot at first. Mostly just quiet. Six months ago, he suddenly got interested in some of the old junk in the barn." Ben kicked a metal harness, and it scattered into pieces across the cracked dirt. "That's why I'm going through this stuff. Something in here might give me a clue as to what he's up to."

A hot breeze rose and tugged at my hat. My lips were dry and cracked, thirsty from all the work I'd done in the past couple days. Still, I felt bad for not visiting Ben sooner. He needed help and I'd ignored his pleas. I picked up one of the pieces of the harness, wincing at the pain the movement caused me. Ben's eyes lost focus and a light flashed in them. He bit his lip at what he saw, but didn't say anything.

"Why do you do that?" I asked.

"Do what?"

Gesturing at his whole body, I said, "All of that. Arms, hair, eyes, ears. Every time I see you there's less of you to see."

He cocked his head to one side. "We do what we do to get ahead." He scratched the back of his neck. "Or at least keep up."

"You do it 'cause everyone else does."

"Something like that." His eyes flashed again, and he smiled. "It's better, though, you know. I mean, you got your arm. Don't you think it works better than flesh and bone? It's just science, man. Full upgrade all the way through."

I looked at my massive metal arm. "I hate this damn thing."

"Do you?"

"It's not the same as what you got. You got a choice. When you upgraded it was because you looked at what was out there and you wanted it."

"I was a stupid kid sometimes, but yeah."

"Mine was done to me by people I thought I trusted with the sole purpose of making me a better soldier."

"So, replace it." He held up his metal hand and wiggled his fingers. If they didn't shine in the sunlight, it might be hard to tell that they were fake. "Modernize."

"That's just it, though. Once you get into that upgrade loop you're stuck in it. Better arm might be nice, but how long till I want better hearing or eyesight." I pulled off my hat and ran my fingers through my hair. "Better hair."

He seemed to consider that for a moment. "End is the same, though, isn't it, whether you choose it or not? You accept what you are or you don't. Seems like you don't."

"Did Francis accept what he was?"

"Nobody but nobody understood what was going on in my brother's head."

"Is it possible he met someone six months ago?" I asked. "Could someone have finally figured him out?"

"Dunno." Ben hesitated, like he was considering his words carefully. "He'd always been pretty secretive. He'd be on his optics pretty much all the time messing around with the tech. I tried to stop him a few times. I'm supposed to be in charge, right?" He looked to me like he wanted an answer, but I didn't give one. "Well, it didn't go well. He fought. Little guy's fierce too. You ever met someone stubborn as you, J.D.?"

"Nope."

"Well, you should give Francis a look. He's got some chops."

"So he stayed on the optics?"

"Yeah. And I didn't have the heart to just shut them down. So, he could have been in contact with anyone. His tech was top notch. Ma always got him all the best stuff right from the start." Ben pulled a cheroot from a hidden compartment in his metal hand and lit it using a flame that snapped up from his thumb. He nodded at the house and started walking in that direction.

I followed. "So he might have contacted someone out there. You think there might be foul play? Was he kidnapped?"

"Maybe." He shook his head. "I don't think so, but maybe."

We walked in silence for a minute before something clicked in my thick skull. Ben was hiding something. There was some piece of the puzzle he was holding back. "Francis contacted me yesterday," I said. "He wanted to show me something."

Ben seemed more worried at this. "Can you call him back?"

I shook my head. "Not that I can figure. He covered up the call so when I call back it doesn't go anywhere."

"He wanted to show you something, but didn't give you a way to get back to him?"

"That about figures it."

"See, it's things like this. He's been more and more erratic like this for a while now."

"He's a kid."

"He's a smart kid. Really smart." Ben took a drag on his cheroot.

"Tracking a tech trail isn't really my thing. Why call me and not the sheriff?"

"I think you know."

"You think he's into something illegal. You don't want him sent away."

Ben nodded.

We reached the house. Ben poured two glasses of lemonade from a chilled carafe sitting on a small table on the porch. He offered me one and I gladly downed it. The drink was sweet and tart, and the icy chill swept through me in a wave of relief. It was just what I needed.

"So, what do you say?" Ben was looking at me with stubborn defiance. It was hard for him to ask for help. If he was coming to me, then I suspected there wasn't anywhere else he could turn.

"Yeah, I'll help." I held up the harness I'd picked up earlier. "But you have to tell me what this does."

He studied my face for a minute, then looked down at the harness. "I don't know."

I held it up, spreading it out with my huge metal hand. "See the shape of it?"

"Horse?"

"Yeah." I handed it to him. "What's all this tech good for on a horse?"

He squinted at it. "It's neural tech, but I'll need to mess with it to figure out how it works."

"Do it," I said. "And I'll help you find Francis."

"You were going to help, anyway."

He was right. There was a weariness behind his eyes that made me think of how harsh life had been to him. It made me wish I could be there for him, help him out more. But I hadn't done anything for him. Four years ago, he had been the rebel of the family. He could have left once tragedy hit. He didn't. I'd help him find his brother if I could.

"He's out there." I slapped Ben on the back. "We'll find him, Ben, but right now I have someplace I need to be."

"Where?"

"You wouldn't believe me."

Chapter 18

As the scarlet sun kissed the western horizon, I closed the solar panel in my arm. The battery wasn't charged up enough, but it would have to do. I leaned back against the WRONG WAY sign outside of the Swallow Hill dead zone. Josephine's floating tank loomed back in the ruins next to the black asphalt of the ancient road. My skidder and Zane's car sat next to it, barely squeezing into the secluded area.

"It won't hurt," Zane said.

"It'll probably sting a little," Abi said. She punched me in the shoulder, then winced as if it hurt her hand. "You can handle it, though."

"You sure this needs to be done?" I asked.

Zane looked annoyed at the question, which wasn't surprising since it was probably the twentieth time I'd asked it. "Yes. It's the only way to collect enough information to put an end to this."

Abi smirked at me. "It's not a big deal. It's only one side, so you'll still be able to see everything all normal-like."

I looked at her. "Why are you here?"

She bit her lip. "Auntie said I could—"

"She didn't, did she?"

"Implied that I could help." Abi held up a can of spray paint. "Nothing dangerous, see?" With that, she darted away, moving down to the edge of the dead zone.

The coin sat in my palm, its little tendril wriggling. I couldn't believe what I was going to do, but Ben was right. There was a choice. That made all the difference. Zane's earpiece was an upgrade, but it was a minor one. It would come out when I wanted it to—if I wanted it to—and the information it gathered could be critical. Zane wasn't going to be able to track down who was behind Swallow Hill until he was able to upload some data from the actual town.

"It's harmless." Zane tapped his own ear. "Everyone has one these days, and this one is proven technology. Nothing crazy about it."

"Doesn't look harmless."

"Neither do you." Zane smiled at me with his quirky grin. "Just stick it in your ear."

I stuck it in my ear. Nothing happened.

"It's backwards."

I pulled the device out and looked at it. The flattened metal looked benign enough, but the wire sticking out of one side was intimidating. I flipped it around and stuck it in my ear, wire side in.

The tendril wiggled and probed around, tickling me as it searched out my inner ear. The metal coin pressed itself in firmly, shaping itself as it fit closer and closer.

Then there was pain. A sharp pop rang in my ear, followed by a rushing sound of fluid. Twin needles dug deep into my skull under the earpiece. I clawed at it, trying to pull it loose, but it wouldn't budge. It was buried too deep. The needles turned to snakes, streaming under my skin. One dug down to my jaw and one to my right eye.

Each feathered out in a wave of tiny pricks. My right eye went blind.

Gasping, I blinked and stared at the ground. I was on my hands and knees, though I didn't remember dropping. The pain eased into a throbbing warmth, then to nothing. Each breath rushed like a tornado through my head. Vision returned to my eye.

"Well, it might sting a little," Zane said.

"They're late." Tucker was behind us. His voice boomed through my skull.

I twisted around, wrenching my bad ribs. Tucker stood there in black fatigues with two rifles strapped to his back and a bandoleer of grenades dangling across his belly. He tossed a black backpack to the ground. There was no evidence that he had arrived in a vehicle. He seemed to have appeared from nowhere.

"They'll be here," I said. My own voice felt like it was piercing holes in my right eardrum. I stood up and faced Tucker, but the quick movement made me nauseated. The world seemed to spin and my right eye dodged in and out of focus.

Zane put a hand on my shoulder. "Give it a minute, J.D."

"If they don't show, then I ain't going." Tucker spat on the ground. "We had a deal."

Out of the corner of my eye I saw Abi approaching. The image in my right eye zoomed in on her face, flickered her name on the display, and performed all manner of irritating distractions. No wonder nobody ever paid attention when people spoke.

Tucker lowered his voice to a growl. "Maybe you're wasting my time, J.D. Maybe I'll just get paid by pushing over your money man."

My jaw clenched so hard it hurt.

"Maybe I'll take that heap of spare parts your girl brought and see what it's worth on the open market."

"Hey!" Abi stepped up next to us. "That's not yours to take."

Tucker gave her a wolfish grin. "Looks like salvage to me."

Abi's jaw worked. Apparently unable to find sufficient words, she threw an empty paint can at his head. He ducked to avoid it.

"I missed this, old boy," he said to me amid guffaws. "You've made some great friends, partner."

Abi narrowed her eyes at him.

"Tuck was in the war," I explained. "He's not quite right."

"I don't trust him," Abi muttered so quiet I could barely hear it, even with my newly enhanced ear.

"Well," I said. "You probably shouldn't. But Tuck and I were in the war together. There's a common bond. Ain't that right, Tuck?"

Tuck held his belly and laughed a little more. "You remember the spider? Aw, hell, that's what it's all about, right?"

"Spider?" Zane asked.

"Yeah." Tucker gestured at Bessie. "'Bout that big. Mean sonoffa bitch."

Abi said something, but I couldn't hear what.

"Twin rattlers on top," said Tucker. "Rattlers, you know, the big guns?"

Zane's brow furrowed.

"You get the idea. Anyway, thing was coming in—"

"Excuse me," Abi spoke up.

"Thing come in blazing, and everyone was running from it because, hell, you don't mess with those things.

Someone builds a spider for war, they likely mean business, you know?"

"Yup," I said.

"So, J.D. here saw it coming and—"

"Hey!" Abi stepped up and waved a hand right in front of Tucker's face. He blinked and looked down at her. She seemed to shrink into herself a little, but pointed at a screen on her wrist. "They're here."

Then they were. Two roaring vehicles, just bigger than my skidder, came bounding over a rise a short distance away. They were wheeled vehicles, antiques gone out of style long before my day. These were nothing like the flimsy flyers of modern times. Full combustion was an extravagant luxury and had been for years, ever since cheap antigrav. These were fancy six-wheeled transports that would have been considered status symbols to a certain class of middle-aged man. These were recreational vehicles that rode much like motorcycles, but with more stability. There was no armor on the two six-wheeled vehicles. They weren't machines of war, but they were what we needed. Low-tech and fast.

Legs rode atop one of the six-wheelers, and Rosa brought the other. They both landed hard, sending sparks behind them as metal struck the road. When they were only twenty meters away, they slammed on the brakes and skidded to a stop in front of us. Legs bounded off, rolled, and stood in front of me seconds before the last trace of the sun dipped below the western horizon.

"Sunset!" He grinned like an idiot.

"Where's the rest of it?" I had to shout over the noise of the roaring engines.

Rosa slid off her ride and popped open a storage compartment. I nodded to Tucker, who put on his handsomest, slimiest smile and sidled up next to the woman to inspect the goods.

In the distance, another vehicle was only a dot on the horizon.

"That's my ticket home," said Legs. "Now you just remember, grab 'n' go. All right?"

"That the strategy they're using these days?" I asked.

"Worked for our game, right?"

"Son," I said. "That was a shit strategy for that game."

"But it worked."

"We won. Doesn't mean it was a good plan."

He scrunched up his face like he was thinking. "They say no plan survives contact with the enemy, don't they?"

I nodded.

"Then you might as well start with a shit plan."

Tucker gave a cry of excitement. He pulled a dozen orange canisters from the six-wheeler and grinned like an idiot. "Incendiaries," he said. "My favorite!" He attached the grenades to his belt in a neat row.

Zane's lip curled up in an expression of mild disgust. He shook his head and offered Legs a thin data stick. "Payment."

"Thank you much."

"It's ten thousand stars plus a little extra for your silence."

Legs smiled. "They've been trying to buy that for ages. Turns out I don't have any left and it'd take the Milky Way to buy it if I did."

Rosa rolled her eyes, grabbed Legs by the ear, and dragged him away. The two walked over the same rise from which they'd arrived and soon the flying vehicle dipped down, presumably to pick them up.

As Zane turned to leave, he stopped and leaned close, whispering in my ear. "If you find the tech that's causing this, get it. Don't let Tucker pick it up and don't just blow it to smithereens. We need it to stop what's coming next."

I opened my mouth to respond, but he had already moved past and was whistling Dixie on the way to his car.

Abi said, "J.D.?"

"Abi."

"You know you don't need to do this, right?"

My aches all weighed down on me. "Well, I was just about to say the same thing to you."

"You could tell the sheriff if there's something wrong going on over there. Why do you need to take care of it yourself?"

"You don't need to be here," I said. "Zane's my getaway driver. You're really not needed."

Silence wrapped itself all around us as the sky slowly dimmed. Zane and Tucker organized the contents of the six-wheelers, arranging things so Tucker would be able to get what he needed quickly.

Abi broke the silence with barely a whisper. "I want to help those people."

"So do I." I put an arm around her shoulder and she leaned into it. "Hell, I want to help all of them. That's not how this world works, though."

"Then why are you doing anything?"

"Can't help it." I sighed and faced the girl. "I've got buttons that can be pushed and they've been pushed. I pretend like there's a choice, but there not. Not really. This has got to be done and it's got to be done now."

Abi's brow hardened in determination.

"Look," I said, "what you pulled with Tucker earlier, that's not a good idea."

"I can handle myself."

"I'm sure you can." I nodded to Tucker, who had stripped off his sweat-soaked shirt. "But so can he."

She stepped back. "Quit it, J.D."

I gave her a questioning look.

"Quit patronizing me. You treat me like a little kid and I'm not. I've been through plenty of shit to know what I'm doing."

"It's not—"

"I'm more than you think," she said. "I can shoot. I can handle a knife. I'll do whatever it takes. Do you think Aunt Jo would have let me out of her junkyard if I wasn't ready?"

"Did she?" I asked. "Let you out?"

"She wouldn't come herself."

"That's not what I asked."

"I'm ready."

"There's ready for life and then there's ready for this."

Tucker slammed the compartment lid. "Go time!"

I mounted the second six-wheeler and tipped my hat at Abi. "Get back home."

She didn't say a word and I didn't listen. My gaze locked with Zane's and he smiled his crooked smile. He held his hat against his chest and the red sky framed hair that was quite a bit messier than I ever thought a city boy's hair could get.

With a twist of the accelerator, the six-wheelers blasted through the no-fly zone at the edge of Swallow Hill's disturbance without so much as a sputter. The augmented eye in my head flickered and my ear buzzed, but soon we were cruising at unsafe speeds down a broken and twisted road.

Chapter 19

Nobody expects antiques to show up in combat. The six-wheelers were antiques, once owned by wealthy hotshots trying to impress everyone with their ancient tech. They were noisy, smelly, loud, and uncomfortable. Despite that, there was no way the defenses outside of Swallow Hill would expect them.

Just after sunset is a tough time for tech. Targeting systems have trouble picking out movement in the dim light. The heat signatures of bodies tend to blend into the background of the still-hot earth. Despite all our noise and smoke, we managed to slip past the perimeter defenses. Those ancient turret towers blinked eerily in the cooling eve, but they didn't attack.

Not everything ignored us.

The first shot from town pierced the front left tire of my six-wheeler. The crack of the shot echoed off the hills behind the town, fading like the dying light of day.

The vehicle fumbled, swerved. I managed to regain control. Signaling with one hand, I ordered Tucker to start his circle early. I was fifty meters ahead of him and we'd planned it so I'd draw fire while he made his approach.

I hit the gas, twisting the accelerator hard and trying to maintain control as the vehicle lurched forward. Something smelled like burning tar, and black smoke belched out of the back of the vehicle.

Another shot whizzed by, foiled by a last-second swerve. I tucked my head down and moved the vehicle to the side of the road. My vision doubled. I closed my modified eye.

The bank was in sight, looming at the edge of town. There were a few people in the street, but nobody close to that sturdy structure. That was good. We'd have a shot at taking care of things before the area got too busy.

The old man in the overalls standing on top of the bank tracked my movement. So that old bastard was guarding the town. I swerved again, then back. Vertigo washed over me. My six-wheeler lurched into the ditch. The uneven ground would make me harder to hit.

A crack of another shot, and the engine in front of me was belching black, oily smoke. Blinded, I wrestled the machine, trying to keep it on course. I closed my eyes tight and ducked below the smoke as best I could. The engine squelched and screamed, but still somehow kept running.

It wouldn't hold much longer. I blinked through the tears and smoke, but still got nothing but a blur. I twisted the accelerator all the way up again, reached back and grabbed my pack from the storage compartment, and jumped.

My metal arm hit first, taking the brunt of the impact.

Not all of it. I skidded along my elbow and the side of my leg. When I'd slowed down enough, I rolled and stopped in a crouch. My pistol was still in my holster, but it'd be useless at this distance, so I left it there. Far to the right I could see Tucker still on his six-wheeler, bounding across the rugged dirt. Hopefully my distraction would work.

From the supply bag I pulled out a pair of fist-sized steel cubes. When I smacked the button on top of each of them, they unfolded into man-sized robots, much like the ones Legs had back at the Cinco Armas compound. Only, these were flimsier and unarmed. As they rose, a holographic image flickered to life, making the things look like gun-toting, hollering cowboys. I slapped the two bots on the back, setting them trotting forward and made my way around, circling closer to the bank at the edge of town under cover of rocks and brush.

Another shot echoed, making a crater of my six-wheeler. The explosion set the bots staggering backward and my ears ringing.

It was going to be bad news if that turret fired even one shot at old Tuck. His payload was considerably more volatile than mine had been. I looked back at my two decoy bots.

One of them was missing a head; the other was walking around in a tight circle like it thought it could bite off its own ear.

I swore.

Standing, I took off my hat and waved it in the air. "Hey!" My voice was harsh from the smoke, but I still had a good volume. "Remember me?" My sore feet took me forward, around the jagged, smoking hole that used to be my six-wheeler.

The man took aim and fired. The shot went wide.

"Shit!" I put my hat back on and broke into a run.

Tuck swung wide and ran into some rough ground. He dropped into a ditch, out of sight. The old man focused on me.

I dove for cover. Another shot rang out. Then I noticed. It was just like those bots that Legs had me fighting. The old man didn't just fire as quickly as he could. He fired every six seconds. Exactly.

One, two. I leapt out of cover and sprinted for the next cover. It wasn't far. Three, four. I dove. Five, six.

Crack. A shot rang out.

One, two. Running hard, my heart racing. Tucker's six-wheeler jumped out of the ditch, only to dip back down below on the other side of a rise. Three, four, five.

Dive.

Six. *Crack.*

Gasping for breath, I sprinted again. One, two, three, four. I wasn't going to make it. Five, six.

Crack. My arm clanged and I spun. Stumbled. Fell. Wind knocked out of me.

One, two. Gasping for air. Three, four. A football-sized stone right in front of my face. Five.

I snatched the stone up in my giant hand and threw it as hard as I could.

Six.

Wham! The stone hit the old man. He toppled and fell in a heap.

He didn't move. Tuck and I met at the bank and I checked the old man's vitals. Dead. Shit.

"Shoot anyone who comes around that corner," Tuck said.

"What?" I grabbed his shoulder. "No, Tuck. I'm not shooting anyone."

"They'll have heard the shots."

I shook my head. "I don't think they have."

Tucker didn't seem affected at all by the old man's death. He popped open the storage compartment on his six-wheeler and snatched up two spray cans. "Foam door," he said with a little giggle of glee. He sprayed the wall with a sticky yellow foam that immediately started eating into the stone surface.

"Acid?" I said. "I thought you were an explosives man."

He grinned. "Explosives are nice if you don't have the good stuff. And this ain't acid."

The stuff hissed away at the wall. It'd already cleared a few centimeters, and some bare metal was starting to show. Tucker applied another layer as inert sludge sluiced down and mixed into the dirt. While we waited for it to work, I took out my glow cube and did a forensics scan on the old man. The way he had moved had been odd, almost robotic. Maybe a scan would tell me why.

"Looks like acid," I said to Tuck.

"It ain't acid. It's nanomachines, like that shit you got running around in your blood." His whisper was getting louder.

Peeking around the corner, I got a good look at the townspeople. Had they heard the gunshots? There was a couple sitting on the bench, but when I saw them another wave of vertigo hit and I staggered back.

"J.D.!" A female voice hailed me from around the corner. Shit. Someone had seen me. I recognized the voice. It was Trish, my old deputy and the current sheriff. "You get your ass out here pronto or there's going to be a reckoning."

Tucker's eyes got wide. He shook his two cans and applied another layer of the foam door. It was nearly a forearm's length in, so it had to be close. "Stall her," he said. "I'll get in and grab the goods."

"Don't grab," I whispered, remembering that Zane wanted to get his hands on the tech. "Just wreck it."

He shook his head. "You know what that's worth?"

Trish hollered, "J.D., you got ten seconds!"

"It ain't worth nothin' if you're dead, Tuck. And we need to disable it."

"I'll hack fast."

I grabbed a fistful of his fatigues and got my face close to his. "Blow it up, Tuck. That's an order."

"Five seconds!"

Tucker's face got red. "You ain't my boss, J.D. Shove off."

"Three, two—"

I stepped around the corner, pistol holstered, but my fingertips brushed the handle.

There stood Sheriff Contrisha Chin in the dying light of dusk. She was a slender woman, but stood with a steady authority that made my words stick in my throat. Her long duster swayed gently in the night breeze and her fitted leather vest looked far too perfect to be the proper gear of a working person. It was hard to tell how much of her was still flesh and bone, but her slender mechanical fingers rested comfortably on the custom-formed handle of a sidearm.

"Hands up," Trish said. The sound of her voice felt like broken glass in my spine. It was an irritating combination of privilege and pitch. "I don't know what your deal is here, J.D., but it's done."

I didn't put my hands up.

She drew her weapon.

Mine was up just as fast.

Our eyes met and seconds ticked.

"Drop the weapon," she said. Her voice, though full of authority, had a quiver in it.

"Drop yours, Sheriff."

Long seconds passed. The timbre of drunken singing came from the saloon and in the distance I could hear the desert coming to life with owls and the things that run from them. Behind me, around the corner, I heard a long creak of metal bending. Tucker was inside, I figured. So in a few seconds, there ought to be an explosion.

"You won't shoot," I said.

She blinked.

"Neither will I, though." I lowered my weapon. "This isn't what you think. There's something going on here that..."

Behind her, in the yellow light cast from the window of the tavern, a man sat in a rocking chair. I had to blink a few times to understand what was happening, but once it clicked, I holstered my gun.

Two images of the man hit my brain at the same time. In fact, the town itself—what I could see of it— seemed to have a dual nature. My left eye picked up what it always had. There wasn't any fancy augmentation and it hadn't been hijacked by Zane's tech. The right eye saw something entirely different.

To the right eye, the town was beautiful. Buildings had immaculate façades, with fresh paint and clean brick. The signs were bright and polished. The bank fit in this view of the world. It wasn't out of place because both the architecture and the cleanliness of it blended perfectly with the building next door. The man in the chair was well dressed, with a crisp suit coat and a black top hat.

I holstered my weapon and held my hands in the air. "Don't trust your eyes, Trish."

Trish scowled something fierce and my mistake hit me. She couldn't hear what I was saying any better than she could see what was going on. She might be hearing something completely different or she might not be hearing anything at all. Was that how it worked? Or did everyone hear and see the same lies?

Trish dropped her weapon and closed the gap between the two of us faster than I could blink twice. Her fist shot at my face—

I deflected the blow with my metal hand. The metal-on-metal clang rang out in the empty street.

She was too fast. Her leg had come down behind my foot so when I tried to step back I stumbled.

Instead of dropping, I rolled away, coming up with a backhand swing of my huge left hand.

I missed, but took her balance. When I followed up with a right, she took it hard in the stomach. It didn't faze her one bit, but it damn near broke my fist.

Two gunshots sounded from inside the bank.

The vision in my right eye flared. For a moment the eye was blinded. Everything went white as a sheet, then black as night. It was followed by a staggering headache that only got better when I covered that eye.

Tucker revved the engine on his six-wheeler.

Trish staggered back away from the bank. My right eye was recovering, so hers must be too. The image coming back was normal, no longer the false overlay I'd seen before. She would get the real thing too, which was good; she would figure out what was happening. I ran straight for Tucker's six-wheeler.

Only, he didn't wait for me. By the time I got around the corner, he was fifty meters away.

My shoulders slumped. Mission was accomplished, but I'd been abandoned.

The gaping hole in the bank was right there next to me. I stepped inside, careful not to touch the edges of the hole where the wall was still being eaten away. A light flickered in the blackness of the bank, illuminating like lightning the grisly scene inside. The smell of burned rubber and blood hit me as I stepped into the building.

The vault door had been opened without damage or force. The massive black metal door hung loosely on its hinges. Inside the vault, a snake pit of wires haphazardly covered everything. Color was washed out by a flickering light, but the walls glistened wetly.

The thing in the center of that room had once been a girl. She had been shot in the head and the heart, but it was hard to believe that she'd even been alive at the time of the shooting. So much of her was missing. Her arms, legs, and half of her torso had been completely replaced with writhing wires. Her hairless head was missing half of its skull, with the back half replaced with lobstered steel and bundled conduits. There was a short console just in front of her. In it was a cube-shaped slot, the same size of my glow cube. The slot was empty.

My knees went weak.

The sound of a pistol cocking perked up my ears.

"J.D." Trish's voice was a calm drawl. "If you don't think I'll shoot you right in the back of the head, then you just go right ahead and move."

I sure as hell didn't move.

Chapter 20

"I'll handle him, Flores," Trish said to Swallow Hill's sheriff.

The three of us stood in the tavern with a rather dumbstruck barkeep. It was hard to blame him. The whole place had suddenly turned shabby in his eyes. He was no doubt questioning his own sanity. Sheriff Flores had the same look in his eyes, but Trish seemed to take the change without much trouble.

"It's my town," Flores said. "My jurisdiction."

"That's not a jurisdiction I recognize. Anyway, seems you might have more important things to tend to here." Trish nodded to the street, where people were starting to gather.

Flores looked around, eyes lingering on the shabby décor of the tavern. His lip turned up in disgust. "That man's responsible for this. Stringing him up is part of fixing it."

"He's my bounty and I'll see it through." She sat down at a small, wobbling table in the tavern. "I don't know what you did, J.D., but you've sure as hell done it."

"So, that's it then." Tension seemed to ease out of my shoulders. I slumped into my chair and breathed deeply. "It's done."

"Seems like. Your partner left you behind, old man." Trish signaled the barkeep for two whiskeys and he promptly brought them over.

Sheriff Flores stood impotent for a moment before storming out. I didn't envy the man his task of explaining to his people why their whole town seemed to have gone to shit over the course of the evening.

I had an e-cuff on my metal arm. It was latched on hard and it sent a signal that shut down all of my tech. Standard law enforcement when a dangerous criminal is half machine. It was humiliating and a little painful, but it kept my nannies from pre-processing alcohol, so the whiskey wouldn't be a waste.

Trish downed both shots, one after the other, and showed her teeth in a grimace. "Good stuff."

"Best around," I said. My mouth felt mighty dry.

Trish narrowed her eyes at me and shook her head. "I can't figure it out, J.D. You're going to have to clue me in. What the hell happened to get you mixed up in all this?"

After a few minutes of silence, Trish ordered a couple more whiskeys, this time pushing one my direction.

"For old times, then," she said. "Back when you wouldn't tell me a damn thing."

"I was done." I downed the shot. "Done with all this, but I suppose it wasn't done with me."

Trish folded her arms and looked me over.

"Trish, there's tech outta control around here. Until we hit that bank, something made your eyes see what wasn't there and your ears hear what wasn't said. Someone was messing with people's headgear and people were getting killed because of it."

The only movement she made was to raise an eyebrow. Hell, she was good at this.

"I wasn't going to come to you," I said. "I know you'd want me to, but you're as vulnerable to all this as anyone."

She sighed. "What led you to all this, J.D.?" She ordered another couple whiskeys and pushed one to me. She sipped hers.

I downed mine in a gulp and slammed the glass down. The first shot was already making my head swim. One of the side effects of nannies that preprocess all of your alcohol is that your liver doesn't build up much of a resistance.

Tapping my right eye, I said, "Seen it myself, with my own eye."

"Well, I'll be damned." She squinted at me. "You went and got eye augments."

"Just the one."

She looked at me like I was just about as crazy as a housecat hunting longhorns. "Nobody gets just one. You'll give yourself a headache."

"The ear too. I can hear what's changed because I only got half."

"You're paranoid, J.D."

I nodded. "Sometimes that's not such a bad thing."

She leaned in close. "What happened out there? One moment it was a nice little town and the next it was Shit Town, Texas."

"It's always been Shit Town, far as I could tell. The tech"—I tapped my augmented eye—"tricks people into thinking everything is just fine."

"Doesn't make sense. Why would they do that?" She looked around the tavern. It was as rundown and shoddy as the first time I'd visited. "People would be able to feel the difference. Smell it. Taste it."

"Folks look for a lot of ways to deal with their positions in life." I nodded to the whiskey. "Like I said, that's some fine whiskey. Smell or touch might tip folks off, but how often have you had trouble finding the source of an odor? Since when do you notice when something's rougher or smoother than it should be?"

"I suppose."

"Folks will do what it takes to convince themselves that everything is right."

"Like break the law?"

"Sometimes."

"Who's your partner?"

"Just look at the tech in that bank, Trish. It ain't no bank. It's something worse. There was a kid in there and..."

Trish didn't seem to be listening.

She took a sip from her whiskey and ordered me another, which I downed as soon as it hit the table. The room spun. Whiskey. The warm blanket of intoxication was wrapping itself around me and I welcomed it.

Trish shook her head as if to clear it and looked around the room. Her tone turned conversational. "What've you been up to lately, J.D.? I mean, besides robbing banks."

"The Hopi have been good." I tried my damnedest to focus on her face, but it was getting harder. "I'm a little bit of a handyman. Horse wrangler." I chuckled to myself. "Spiritual leader."

"I've always thought those folks did fine out there, but if they've got you as a spiritual leader, there must be something horribly wrong."

"Indeed."

"What do you tell them? Transcendence of shooting squirrels?" She wasn't looking at me. She squinted hard at the bartender.

I shook my head. "Hey, you gotta watch out for squirrels." There were eight empty shot glasses in front of me. Had I drunk eight shots of whiskey? Maybe. I was seeing double. Holy shit, had I drunk sixteen? "Had some visitors from up north. Navajo."

"No kidding, really?"

"They wanted to meet with my tribe's spiritual leader yesterday."

"You didn't go, did you?"

I shook my head. "Why would they pick me? I'm about the last person you'd want negotiating or leading spiritually. I'm a warrior, as far as they care. A failed, retired warrior."

"Any warrior who lives long enough to retire must have something like worthwhile wisdom."

A long while passed in silence. Trish watched me the way someone watches a dog that might need to be put down. I sat there, stewing in my own sense of failure. I'd failed my tribe and my town. I'd failed to catch a horse and I'd failed to rob a bank. Hell, I'd even failed to keep sober.

It was some damn fine whiskey, though.

Some men entered from outside and sat down for some poker. They were the same men I'd seen earlier, but the man in the nice suit wasn't there. These men all wore shabby, threadbare clothes. Trish watched them closely.

"Why aren't they upset?" I muttered under my breath.

"Come again?"

"Trish," I said, "tell me what you see over there?"

"Some fellas playing hold 'em."

"What are they wearing?"

She looked for a good long while. "I don't see anything special about what they're wearing."

"Describe the farthest guy to me."

"Short beard, brown eyes, augmented. Missing a finger on his left hand. He's wearing a leather duster and a button-down shirt."

"Is it shabby?" I was whispering, but my whispers might have been louder than I intended. A couple of the men were casting glances our way.

"What?"

"Are his clothes shabby?"

She didn't get a chance to answer. Her head cocked to one side. She stood up and checked her weapon. "You're coming with me, old man," she said. Without waiting for an answer, she grabbed my arm and yanked me to my feet. I swayed there for a moment, but didn't get a chance to gain my balance because we were out the door.

My metal arm was dead weight. I staggered, half dragged by Trish. Alcohol sloshed around in my belly and my head felt like it was on backwards. There were lights outside, around the corner of the bank. Drones hovered above casting a brilliant day-bright glow over the area. In the distance, I could hear a familiar buzz, but I couldn't quite place it.

"What is going on, J.D.?" Trish asked in a rushed whisper.

"Is it coming back?" I tried to pull her to a stop. "Are things changing back?"

She looked, wide-eyed, around the town. Shit. It hadn't even been an hour. All that work and whatever had this town in its grip had already recovered. There must have been a backup already. Folks were moving on as if nothing had happened.

The buzz stopped.

It was Tucker's six-wheeler.

Trish pulled me again, rounding the corner of the bank. There was an extra body in a heap near the spot where Tucker had made an impromptu door. A deputy right next to the body of the old man. Trish dropped my arm and rushed to the guy.

"He's alive," she said. She drew her weapon, stood up—

A crack of a gunshot rang out in the night. Trish's head snapped back, and she landed right next to the deputy.

The buzz of Tucker's six-wheeler started again, its odd warble echoing off the hills. I leaned heavily against the wall, trying to make my way over to Trish, but the ground kept swaying underneath my feet.

"Step to it, if you want a ride," Tucker said as he hopped off his six-wheeler wearing a metallic mask over his face. He pulled a duffel bag from the trunk in back and disappeared into the bank.

I fell to my knees in front of Trish. She was still alive, breathing in short gasps. A three-pronged dart stuck out of her forehead, pulsing every couple seconds. No doubt it was a fancy model of the e-cuff that I had on me. She was awake, but the only thing she seemed able to do was glare at me.

She was going to live. Relief washed over me. My stomach churned on the whiskey, but I held back the nausea and tried to keep my senses about me. Trish had my weapon. I patted her down and found it in one of her coat pockets, holstering it immediately.

"Flores will find you, Trish. Hell, someone'll come tonight to investigate what's going on here now that we've made some noise." I looked up at Tucker as he emerged from the bank carrying a satchel. "This isn't going as we planned, but you'll see it was the right thing."

Tucker emerged with a grim look on his face. He slung the stun rifle over one shoulder and pulled out the other rifle. He turned to Trish.

"We can't let her say anything, J.D." He stepped up to her and leveled his rifle at her head. From that distance with that high-caliber rifle, no armored skin would hold up. Even if the bullet didn't penetrate, her skull would be crushed.

I shifted so my body was between Tuck and the sheriff.

"No witnesses," Tuck said. "That's how we roll."

"No killing either."

"Has to be done. You knew that once this went south. I'm just cleaning up the mess."

Tucker reached into his pocket and tossed a handful of dark cubes into the air. They emanated a high-pitched hum as they hovered up and swarmed around the drone.

"No witnesses, J.D."

His shoulders tensed.

Before I could think what I was doing, I grabbed at his rifle. He ducked back, throwing me off balance. His knee came up into my hip hard, doubling me over and sending me sprawling to the ground. The man was faster than he looked.

The muzzle of his rifle pressed into the base of my neck. Tuck breathed hard, uneasily. He swallowed.

The flying cubes, the drone, and the entire night sky lit up in a series of explosions.

Then there was darkness.

"Dammit," Tuck said. "Dammit, dammit, dammit."

Voices. Shouts of townsfolk looking to investigate.

Tuck kicked my ribs hard. Bolts of electric pain radiated from my gut; when I recovered, the gun was no longer pressed against my neck and I was still alive. The six-wheeler buzzed and by the time my eyes were adjusted enough to see it, he was far away.

The duffel bag. It must have been the bulk of the explosives we'd gotten from Court. How much time did I have?

I grabbed Trish and the deputy, dragging them as best I could by their shirts. We inched our way down, away from the bank.

The bank lit up in a column of light. It wasn't so much an explosion as it was a column of pure brilliance. The heat of it struck us in waves, singing the stubble of my beard. There was no concussive blast. This was pure destructive heat.

Right about then I vomited. I can't say that I threw up directly on Trish, though it wouldn't be honest to say that I'd entirely missed.

When I was sheriff there were plenty of times when an outlaw would do something for good reason. He'd come to that point where he could put himself at the mercy of the law or he could run. The mercy of the court wasn't an easy thing to deal with, but running always made things worse. They'd break more laws and make their case of justified law-breaking that much harder to argue. Hell, I'd sent more men up to Iowa than I'd care to admit in just that circumstance.

Trish glared at me from where I'd propped her up against a rock. Oh, she was not happy. Taking her hand, I pressed her thumb up to the e-cuff, deactivating it. The jolt of all my tech waking up to find itself in a poisoning emergency caused me to stagger back. Vertigo took me again as my eye adjusted to the false feed.

An outlaw's situation always got worse when he ran.

I ran.

Chapter 21

Nothing sobers a man like a nice long jog under the stars. The Milky Way stretched across the belly of the sky, mocking my steps for their insignificance. There were times when I woke to find I was still walking. There were times when no matter how hard I pushed, there weren't any more steps to be had.

Trish didn't follow—or at least, she didn't find me. Townsfolk gave chase for a short time, but they were easy to lose. It wouldn't have been hard for an experienced tracker to find me. Trish was good at a lot of things, but she was no tracker. Maybe she hadn't bothered to try. Whatever the case, I walked all through the night, the whole time debating the benefits of collapsing right there and giving up.

The pains of my life slipped back in, one at a time. My ribs ached first, a dull poke in the side that expanded as I walked. My legs, my back, my belly—everything took its turn. Each overshadowed the last. By the time I saw my skidder illuminated by the rising sun, my head was hurting worst of all. Light seemed to shine unfiltered directly into my skull, toasting my brain with its radiance.

Still, every time I stopped, there I was starting again.

Then I saw him. Francis, standing at the edge of the dead zone, watching me with cold, emotionless eyes. His black duster hung off him like someone had tossed it on a coatrack. His hat was a size too big and a gaunt face framed his hollow eyes.

"Well," said Francis, "what did you think?"

I squinted at him. He was only visible in my right eye, so I knew he wasn't really there. A projection, then. But how would he project here?

"It's peace. Just like we wanted." A lizard smile crept across Francis's face. "Peace that lasts. Doesn't need a war to make it or lawmen to keep it."

"Francis," I said, "your brother's looking for you. Go home."

"Home? No, I don't think so. The lab's better here and these people are nice to me."

"You've done enough. These people need to be set free."

His expression got real serious. "These people want this. They're happy. They've been this way for a long time all on their own. I'm only here to help."

"Generous of you."

"Don't you see? It's what we—"

The buzz of the dead zone rippled through my body. It felt like freedom. How long would that last? Trish would come after me. There were important things I needed to do before I let her catch up to me. I'd need to learn more about what was happening in Swallow Hill if I wanted to have any chance to clear my name. My tribe needed me to help smooth relations with the other tribe. I dreaded it, but it had to happen. I needed to make sure they were safe before I left.

If I left.

I'd promised Ben Brown I'd help find his brother. Now I knew. He was somewhere around Swallow Hill. He was involved.

I had no delusions that I'd be cleared of my crimes. I'd left the law behind when I robbed that bank. That was enough to get me sent north. Justice had a funny kind of severity out here in the outlands. I'd see a few years of hard labor even if Trish vouched for me. But why would she?

Affairs needed to be in order before they caught me.

When I left the dead zone, my arm and all of my tech snapped back to life. The aching pings of warning that my arm had been sending me came back full force, double what they were before, despite the charge I'd given them earlier. My vision wavered again, but it wasn't as bad as before. I was getting used to it.

"Ben," I said into my headgear.

"Yeah."

"Got a lead on your brother."

"Uh-huh." He didn't sound convinced.

"I'll stop by later today."

"Fine."

Moments later, sun swiftly rising, I set my jaw and forced myself to move.

There was a line that someone had painted on the ground. It ran in clean, blue paint right along the edge of the dead zone. Perpendicular lines radiated out from it every twenty meters or so. I resolved to ask Abi about it when I saw her next.

That was one more thing on my list.

My skidder smelled of piss. It was an overwhelming surge of musk and stink that almost had me retching again, but I held it back.

Once I was in the sky, moving fast, nothing smelled like nothing.

I'd told Ben I would meet him early, but he'd have to wait. The one place I knew Trish would come looking for me was Underpass, where she knew I lived. If I was going to help my tribe, I needed to do it soon. It had to be first.

I tried to contact Zane through my headgear without any luck. He was the key to getting things cleared up, even though I couldn't decide how much I could trust him. Had he given me bad tech? What was his motivation in all this? I knew he worked for Goodwin, but that didn't tell me much.

Mina saw me coming from far away. She looked up from picking tomatoes in her garden and scowled something fierce. As soon as I landed, she dumped her tomatoes into a basket and ushered me inside. Once we were in her tiny house, she left without saying a word. When she came back a minute later, her eyebrows were knit together in worry.

"I've covered your skidder so they won't see it." She looked me right in the eyes for a moment, sniffed the air, and started brewing a pot of coffee. "What kind of trouble are you in, anyway?"

"Mornin'," I said, tipping my hat.

"They've had that deputy out here looking for you."

Mina's coffee pot started bubbling and I just about found religion. Once it was finished brewing she poured a couple cups and handed one to me. I spent a full minute just breathing it in, and when I took a sip my headache faded.

"Much appreciated," I said.

She smiled. "You're not too popular around here, you know."

I took another sip of coffee and closed my eyes. The warmth sank right down into my chest and threatened to put me right to sleep.

"Chief says you were supposed to meet Ayze yesterday. Said you'd agreed to it." She kicked me gently in the shin and my eyes snapped open. "I've never seen the chief angry, J.D., but he was close on this."

I nodded.

"I had to fill in for you."

"How'd it go?"

She glared.

There was a tap at the door and Mina stepped over to answer it. She opened the door just a crack and whispered something to someone outside.

She turned to me and grinned. "You're lucky. Ayze is due to leave this morning to travel back north."

"Lucky me."

"Not so lucky." Mina frowned at me. "Deputy Green just arrived. He's looking for you."

I raised an eyebrow. "Already?"

"We'll have to get over to the Kiva without him seeing you." She peered at me closely. "First, we need to get you cleaned up."

"What? Why?"

Mina opened a trunk at the foot of her bed and pulled out a straight-edge razor. She found a cup with soap and an old brush. She handed them to me and brought a mirror over.

Gaunt and pale, the haunted face scowling back at me in the reflection was one sorry son of a bitch. The beard stubble was wild enough to be considered shaggy. My hair was dirty and lopsided, but I always wore a hat, so I didn't think it would matter.

Mina started combing the tangles out of my hair and working some kind of oil into it. While she did that, I played obedient and shaved.

"Why all this fuss, Mina?"

She didn't answer, but instead tried to brush the dust off of my shirt. It didn't work. When dirt is rubbed in that hard, there's nothing that's going to get it out.

"This won't do," she said. She opened another short trunk and pulled out what looked like a leather poncho decorated with tassels. She draped it over my shoulders and stood back to eyeball me. "Much better."

I scowled at myself in the mirror. It felt good to have a shave, but unnatural to have my hair combed and parted down the middle. Also, the leather tassels felt odd.

"Isn't this women's clothes?" I said, indicating the poncho.

"Well, I'll let you borrow it." She rushed to the door in response to the sound of a light scratch. After a short discussion with whoever was outside, she waved me over. "C'mon, J.D. It's time to move."

I grabbed my hat from the table and just about got it onto my head before Mina slapped it away. She met my eyes and shook her head, so I carried it with me.

Outside, Marcus motioned frantically for us to cross to another building. Mina crouched low, so I followed suit and the two of us crossed and found a spot between some boxes to wait for the next signal.

"What's this all about?" I whispered.

Mina just shook her head.

Marcus waved us on. When I glanced back over my shoulder at him, I could see him approaching, hailing someone I couldn't see. We crossed to another building, circled around it to where a fenced-in area held a couple of goats. We hopped the fence, tiptoed carefully through the muddy pen, and hopped out again next to Vincent, the gray-eared donkey.

Mina untied the donkey from the fence and started leading him.

"Hide behind Vincent," she said.

I crouched down and tried to stay behind the creature.

"Just stay quiet," Mina whispered to me. "We're almost there, but we gotta cross this field and Deputy Green is talking to Marcus on the other side."

The donkey was damned slow and plodded at his own pace along a worn path. My back started to ache from squatting down behind the thing, and I don't think it did a very good job of hiding me, considering my legs would be fully visible. There were some decent scrub bushes that might help, but it was hard not to feel foolish and completely exposed.

"Shit." Mina handed me the lead. "He's coming this way. You take it the rest of the way."

Mina dashed off, leaving me with Vincent.

At first the beast kept on its painfully slow pace. It plodded forward, trundling from side to side.

Then it stopped.

"Move it, Vinnie," I said. I crouched down low and peeked under Vincent's belly. Mina was talking to a man with a deputy's star pinned to his hat. He was young, with a small paunch of a belly under his sloppily buttoned shirt. His hat didn't seem to sit right on his head, and he rocked back on his heels when he spoke. Mina had managed to get him facing away from me.

I slapped Vincent on the butt. He took a step to the side, away from me, but refused to move forward.

Vincent reached down and took a big bite from a tuft of dry grass. He chewed it with slow, mocking deliberation, as if trying to drive home that he wasn't going anywhere.

The lead was still in my hand, so I thought I'd try to use it. I pulled it forward, ahead of the donkey, and tried to motivate him with a few short tugs. He still didn't move forward. Instead, he just rotated his back end around away from me, effectively diminishing my cover.

Soon, I was right in his face. Vincent's bottom was facing the deputy and the damn donkey just stared at me and chewed his grass. He finished, swallowed, and took another big bite.

I cussed at him through my teeth.

The grass was what he wanted, so I pulled up a big handful and held it in front of his face. It almost worked. My back ached and my knees were starting to feel like they had knots in them. The donkey finished his mouthful and turned to where I was holding out more for him. It gave me a little more room to hide, which was good. The donkey took a step forward, and I tried to move with him, but my knee seized up and I wasn't fast enough.

Vincent's square teeth dug into my thumb as he snatched the handful of grass from my hand. I tugged hard as I could, but again, he wouldn't move.

"Need some help?" someone whispered right behind me, nearly sending my heart into a fit.

It was Haley in her soft sneaking shoes. She grinned at me, obviously proud of herself. She took the reins from me, made a kissing sound, and led Vincent slowly the rest of the way across the field.

Once we were all the way to the Kiva, I turned to her. "Thanks," I whispered. The door was at the bottom of a short stairwell, and I opened it as quietly as I could.

She grinned at me and did a little curtsey. "Do good, okay?"

I nodded. "I'll try."

She leaned in close to whisper, "Make him fall in love with you."

"Wait, what?" The door swung closed and I was in Broadfeather's decorated home.

Chapter 22

The Kiva was a structure of natural stone set deep into the earth. The door opened into a single room. There was little natural light in the building, with narrow windows near the ceiling being the only ventilation.

The haze of tobacco and incense hit me in a swirling mess of too-strong and too-sweet. My augmented eye adjusted quickly to the dimness. Broadfeather sat cross-legged on the other side of a tiny fire pit filled with glowing embers. He wore his full fancies, including a feather headdress and colored leathers. In his hand he held a long, intricately carved pipe. It was an ancient thing, worn smooth through time and use. The pipe trailed several strings of beads, which Broadfeather held high enough that they didn't brush the ground.

There were others arranged in a small circle around the embers. A few I recognized from the tribe; others were unknown to me. Strangers. This was our peace pipe ceremony, then. They expected me to be here for this, to run the ceremony. I'd failed. Worse, I was walking in as it was halfway through. Nobody looked up in my direction, but I found an empty spot in the circle and knelt there.

The peace pipe ceremony was sacred to my people, but it was not known well. Not anymore. For years, the faith practices of Hopi and other tribes were forbidden. Generations without practice left gaping holes in our understanding. When America finally fell, many of my people died as well. Traditions barely survived in the minds of those who lived. We did our best, though. We used red willow bark and tobacco, mixing for a sweet smoke that lingered but did not muddle the mind. There were no hallucinogens in this smoke. Nothing that would really alter the mind. I had missed the first part of the ceremony, when the spirits of earth and the sky were acknowledged.

The chief passed the pipe to his left, handing it to a broad-shouldered woman I did not recognize. The woman, with a grim look upon her face, smoked the pipe then passed it on.

Some of the men and women chanted when the pipe came to them. They would thank the earth or pledge to protect it.

I would be expected to say something. Broadfeather had described me as the new spiritual leader of the tribe, so whatever I said had to be profound. My knees ached. The lump in my chest started to pound. It was unlike any adrenaline rush I'd ever had in a fight. This rush threatened to pull me apart and send me running.

"Oh, great spirit, I thank you for the water from the sky," said Edgar Buck. His best leathers were laced with feathers he had collected during his own time in the wild. "And for the creatures of the earth." He held the smoke in, giving long pause to consider his words. He passed the pipe.

The spirit was meant to move the words of the ceremony. It wasn't rote memorization. There were no right words or wrong words. This made my predicament so much worse. Haze filled my head the way the smoke filled the room. I couldn't think of a word. Not one damn word.

The pipe made its way around the circle. Next to me, a person who defied gender sat with a look of absolute serenity. This must be the two-spirited one, then. Her lids were half closed. The pipe came to her.

She licked her lips and breathed deeply. "Peace at all costs," she chanted. She passed the pipe to me.

The pipe was lighter than it looked. I ran a hand along the smooth wood. The feathers hanging from the bowl were old, ragged, but those on the pipe itself were much newer. Brighter. I closed my eyes.

"Oh, earth spirit," I said, "give us protection that we might seek peace."

Broadfeather pointed the pipe upward to the sky, emptying the bowl and cleaning it. He then separated the pieces and stored them in a red bag made especially for that purpose. After he was finished, people stood up without word and many of them left. Broadfeather, the two-spirit, and myself remained.

The chief said, "J.D. Crow, this is Dibe Ayze."

Dibe's dark hair was pulled back and braided with black feathers and white frost aster flowers. Her slender body was bronzed and oiled, seeming to shine in the dim light of the fire's embers. The garment draped across her shoulders was loosely gathered around her waist. Her broad shoulders and strong back were undeniably masculine, but I couldn't think of any word to describe her other than "beautiful."

The sound of shouting came from outside. I couldn't make out the words, but somewhere not far away there was a commotion. I tensed. My time here would be short.

"You are a man of peace?" Dibe asked.

I nodded. "I hope there are many reasons for our tribe to find peace."

"If someone came to hurt you, would you fight?"

"I expect so."

"What if they came to hurt your people? Then, would you fight?"

I nodded.

"Then you are no man of peace, Mr. Crow."

Was she right? These past four years I'd lived without violence. I'd stopped being the sheriff and had started living a life of relative peace. When people needed help, I was there for them. I helped my tribe rise from poverty and starvation into something that could eek out a living in the harsh desert. It was a struggle. Every day tried to lead me back to the violence I'd left behind. Apart from the past couple days, I considered myself successful in my quest for peace.

But was I?

"Dibe," I said, "there aren't many of us out here. If someone came to hurt you, I'd stop them. All I hope for is that you might do the same for us."

"In the north we survive by not poking bears," Dibe said.

I shook my head. "But if they come to you, do you feed them? There might be no reason to fight, but that doesn't mean we shouldn't be ready for it." Another shout rang out, this time just outside the door. I took Dibe's smooth hand in mine. "Please, consider my words. We must stay together in this."

Broadfeather slipped outside, leaving us alone in the hazy room.

"Bring your Hopi north," said Dibe. "They would be welcome."

North. The Navajo Nation. It would mean safety, but at what cost? Would they allow us to continue to be our own tribe? "We'll consider it. Hopi lived on lands up north long ago. Before the earth broke."

"The sky is cooler. There is water." Then it came. "Merge your tribe with ours, Crow. Broadfeather will not do it, but you would be chief one day if you desire. There are so few of you. Come join Navajo and be part of something larger. It will be safer for your people."

Safer. Could there even be such a thing? All it would cost would be the traditions of my people. This last scrap of Hopi would be dissolved once and for all. We'd follow their traditions. We'd live under their rule.

"I'll think about it." With that, I turned and pushed back into the blinding sunlight. The scene outside was not one of peace.

Deputy Green pointed his gun at Mina. She stood between him and Broadfeather's hogan, making no secret of her defiance of the lawman. At Green's feet was a limp figure, but the angle made it hard to tell who. There was blood on it and blood on Green's shirt. Broadfeather leaned heavily on his walking stick, a somber look on his face.

"Just let me serve my warrant," said Green. He turned to me, "Mr. Crow, I'm afraid you're going to have to come with me unless you want this getting ugly."

"Point the gun at me, Deputy," I said. "The lady's got nothing to do with it."

Green's gaze darted from me to her and back. His gun hand shook. He took a step back, but the gun stayed on Mina.

"You know a bullet from that gun will kill her, just like it'll kill me. We don't have the skin you folks seem to like." I kept my voice low and mellow.

"Hands up," said the deputy.

Mina said, "He found your skidder, J.D. I'm sorry."

"Don't be." I raised my hands very slowly, feeling the pinging ache from my metal arm. "We knew he'd find me eventually."

The deputy reached into his pocket and pulled out an e-cuff, but he fumbled and it fell to the dusty ground. He looked at me with panic in his eyes.

"Well," I said. "Pick it up." My arm was getting tired.

He gestured to Mina with his gun. "Back up," he said. A bruise was forming on his left eye and I wondered if maybe he had reason to be wary of her.

Mina backed up, moving several steps to the side. The heap at Green's feet shifted and I saw that it was Marcus. He was bleeding from his nose and his eyes were closed.

Mina said, "After he found your skidder, he got the sheriff on the line. She'll be here soon."

Green reached down slowly and picked the e-cuff up off the ground. At the same time, I started walking forward, one slow step in front of another.

"Stop." Green tensed up. For a moment his gun was steady.

"Let the lady go." I stopped moving forward, but started circling slowly to the right. "Someone ought to check on that kid too."

Green glanced down at Marcus. "He came at me."

"Sure."

"It had to be done."

"He's a kid." My voice was just short of a growl.

"Enough," he said. There was a hint of fear in his eyes. The man was out of his element. "Move."

Nobody moved.

"Move!"

The door opened behind me. Dibe stepped out and took everything in with an air of serenity.

Green faltered and took a couple steps back. His weapon drifted to the side, no longer pointing straight at Mina. If I drew on him, it'd be over before he even knew what was happening.

But I didn't draw.

Dibe put a hand on my shoulder. "The way of the peaceful man is difficult, friend." He stepped in front of me and walked over to Marcus. He rolled the boy onto his side and stroked his hair. Almost immediately, the boy's eyes fluttered and focused on him.

"There," said Green. "Now will you come?"

I nodded.

Green tossed the e-cuff my way. I caught it in my right hand, the one it wouldn't affect. The deputy tensed and pointed his weapon at my head. He fingered the trigger nervously.

"Relax, son," I said. "You forgot to activate it." I thumbed the e-cuff and slapped it to the back of my metal hand. As soon as I did this, the familiar thrum buzzed through my body and all of my tech went dead.

On the way back to Deputy Green's cruiser, I managed to catch Dibe's eye. I don't know for sure what I saw there, but I suspect it was respect. I'd handled the situation without violence. I think she knew that I could have fought my way free. Her method of non-violence might have some merit. It might, in the end, win the day. So, at least I had done that right. I'd gained the two-spirit's approval.

A shame it wouldn't last.

"Get in," the deputy said, poking me in the ribs with his pistol.

I didn't get in. "You're new at this, aren't you?"

"I said, get in."

"Fella like you shouldn't be out wrangling real criminals. What kind of trouble is Trish in that she's recruiting folks and putting them in the field without any real training?" I raised an eyebrow at him. "You ever shoot that gun?"

"I'll shoot it just fine if you don't get into that seat."

"Can't open the door." I nodded at my limp left arm and tried to show that my right was weak too. "I'm cuffed."

Green sighed and reached in front of me to pull the door open.

I grabbed his gun hand, slammed it against the cruiser, and sent the pistol flying. At the same time, I stomped on his foot and shoved him back. Green landed hard on his ass, spitting angry and cursing up a storm.

I dropped a knee in his gut, punched at his head twice.

While he was stunned, I ripped the e-cuff off of my hand. Since I'd enabled it, it was tuned to me and allowed me to disable it with no trouble. I reactivated it and stuck it right on the back of Green's neck, where it attached to his enhanced skin. He twitched a little, then dropped face-first into the dirt.

"Son, I'm really pleased to have been able to teach you this lesson." I stood up and stretched. "E-cuffs don't disable non-augmented limbs, so it's best to tie a man up if you don't know his status. Also, never bludgeon a kid if you want cooperation from those who care about him. Pisses a man right the hell off."

I turned to leave, thought better of it, and kicked Green in the ribs hard. "Right the hell off."

My skidder was only a short distance away, and I ran to it and kicked off high into the sky. Once I was up there, I took a deep breath to calm myself.

"Zane," I said, touching my ear.

"J.D." He sounded surprised.

"Let's meet."

Chapter 23

"That is one fetching outfit," Zane said as he drifted casually up in his red car. "And did you shave?" He hopped out and reached up to touch my face, pulling back only at the last second. The look on my face must have pulled him up short. "They don't really get you, do they?" he asked.

"They try." I pulled uncomfortably at the outfit Mina had picked for me. It really did look ridiculous. "I don't think they really know what it means to be two spirited. They make so many guesses at the traditions, and, well, I think they thought I would fit."

"But you don't."

"No," I said, rubbing my smooth face. "Not really."

We were under the dead oak for which Dead Oak was named. It was once a majestic testament to strength and nature, but somewhere along the way it had stopped turning green. Its claws scraped at the morning sun, but no life sprung from its buds. Dry heat was quickly moving from unbearable to oppressive. Zane was just as immaculate as always, wearing another crisp black suit and sporting a neatly trimmed beard. I blew the smoke of the last stub of a cheroot through my nose and stubbed it out against the tree.

"What aren't you telling me?" I asked

His tone got serious. "Did you bring the tech?"

I shook my head. "There was a kid in there."

"In where?"

"The machine in the bank. She was..." I gestured, trying to wordlessly convey something that was difficult for me to say. Then I had an idea. I used my glow cube to pull up the scan of the old man. "This look like anything to you?"

Zane winced. "A Kiva."

"What?"

"He's hollowed out. The girl you saw in the bank probably was too. It's possible to remove a person. Their identity. Everything. Leaves nothing but a Kiva."

"Seems there wasn't anything left."

"The human brain is an amazing thing, you know." Zane lips were pressed into a tight line.

"Who would do that?" I poked him in the chest. "And why do you want the tech that makes it work?"

"We need to be able to counteract its effects."

"Or replicate them."

Zane's expression turned flat. "Replicate?"

"Tell me something, city boy." I stepped forward and talked right into Zane's face. "Can you guarantee me that Goodwin won't use that tech once he has it? Can you look me in the damn eye and tell me that there ain't nothing but good intention in what you're planning with it?"

Zane looked at me. He looked hard, right into my eyes. "Yes," he said.

I met his gaze. Held it for a good long time.

"No," he finally said. "But if Quintech's the only one to have it, then it'll be worse. They'll own the whole damn continent before you can so much as spit."

"It'd be better if Goodwin owned it?"

Zane shook his head. "Balance of power. You know what that means?"

I nodded. It made some kind of sick sense. If only one organization had the tech, then they'd take over easily. If two had it, there'd at least be some resistance. "War," I said.

"Stability. Stable is good." Zane rubbed his temples. "It's a damn game. People like you are just caught up in it."

Part of me wondered if he was just caught up in it as well. How much was Zane a puppet and how much puppeteer? The Quintech Corporation sounded familiar though. They built my arm and a lot of the tech in Josephine's junkyard. Somehow there wasn't much talk about them, though.

"So why meet here?" Zane asked. He looked around the central square of Dead Oak. There wasn't anyone around. Folks tended to stay inside during the hottest part of the day, which in this season meant most of the time the sun was up.

"Sheriff's after me." I nodded to the station. "When a manhunt's in full force, there's just one place guaranteed to be just about free of lawmen."

"Right here."

"Yup." I stuck a thumb out and pointed to Josephine's junkyard a short distance away. "And I got some business."

"Your skidder's broke?"

"Something like that."

He looked back at me. "Where's the tech, J.D.?"

"I don't—"

"Tucker got it, didn't he?"

I didn't say a word.

Zane climbed in his ride and started floating upward. "Thanks." He sounded genuine. "For..." He took a fresh cigarette and lit it. "Just, thanks, J.D."

"Zane," I said. I took off my hat. Now that he was leaving, something just pulled at me. "Zane, I got a favor to ask."

That quirk of a smile crossed his face. "Name it."

"Boy I know disappeared. Brilliant kid named Francis Brown. See if you can find anything on him." I bit my lip. "If it ain't too much. Kid's involved in this somehow, if that makes a difference."

"It doesn't." He sighed. "I'll look into it, but it won't be easy. We're not set up to track down kids, especially those who don't want to be found."

"Can you see if he has connections to that Quintech?"

Zane winced. "Goodwin and Quintech aren't exactly on friendly terms."

No, they wouldn't be. "Be creative," I said.

Zane shook his head. "I'll see what I can do." His ride lifted up into the sky and disappeared on the horizon. I watched it go and wondered if there was something more I could do to understand the man. Something in me wished that he understood me.

How could he, though? I hadn't told Zane the real reason I was in Dead Oak. Truth be told, I was there to finish things. The fight with Green had me on the wrong side of the law, and things were only getting worse. The law was after me, and if I kept running, someone was going to get hurt. Hell, Deputy Green had already done more than his share of suffering. My part in the business was done. Maybe there was a chance that I could convince Trish that I deserved to stay free. It didn't seem likely, though. She knew I was a good man, but a lawbreaker's a lawbreaker.

Still, it wouldn't be honest to leave without helping Ben find his brother. I started strolling over to the junkyard, tapping my earpiece to try to get Ben on the wire.

All I got was noise. It wasn't the noise of no connection. There was an open sound to it, like wind blowing across an open bottle. The sense I got was one of a silent urgency, like a heart beating faster and faster.

There's a hell of a lot that this kind of silence can tell a person.

My heart beat faster and I picked up the pace. Something didn't feel right. The heat of the day was searing and intense, but nobody was around. Nobody. Dead Oak was a small town, but not an empty one. Even in the brutal heat there ought to have been someone around.

That's when I heard the sharp crack of a rifle.

I broke into a run. There was no doubt that the sound had come from Josephine's junkyard. Could be she was just up to some target practice. Could be she was doing a little rat hunting.

Something smelled off.

More gunshots rang out as I reached the huge steel doors. I shouldered one, but it didn't budge. Drawing the tiny pistol, I pounded on the door with my metal fist.

"Jo!" I hollered. "Open up!"

The wall around the junkyard was too slick to climb and too tall to jump. My skidder was back near the old oak in the center of town. It would get over the wall easy, but would it take too long?

A scream came from the other side of the wall.

I stuck my metal fingers forward and jammed them hard between the two doors. Thick steel gave way, and with a grunt I twisted and tore the door open enough to squeeze through.

Something darted past, ducking behind a stack of junk, disappearing before I could properly get a look at it. Moving through the stacks of metal, I kept my gun up and steady. I forced my breathing to slow so I wouldn't throw off my shot.

A narrow aisle between stacks of junk opened into the main courtyard, and when I got there I could see that the gate on the opposite side of the yard was wide open. There was a coyote there, across the yard, hackles raised. Keith was a few meters away from it, backing slowly away. He had a rifle pointed at the creature. His mouth twisted up in fear as he kept pulling the trigger of his empty gun.

I sighted it in, wide stance, steady grip. It was too far for a proper pistol shot, but if I was careful with my aim, it wasn't beyond me. I let out a breath halfway, held it, and fired.

Missed.

The coyote turned to me. It fixed its yellow eyes on me. Half of its head shone with polished steel. It wasn't just a genetic creation. It had been modified. Upgraded.

Keith took advantage of the distraction and ran.

Thundering shots rang out from inside Jo's shack. The flashes lit up the inside like lightning strikes, illuminating red smears around the door and window.

The coyote ran after Keith.

My hand shook. Try as hard as I might, I couldn't stop it. I dropped to one knee and let the pistol fall to the ground. The smell of piss and blood baking in the sun hit me hard. It was the smell of war in the desert. The smell of wild animals marking their land. My heart raced and my breath came only in sharp gasps.

All my pain came back at once. My rib, my arm, all of it just ached. It told me to curl up where I was and wait for it to be finished. There wasn't nothing for me to bring but pain and suffering.

It was only through sheer stubborn willpower that I stood up.

Keith had been unarmed, so I ran after him. My legs pumped with strength I didn't know I had left. Adrenaline made my ears rush with the pounding of my heartbeat.

His scream pierced the night. I ran right instead of left, circling around a stack of junk. On the way past, I jammed my metal hand into the heap and pulled out a hunk of crumbled steel the size of a football.

The coyote had Keith's leg in its jaws. Blood sprayed as the creature shook and Keith kicked. He pounded at the coyote with the butt of his rifle, dislodging the jaws in a bloody spray. He staggered back and fell backwards into the piles of junk. The coyote's gaze locked onto Keith's neck and its muscles tensed.

I threw the metal. It slammed into the coyote, sending it flying. Keith scrambled backward while I moved in.

The coyote ran away.

Keith sputtered incoherently.

"You good?" I asked.

He nodded and pointed back to the shack. I understood right away and ran, hoping I wasn't too late.

But I was.

The door of Josephine's shack hung open, the jamb splintered where the locks had been engaged. There were prints on the ground—reddish brown marks made of blood and mud. I knelt down by one, horrified at what it might mean, but afraid to keep moving. The print was a giant coyote's, just like the one outside of Underpass. That wasn't much of a surprise. The coyote I'd fought had been the right size for it. There were at least three sets of tracks, but one was bigger than the others. That one was the bloodiest of the three, by far.

My right eye flashed to life, modifications kicking in and showing me details I'd have missed with unaugmented vision. None of it was useful, as far as I could tell. Just an annoyance. My ear picked up a noise: a sobbing whimper coming from the shack.

The floor was slick with half-dried blood. The smell of blood-mixed-with-shit hit me hard. It stopped me. Stubborn as I was, it stopped me.

The sob came again, off to the right.

I breathed in the stink, forcing myself to be strong against it. Nausea hit, but I ignored it. I forced it down and stepped inside. My boots stuck to the thick blood. There was just so damn much of it. Too much. Could it all be from one person or were both women dead?

Josephine had slid all the way back in the corner, rifle still gripped in one hand. Her belly had been torn open, insides strewn about. One of her legs had been chewed nearly off and the blood still weakly dripped from the wound.

Her eyes moved.

She didn't exactly focus on me. Her eyes pointed in my general direction.

"Jo," I said. Setting her gun aside, I took her hand. "I'm sorry, Jo. I'm so sorry, I shoulda—"

Josephine shook her head. Her mouth opened, like she was going to talk, but there weren't any words. Hell, I don't even know if her lungs still worked properly. Her hand gripped mine, surprisingly strong. One of her eyes seemed to focus on me for just a second.

"Abi," I said. "Where's Abi?"

The mechanic closed her eyes. For a moment I thought I'd lost her, but her grip stayed strong. When she opened her eyes again, they were full of hard determination. She looked at me with both eyes focusing and then looked down at the ground.

There was a trapdoor underneath her.

"Is that where she is? Is she safe?"

In response, Josephine let out one last whimpering sob and slumped to the side. Her eyes stared off into the great beyond, and whatever freakish technology was keeping her alive finally let go. I held her hand a moment longer, trying to find strength in myself that just wasn't there.

In the end, though, she needed to be moved. I crossed her arms over her chest and dragged her body into the center of the room. With a few quick movements I pulled together the biggest chunks of her and covered the whole mess with a blanket.

The trapdoor was a safe. It was heavy steel, but not locked. I heaved it open to find a tiny compartment below. Abi barely fit, curled in a ball and crammed in amongst some metal boxes. When the light hit her, she looked up. Tears streamed down her face and blood soaked her clothes. The safe had leaked. The poor girl had been right there when her aunt had been torn to shreds. Hell, Abi probably didn't know whether or not she'd be able to get out.

I helped Abi up and half carried her to the door. We blinked at the piercing sun as we stepped outside. Both of us were covered in gore, but at that point I didn't care. My brain felt numb.

My right eye flashed blue and a series of text messages appeared that were too quick to read. My eyes kept trying to track the words, but wherever I looked the words seemed to float in front of me. Finally, I stopped flailing around and stared straight forward.

It was a call.

Francis Brown appeared in front of me out of nowhere, visible only to my modified eye. The boy wore fancy duds and no expression on his gaunt white face. The white suit he wore was pristine, even though he appeared to be walking through a wind-whipped section of the courtyard. His blond hair was long, tied back in a ponytail. His eyes glowed white.

"You took something of mine and I've taken something of yours," he said. "Now we're even." His voice was dull, lacking affect.

I blinked. His words made sense in the way that the words of a foreign tongue sound like words with no meaning. The boy looked me up and down for a minute as I shuffled Abi farther away from the shack. The image of the boy walked alongside us, looking us up and down the whole way.

"Aren't you happy, J.D.?" He straightened his string tie. "This is your kind of justice, isn't it?"

I looked at him, incredulous. Without a word, I scooped up my pistol, swore at the damn thing, and holstered it.

"Sure, it's a little more creative than what you're used to doing, but isn't it nice that we're on the same side? Isn't it nice that we can both work together for justice?" The hint of a smile touched the corners of his mouth. "She was a thief, J.D., She killed people and stole from Quintech. Important stuff too. Now justice has been served."

The doors I'd twisted apart weren't going to close anytime soon, so the junkyard wasn't safe. Francis talked like the attack was done, but I trusted that kid just about as much as I trusted a coyote in a chicken coop. We needed to leave, and soon. There wasn't any sound of activity outside the door, but I poked my head out all cautious anyway. Nothing. I led Abi through and we started making our way to my skidder.

Abi walked the walk of the half dead. She shuffled when I led her, but she didn't talk. I could have walked her off a cliff and she wouldn't have hesitated.

About halfway to the skidder, things got ugly. The yip-howls of the coyotes rang out around the bend. They were getting closer. The image of Francis still looked at me with cold, emotionless eyes. He'd stopped talking and seemed to regard me the way an intellectual regards a curio. His head cocked to one side and his eyes tracked us closely.

"You're in no danger, Mr. Crow," the boy said. "No danger at all."

"Who else did you attack, boy?"

"I'm not attacking anyone. This is justice, plain and clear."

The coyotes rounded the corner. There were three of them, one much larger than the rest. Only the biggest had part of its skull replaced with steel. The others had what looked to be leather harnesses cinched tight across their necks and torsos. The largest one stopped and perked its ears up, looking at Abi and me.

My fingers lingered near the grip of my pistol. The hand shook. The taste of bile rose in my throat and suddenly all I wanted was a stiff drink and a night of oblivion.

It wasn't going to happen.

The coyotes edged closer. They crept up like sneaky hunters, but in broad daylight they weren't any stealthier than I was in my boots. Still, they came closer and the big one's shining metal teeth shone as its lips pulled back in a near-silent growl. Blood caked the fur of its muzzle and crusted over its paws. The creature's hideous form edged closer and closer, faster and faster.

"Call them back, Francis," I said.

"I've got no responsibility here. Nature does what nature does."

"That ain't nature, kid." I pulled Abi faster, but she wasn't going to move faster than a walk unless I picked her up. That would leave me vulnerable to an attack. "Them things are too far gone from nature for that argument."

"They're simple creatures all the same."

"And you can call them off. Makes this your responsibility."

"Does it? So, if I can stop a war, I should do that too, right?"

The smallest of the three coyotes closed the last few meters in one quick lunge, nipping at my ankle. I felt it tug hard on the leather of the boot, even getting a tooth deep enough in to find flesh. A kick sent it scampering away, but by then the other small one had circled around and was moving up on me.

"Don't you even," I said, glaring at the creature. It hunched its shoulders and slinked back a few steps.

The big coyote took the opportunity to attack. It dug its wicked metal teeth into my calf. Needles of pain shot up my leg.

Then the coyote shook.

I didn't fight it. Fighting would make it worse. If I pulled against the coyote's bite, all that would happen was I'd tear the muscle even worse. So, I didn't work against it. I moved with the shake as well I could. It stopped, looking up at me with hate-filled eyes. Warning me. Hating me.

Hate. This wasn't a creature of nature any more than Francis was standing right next to me. There was intelligence in the coyote's eyes. His hackles raised and the fur around his metal harness stood on end.

On the far side of the junkyard a familiar hum shook the heaps of metal. Bessie, Jo's tank rose from the ground with Keith riding in the open top. He had his rifle in hand and opened fire on the straggling coyotes. The one on my leg was the only one that stayed put; the others ran.

"Coyote," I said. I nudged Abi and she walked the last couple steps and sat on the skidder. "You might wreck my leg, but if you do I'm going to crush your skull." I wiggled the fingers of my metal hand.

The coyote let go.

"See?" Francis said. "That wasn't so hard. Justice is that thing that powerful people do to keep the weak in line. It's how we keep the peace. Without a threat like that, there'd be no peace at all."

I limped the rest of the way to my skidder, wary of the too-close coyotes. They didn't attack. My metal hand slid into the console and I painfully straddled the vehicle. Abi was already seated on the back, and she held me tight as we lifted off into the sky.

Chapter 24

"J.D.," said Ben, "I'd say that you look like shit, but you always look like shit, and I wouldn't be giving this particular circumstance proper credit."

Ben was bandaging my leg with something that looked likely to be designed for livestock. It was a fibrous material and seemed to sink into the wounds in my leg as he wrapped it tightly into place. It was bright yellow, but where it came in contact with damaged flesh, it turned red then faded quickly to dull orange. I could feel it working, like a worm crawling under my flesh. The crippling pain of torn muscle faded to a dull ache that matched nicely with all of my other dull aches.

Abi was curled up on a sofa near where Ben had me sprawled out on the floor. Her eyes were shut hard, as if they could keep the whole world out if she only held them tight enough. Hell, I might have been doing the same thing if I thought it would work. We'd checked her over and found no obvious injuries. The damage was all in her head. Worst kind of injury, really.

Ben stepped back and admired his work on my leg. "The hardest thing with the longhorns is keeping them off the injured leg. They don't feel the pain, so they figure it's not injured anymore. Truth is, it's not really fixed yet. Won't be for days." He poked at the bandage. "I'm just happy to be putting it on someone who understands what I'm saying when I say to stay off the damn thing."

"Thanks, Ben." I stood up, testing the repaired leg. It felt fine.

Ben rolled his eyes for some reason.

"We didn't have anywhere else to go," I said. "My home isn't safe and there just aren't many places I'd consider friendly anymore."

"And here I thought you came to help me find Francis." Ben handed me a glass of lemonade.

"That too." I took a sip of the lemonade and then downed the whole glass. It was good, cool, and clean. My whole insides shivered, which felt good considering how hot the day had gotten. "He's tied up in all this somehow. Finding him is the top of the list now."

"Oh, now it's important? You selfish son of a bitch."

I turned on him, poked him in the chest with my finger. "Listen here, son," I said, "you didn't tell me he was a killer. You didn't tell me he was psycho."

Abi whimpered and curled up tighter.

Ben lowered his voice. "Is he?"

"I don't know. Something doesn't seem right. People's lives are at stake." I picked my hat up and put it on. "Maybe even yours," I said in a low voice. "Maybe her too."

"Doesn't matter, though, does it? We still don't know where to find him."

"No," I said. "But it'd be nice to take a look around his lab."

"Lab?" Ben scratched his chin. "I'm not sure what you mean by that."

"He mentioned that his lab here wasn't very good at home. Does he have something in the house or the barn?"

Ben's shoulders slumped. He shook his head. "He would always disappear during the day. I'm not sure where he went."

"If it's on your land, we should be able to find it."

The day was hot. The windmills in the distance wobbled as heat waves rose from the scorched land. It was late afternoon, the hottest time of day. I'd have to endure it if I wanted my search to yield anything.

It had been days since the boy had disappeared. There hadn't been any rain, and there hadn't been very much wind. There was a chance that his trail was still intact, so long as the boy had gone by land. Nothing really guaranteed that, of course. The only way to find out was to walk the perimeter.

"I'll stay with her," Ben said, standing behind me on the porch. "Somebody should be here for her."

I nodded.

He handed me a canteen, which I took and clipped to my belt.

"I'll start my walk at the perimeter's edge, near your cattle path," I said. "If luck's with us, I'll spot his trail before night falls." My leg muscles tightened, so I stretched as best I could. "If I don't find anything before sunset, well, I'll keep looking."

"Did you even hear me when I said to stay off that busted leg?"

"Nope."

My skidder was still nearby, so I used it to fly out into the field. The giant longhorns that Ben still kept on the ranch lived in the barn and grazed anywhere they damn well pleased. Obedient, docile creatures that they were, there was something intimidating about the beasts. They walked along their path, the ground shaking below their enormous hooves. The first perimeter post shined in the afternoon sun. Ben had told me what to look for; otherwise it would have been hard to spot. It was nestled amongst the black windmills and stood barely a meter out of the cracked soil.

I made a quick survey of the area. The ground here was red clay, cracked from the dry heat. Short, scrubby grasses shot up in lower dips of the ground, but most of it was dead or desiccated. Grasses didn't fare well in such heat, except in more protected areas. The path that the lumbering longhorns followed was just a short distance away, and a long line of the beasts was rumbling back home already. What protected field were they coming from? How was it shielded from this brutal heat? There were hills that might shelter them from winds and sun, but the heat of the past few days would threaten even that.

The next post was thirty meters off to the right. The ground was hard, near as hard as rock. It wouldn't be easy to spot a several-days-old trail even in the best conditions. It was a very real possibility that there was no information to gain, in which case, the backup plan was to charge back into Swallow Hill looking for trouble. That was not a great option. It would be much better to go in informed.

After a half-hour I stopped to take a swig of warm water from the canteen. The wind had caked my whole body with silt, making my lips gritty and the water taste like clay. I patted myself down, looking for my snuff or a cigarette. Nothing. The sun beat a fierce retreat now, lower on the horizon, but still hot. There wasn't a damn cloud in the sky.

When I started walking again, my injured leg felt about as stiff as a petrified log. It took ten minutes just to get so I could walk without a heavy limp, but I got there.

Another kilometer passed, nice and slow. Post after post passed, each humming with a subsonic thrum that rattled my teeth and made my fingernails itch.

The first trail I found was halfway around the ranch. As soon as I saw it, I knew I'd made a serious mistake.

They were coyote tracks. Fresh ones, clear as day in the red light of the setting sun. A dip in the land took me to a basin of clay that was still soft. In it, I saw several clear tracks and the smell of the coyotes was a hint of musk in the air.

My pistol still hung on my hip, but there still hadn't been time to sight it in properly or check how it worked. Hell, I didn't even know how much ammo was in it. Might be that there was none. It hadn't occurred to me to get a rifle from Ben while I was at the ranch and now I was a couple kilometers away, on foot, and still wounded.

All the more reason to keep moving.

The sun bled crimson across the sky before dying into dusk. There was no use walking when it was dark, but the moon would be out soon, so I set up against one of the windmills and took a nervous break.

It wasn't long before I heard howls in the distance. They were far off, hidden and distorted by the low hum of the mills. My pulse quickened. The natural fight-or-flight response triggered by the frightening predators of night. Before I could think about it, my weapon was in hand.

Fear is a damn useful thing in certain circumstances, but it can also be a hell of a distraction.

My hand shook, the weapon quaking so badly that I couldn't even justify keeping it out. I holstered it and pulled out a jagged hunting knife. It was a damn fine knife. When the coyotes came I'd take one down before the others tore me to shreds.

"Ben," I said, touching my ear. There was no answer on the other side. Either he was asleep already or ignoring my call. How rude. Youngsters have no manners these days.

It wasn't like I was blind. My right eye was adjusting perfectly to the night, giving me a full view of the colorless terrain. I didn't trust it to help me track my quarry, but it'd at least let me know when I was about to become a snack.

An eerie howl rang clear through the night, answered afar by another. A third howl pierced the night, then a fourth.

Minutes passed in dead silence.

All around, windmills hummed in the darkness. A gentle breeze kept the whole field in a constant state of motion and noise. It made locating the coyotes impossible. There was always movement visible in the corner of my eye.

My muscles ached from the tension. Knuckles were white from gripping my knife.

The coyotes howled again, closer this time. Were they tracking me? Were they getting ready to spring on me as soon as I closed my eyes?

I closed my eyes.

Fear wouldn't rule me. My breath slowed, deep and strong. The cracked ribs still stung with every breath. My body still ached. After a few minutes my heartbeat slowed.

My eyes snapped open. A howl. Close this time.

There wasn't anything to see. Nothing lurked in the shadows or darted between mills. Nothing crept closer in the night.

I was still alone.

The coyotes out there near the ranch couldn't possibly be the same as the ones that had attacked the junkyard. It was too much distance for them to cover in so little time. These were likely run-of-the-mill coyotes out searching for carrion. They'd leave me alone.

An hour passed. The moon came up and it was time to move. I shifted the knife in my hand and stood up. The injured leg seized up. Liquid fire shot all the way up my side, worse than when I first got the wound. The shock of it dropped me back to the ground and curled me up like a millipede. Long seconds passed like that.

Slowly, carefully, I worked my leg until it would move again. I tested it carefully and was finally able to put weight on it.

I could walk, but my modified right eye was making it impossible for my left eye to adjust to the moonlight. My finger found the slight impression in front of my ear: the power switch. I pushed it hard for three seconds, and the augmentation powered down. I felt a pang as the sounds of the night faded to near nothing.

My eyes adjusted to the dark and I started walking.

Finding the trail wasn't going to be easy. Moonlight isn't a whole lot of light, after all. This moon wasn't even full. The night was clear, though, and the angle of the light was good for picking out slight imperfections in the soil. It was plenty to spot crushed grasses or broken cacti. More coyote tracks proved to me that it was at least possible to spot something.

They sure didn't make me feel much better.

The bright eyes of a predator appeared a short distance ahead, glowing in the deep night.

"Howdy," I said, using my knife to tip my hat. There was no reason not to be polite.

The eyes blinked.

"Well, are we finishing this here, then?"

A long minute passed. Another set of eyes appeared a short distance away, then another. Three of them. I had no doubt that they could finish me without any real trouble.

But they didn't. Moments later, the three sets of eyes disappeared back into the night.

By then I was nearly all the way around the ranch. Another half-hour would finish the loop. It would also prove me a failure. I'd have to come back and try again in the morning. The idea of it sapped the strength from me and I stumbled, dropping to one knee.

How long had I been pushing too hard? How long had this been too much? I'd lost sight of reason a long time ago. Nothing but stubborn grit moved me now. Hopeless tasks seemed like all I'd seen for years out in this waste. Hell, hopeless didn't seem so bad anymore.

Still, I kept going.

The last segment of the perimeter went fast. The moon was higher, brighter. The coyotes came back. They were behind me now. I couldn't see them, but I could hear them. They sniffed and scratched at my trail. The wind hinted at their stink.

Running would be foolish, but my pace quickened. The hopelessness of the task choked at me, making my eyes quicker to dismiss the small things that need to be registered to pick up such a tricky trail.

That's why I nearly missed it.

The longhorns' trail cut like a gorge across the moonlit earth. It was like a road crushed into the ground and kept clear by constant use. Nothing grew anywhere near it, so I knew I was in the right place. My skidder was just on the other side of it, and I hurried to it, spitting mad at my own failure.

When I crossed the path, though, my foot twisted on the hard, uneven ground. I dropped again, wincing at the tearing sensation in the wounded leg. I stared at the ground, forcing my breath to slow down. Sweat broke on my brow.

The branch in the path was almost invisible. From any other angle it would have been almost impossible to see. Down near the ground I could see how the plants just a short distance from the longhorns' path were stunted and crushed. It was only about fifteen meters away, but I would have missed it if I hadn't fallen.

I forced myself to my feet and rushed to the impression.

Cracked clay soil sported broken edges and several tufts of grasses were crushed entirely to the ground. It wasn't the lone path of something that had been passed once. This was a trail that had been used for months, maybe years.

Longhorn hoof prints were sunk into the clay. My heart sank. This was just another trail for cattle, then. One of those grass-fed beasts liked to wander from the herd here, nothing more.

I followed the path a short distance, but soon I'd lost it. Once away from the trail, the path feathered out and nearly disappeared. I lost it and picked it up again three times, making good use of some choice cuss words in the process.

Limping back to my skidder, I ignored the yips and howls of the coyotes. There were many more now, maybe dozens. Their eyes flashed in the night as they edged closer and closer.

I jammed my metal hand into the console and threw a leg over the seat. In seconds I was in the air, hovering above the second trail. It was difficult to see from the air. The light of my thrusters made black ink of everything outside of its range. The thrust also crushed plants and scorched the land. It was useless to try to follow a trail from above. The smart move was to get back to Ben's ranch and rest overnight. Hell, the smarter move would be to rest for a few days. My leg wasn't getting better and whatever Ben had put on it wasn't designed to take any kind of continued abuse.

The night had given me all it was going to give. I spun the skidder around and rocketed back to Ben's ranch. Once there, I made my way quietly inside, noting that Abi was curled up at Ben's side on the sofa, just where I'd left them. She had relaxed some and drifted off into a proper sleep. They looked good together. Peaceful. There wasn't much hope in the world, but I suppose there was that.

Soon as my boots were off, I was asleep in the rocking chair. It was by far and above the most comfortable place I had ever been in my entire life, and I swear that is the truth.

Chapter 25

Don't ever let a fool tell you sleeping in a rocking chair is comfortable. It sure as hell isn't. In addition to the burning fire in my calf and the pinging ache of my low battery, I had a kink in my neck and a stiffness in my back that would not go away no matter how I stretched. On the bright side, my ribs felt better, and the stitches on my belly oozed clear fluid rather than blood. Most folks would take a morning assessment like that and rethink their life choices.

Ben handed me a cup of coffee without saying a word. The morning was looking better already.

The brew was bitter and strong. I gave it a minute to warm up my belly.

"How's she doing?" I asked.

"Better." He took a sip of his own coffee. "But not good. You want biscuits?"

We went back into the house and my stomach let me know how hungry it was. Biscuits were already on the table, and Ben hurried to the stove, where he'd been making a heavy beef gravy. Grits were cooking too, next to a pile of sizzling sausages. Ben brought the food over to the table, where Abi already sat wearing some of Ben's old clothes. His shiny leathers with spiked elbows hardly seemed to fit with her wetted-down hair and glassy eyes, but at least she was moving. She perched on her chair and fiddled with a fork, hardly noting my entrance.

Sitting across from Abi, I made short work of the breakfast. Ben similarly ate like a starving man. The biscuits were wonderful, soft and flakey. The gravy and sausages were hot and just the right amount of greasy. Washed down with coffee, it seemed a fitting feast for a king.

Abi hardly ate. She picked at a biscuit, but didn't get far into it before giving up.

"We need to find your brother," I said when I was finished eating.

Ben set his fork down. "Well, sure as shit we do, old man. You just coming to that conclusion?"

"I saw him yesterday, Ben." I tapped my modified right eye. "He called during the attack and..." I glanced at Abi. "And he taunted me after what happened to Jo."

Abi's grip tightened on a spoon.

Ben didn't seem to notice. "And that's why you think he's dangerous?" He leaned forward.

"I shouldn't have waited to find him."

"But you did."

My voice came out louder than I wanted. "I can't do every damn thing."

Ben's jaw clenched.

"It doesn't always have to be me. Plenty a trackers coulda figured out where he went. Hell, the law could probably find him."

He stood up, sending his chair sliding across the room. "But I asked *you*, J.D. You owe this family. You owe me."

I swirled the last of my coffee around in the mug and drank it down. "It's more than that. I don't owe your family, Ben, but it was wrong to wait so long. I thought I had too much other stuff going on and now Jo's dead and Abi's scared as hell."

"I ain't scared," Abi said, barely loud enough to hear.

"What are we going to do, then?" Ben asked. "Can you protect Abi? Can I? I take it you didn't find anything out there?"

"I ain't scared," Abi said a bit louder.

"Nothing," I said. "Hell, half of it was in the dark, so it's worth going over again." I stood up and cleared my plate. "Only thing I found was a spot where one longhorn splits from the herd on a regular basis. Coyotes too. Hell of a lot of coyotes."

At the mention of coyotes, Ben glanced at Abi, like it might frighten her to talk about the creatures. She caught the glance, stood up, and looked him straight in the eye.

"I ain't scared," she said through gritted teeth. "I'm furious."

Ben's jaw worked like he was trying to find something to say.

"Mad as hell," Abi continued. "She didn't even give me a chance." She stuck a finger out at me. "Just like you're not giving me a chance."

"What do you mean?" asked Ben.

"I can shoot. I can fight. Aunt Jo knew that, but soon as those monsters came, she shoved me in the safe." She collapsed back into her chair. "I could have helped. It didn't need to end like that. She said if they saw me it was over."

I put a hand on her shoulder, hoping that it would help comfort her. Some of the tension seemed to ease out of her.

"Tell you what's going to happen," Abi said. "I'll take J.D.'s skidder back to town. I'm going to clean up and get Auntie Josephine ready for a proper burial. You two are going to find Francis and figure out what the hell he's up to. If it's what J.D. said, then you're going to throw him in a jail or take off his head. I don't care which."

"I can't leave the ranch," Ben said. "Not even for a day."

She looked at him like he was stupid. "You don't have it automated?"

His expression was answer enough.

Abi sighed. "Fine, but you can help him for a few hours in the morning, then again in the evening."

"That'll work. Morning chores are already done."

Abi turned to me. "I'll meet you back here round sundown. I'll have Josephine's rifle and a few other tools. You just need to figure out where we're going with them and how to get there, all right?"

I nodded, unsure if there were any other possible response.

She looked at Ben. He nodded as well, but his look seemed to be more of awe than of the confusion I felt. "Good," she said. With that, she stood up to leave.

"How are you going to drive my—"

"I can drive it."

With that, she left and seconds later was in the sky flying away on my skidder.

"Hey," Ben said quietly. "Did you say that one longhorn split from the herd?"

"Yup."

"They don't do that."

"This one did."

"No. They stay together until they get to the grass. It's not just for fun. It's engineered into their genetics. The programming doesn't force them to stay together, but it suggests pretty damn hard."

"If someone wanted to get somewhere a good distance away, and they didn't want to drive..."

"They could ride." He looked at me, biting his lip. "You said there were coyotes out there?"

"Sure," I said. "But they're nocturnal."

"Didn't seem nocturnal yesterday when they attacked the town, did they?"

"No."

"Well, you need a weapon?"

My hand twitched. "Got one."

Ben left for a minute. When he came back he was carrying a shotgun with a short, shiny barrel and a cartridge the size of my forearm. He checked it over, worked the action a few times, and stowed a couple of spare cartridges. He looked at me with a sideways grin.

"Hell of a weapon," I said.

"Haven't ever been sorry to own it."

"I suppose not." I pulled my pistol out of its holster and handed it to him, handle first. "You mind taking a look at this for me? Hell if I know how it works, and I can't seem to hit a damn thing with it."

He took the weapon and let out a low whistle. Turning it over, he pressed something that I didn't even know was a button. A laser sight lit up. Another quick movement and a slick little compartment opened on the side, revealing dozens of tiny balls neatly arranged in a magazine.

"Smith & Wesson BB gun?" Ben smiled. "Haven't seen one of these in a while. Where'd you get it?"

"A BB gun?"

"Well, not like a toy gun or anything. See these panels here that make up the octagonal barrel? Those are accelerators."

"Magnets? Like a rail gun?"

"No, they're not magnetic." He pulled a tool out of his back pocket and used it to check each segmented piece of the barrel. "Gravitic and nucleic, if I remember right. Speeds the ball up to near half the speed of light. Doesn't even matter if it's small when the thing's going that fast."

"Why can't I hit anything with it? How do I sight it in?"

"Maybe you just need practice."

I took the weapon from him and closed it up, switching off the laser sight.

"Use the laser sight. Nobody uses the little metal ones, J.D. Those are just for show." He held the front door open for me. "Plus, the gun will auto track to wherever the laser is pointed. Makes it accurate a hell of a lot farther than a pistol has any right."

Our first stop was the enormous, black shed. Its photoelectric layering made it sit like a black blotch on the dry dirt, but it housed a hundred huge longhorns.

"It's probably not the right path," I said as I peeled the bandages off my leg. The longhorns were already gone, having lumbered their way out just before we arrived at the barn. "Likely one of your longhorns just got a head worm and nobody noticed."

Ben shook his head. "Doesn't seem likely to me." He tore open another first-aid kit and wrinkled his nose when he saw my wound. "Hell, J.D., that's worse than it was before."

It felt like it.

"You gotta stay off it this time. We're not walking out there like damn fools." He stuck a thumb out at the corner of the barn, where a small utility truck sat parked. "We'll take the truck."

"Can't track from a truck."

"Like hell you can't. Maybe you can't track a person, but we're tracking a thousand-kilo beast. This'll work just fine."

He was right. The herd instinct wasn't the only engineered part of those beasts. They also weighed a thousand kilos and stood as tall as the old American Bison with which they'd been spliced. They were a fearsome sight to anyone who didn't realize that docility was engineered into them as well.

Once my leg was bandaged, we climbed into Ben's truck. It was a closed cab, with an open bed that was littered with tools and equipment. I recognized some of the tech that Ben had been working on days ago, including the drones and harnesses. The young rancher jabbed at the manual controls and we lifted off.

When we passed the point where the longhorn's trail split off, Ben clicked his tongue. The clusters of windmills made it impossible to see very far, but the trail was obvious from a few meters up. After the initial split, there was a long stretch of trampled, dead grass. Now that we knew where to look, there wasn't any missing it. This wasn't a trail someone had walked once to get off the property. This was something a giant had walked on a daily basis for years.

"How often did he come out here?" I asked after a few minutes.

Ben didn't answer right away. He seemed to roll his words around on his tongue before saying them. "My big brother Jason and I were busy holding everything together.

The rest of the kids pitched in some, but nobody really had time to take proper care of them. Francis was big enough he should have been working, but he didn't."

"So when Jason left…"

"I had a choice. Work my ass off and keep the ranch or sell out like he did and move to the city."

The trail slid by below us. After a while, the dry patches of prairie grasses got greener and more frequent. Thick cacti spotted the terrain as the windmills thinned out.

"The city's no place for me. I might be hot shit out here, but I know enough not to think I'm nothing in Austin." Ben got a far-off look. "There were some strong words between me and Jason. I regret it, but not enough to call him up. Not yet."

"And Francis in all this?"

"Francis was there at sunup for breakfast. He was there at sundown for supper."

A kilometer went by, then two. At one point we passed over a lone longhorn, but we paid it no mind. We didn't need the steer to show us where we were going. The land swayed gently below us, the rise and fall of rolling hills getting bigger and bigger as we moved west. Windmills covered the land at first, but as the hills got steeper, soon the mills only adorned the tops of the hills. The trail joined up with the wispy path of a dry creek.

The ground had transformed into flowing emerald waves of grass. Hills on either side blocked the furnace winds and shortened the day. Water from some unseen spring must have kept life thriving in this hidden place.

Ben set the truck down at the edge and I hopped out. Brutal heat yanked the air from my lungs. Such heat so early in the day was not a good sign, especially in such a protected valley. I shrugged it off and started making my way forward, following the trail again. From up close it was easy to spot. The earth was soft there, and soon I was able to find some human footprints.

Ben hurried up behind me. "The longhorns have different feeding grounds on the property. We rotate them around, but this one's not on the map. I'm sure of it."

I held up a finger to shush him.

"Wait here," I said. "Keep an eye out."

"For what?"

"Got a bad feeling about this. Something's fishy."

The trail led a short distance to where a grove of mesquite nestled up against the side of a hill. The small trees were packed in tight, hardly passable, but when I got close I could see there was an opening right where the trail went. I had to crouch down and move sideways to get through, but it was only thirty meters until a clearing opened up, revealing a door in the side of the hill.

The door was a black metal slab stuck into the side of the hill at an angle. It resembled the old cellar double doors put in as tornado shelters in the old days. There were no hinges visible, nor were there any handles or locks. Across the clearing from the door was a single black metal post.

"So this is where you've been," I muttered under my breath.

The air above the post shimmered with wavy iridescence. The image flickered in the sunlight, seeming to sway in the warm breeze. At first it was hard to make out the image, but after a short warm-up, it became clear. It was a keypad, floating in the air. Why wouldn't they just make a regular keypad? Didn't make a damn bit of sense.

Regardless, the panel expected some kind of code. I scratched the scruff of my chin a few times, guessed at a few numbers. No good.

There was a slot on the side of the column, however, that looked mighty familiar. It closely resembled that slot on the console of my skidder, the one Jo had installed. Tentatively, I connected my hand.

My awareness slid into the device like it was meant to be there all along. Instinct seemed to slide over the climate controls, computer systems, automated crafting, systems, and... door. It was like opening a fist. The big black door behind me swung open.

Three sharp gunshots rang out in the distance.

The shots echoed into nothing and were followed by a silence so heavy it darn near made the dirt sit up and take notice. My boots felt like they were rooted to the ground. The big metal door hung wide open, darkness greeting me there. But could I go? Was Ben in trouble? Were those warning shots? What if someone had tracked us down and the young rancher was fighting for his life? What if he needed me? Wouldn't there be more shots?

I tapped my earpiece and tried to call Ben, but failed to get any kind of connection.

What if he was already dead and in serious need of vengeance?

My jaw hardened. This was a mission. Back in the days of the war, if I was on a mission, I'd never falter. I'd never hesitate, because I knew that those who were doing their part to watch my back could be depended upon to do just that. Tucker had been the best among them. Used to be he was trustworthy. Turning back to help him and ignoring my own mission would have been a betrayal of the trust he'd put in me.

But Ben wasn't a ranger. No matter how I turned it around in my head, gunshots meant that he needed me. Everything else had to wait.

As I sprinted down the choked mesquite trail, I tried to figure it in my head. Had those been shotgun blasts? I didn't think so. They were too high, too focused. Branches raked across my face, even though I tried to block most with my arm. I drew my sleek pistol and touched the line that activated the laser sight.

When I saw who was there, I lowered my pistol.

Two deputies stood near a cruiser, their backs to me. Ben was on his knees in front of them, facing away. His hands were interlaced behind his head. One of the deputies was shouting at Ben, furious about something. From where I walked, I could see blood on the deputy's shirt. Ben's gun was on the ground a few meters away.

I gave a sharp whistle, but emerged walking fast in their direction.

Both deputies looked my way. One of them was Deputy Green. The other one wasn't familiar to me. I wondered how many poorly trained rookies there were out there. Green jammed his rifle into Ben's back, but the other guy pointed his at me.

"Gentlemen." I didn't slow my pace.

"Stop right there, Crow." Green scowled. "This don't need to get messy."

I didn't slow down. I'd already covered half the distance to the deputies. "The boy's no concern of yours, fellas."

"He shot at us," said Green.

I stopped walking. "Ben," I said, "why the hell did you shoot at them?"

"They were on my land." Ben's response was sullen.

"And how exactly did you expect that to turn out?"

He shrugged.

"Listen here," said Green. "You drop your weapon or Elliot here will put a bullet in you."

Elliot fingered the trigger.

Only a few meters separated us, and I was sure that before Elliot got up the nerve to shoot me I could shoot him. Twice. But there wasn't going to be a damn thing I could do for Ben. Deputy Green had been shamed. Shame is a dangerous emotion in a man with a gun. Shame's near as dangerous as rage and by the look of it, Deputy Green had a nice helping of each.

"Takes a brave man to wear a star," I said, my voice low and slow. "Doesn't take clever or good, but it sure as hell takes brave."

I lowered my weapon to the ground and placed it gently in the wavy grass. In the distance, on the path back to the ranch, I saw the lone longhorn making its way closer. I squinted at it for a minute, but it was far enough away that it didn't matter.

"Elliot," I said, "you'll be wanting to take your finger off that trigger. It'd be a shame to shoot an unarmed man. In fact, I'd be mighty disappointed to know I'd been shot by accident."

Elliot glanced at Green, who nodded. He slipped his finger off the trigger but kept it close. Beads of sweat ran down the man's forehead and dripped right into his eyes. He blinked it away.

"Now, Deputy Green," I said, "it's your turn. Please remove your weapon from my friend and point it at me. I'm not going anywhere, and he's unarmed. Good. Now, Ben, stay in Green's field of vision and don't..."

There was a vibration that I felt in my boots. A rhythmic pounding getting steadily stronger. I squinted again down the trail.

"Ben, would you say that the longhorns you have here are particularly aggressive?"

Ben shook his head and looked at me like I was stupid.

"Prone to frolicking?"

"What?"

"Would you say they're prone to a good frolicking run from time to time?" I took a step backwards.

Ben's eyes got wide. He craned his neck and saw what I was talking about.

Green wasn't having any of it. He took a step forward and jabbed his rifle in my direction. "On you knees, then," he said. "We'll do your e-cuffs right this time." He reached into a pocket and took out one of the sleek little orbs. He thumbed it, activating the device.

The longhorn disappeared behind a rise. It was close now, and coming fast. Its thundering hoof beats were shaking the ground, making pebbles dance. Elliot looked around nervously, but Green was not allowing any distractions.

Green wanted me to drop or some such, but all I could think of was the thousand kilos of quality Texas beef headed our way.

The beast let out a deep bellow and crested the hill. The sound was fury and pain all mixed up in a roar that shook my chest. Green and Elliot turned, got off a few shots, which didn't seem to slow the thing at all. The longhorn lowered its head and charged their cruiser.

Horns slammed into the car, sending it screeching sideways and flipping it over. The monster shook its massive head.

"Run!" I gestured madly for the deputies to get out of the way. Green did as I said, bolting straight for the mesquite.

Elliot stood his ground, firing rapidly without any real consideration to aim. He hit plenty of times, but it did no good other than to anger the already furious beast.

Ben scrambled to his shotgun and snatched it up. He raised it at the beast.

Another furious bellow. Mad eyes focused on Elliot and it charged.

I dove at the deputy to pull him out of the way.

One horn cracked into my metal arm, sending me spinning. The other pierced Elliot's sternum, passing through him like a shish kebab through an onion. It shook him hard, tearing flesh and bone apart until Elliot's body went flying off into the grass.

I tried to regain my feet, stumbled, then staggered over to Ben's truck.

Ben's shotgun roared twice as the bull turned its massive form around. Ben took careful aim at the thing's head.

"You're too far away," I shouted at Ben. "It won't work!"

"Then let it get close." There was a dead determination in his eyes. He widened his stance and aimed down the shining barrel of his gun.

The longhorn pawed at the ground. Crazed fury still boiled behind its eye and its gaze damn near bore a hole through Ben.

I jumped up on the truck.

"Hey!" I banged my metal fist into the roof of the vehicle as hard as I could, over and over. The longhorn turned to me at the noise. "Ben, get out of here."

"I ain't leaving."

"Get!"

He seemed to falter for a second. The longhorn shook its head, snorted, and pawed at the ground.

Ben stood his ground.

The beast charged me. Its thundering hoof beats shook the truck, almost enough for me to lose my footing, but I held. On top of the truck I was too high for the deadly horns, or so I hoped. I crouched down, gripping the edge of the vehicle with my metal hand.

Primal rage erupted inside of me and I let it out in a war cry, my bellow meeting that of the charging bull.

At the last second, I launched myself into the air. The bull slammed into the truck, sending it tumbling away.

I twisted myself around in the air, hoping my estimate had been right.

It was. I landed on the back of the beast, grabbing big fistfuls of the shaggy hair.

The longhorn reared up. My boots dug in hard. Its front hooves came down hard, knocking the wind from my lungs. I held, but the beast didn't let up. It kicked its hind legs then shook. My leg flew free, but I was able to get it back in place before the next big kick.

My hat started to fall, so I grabbed it with my hand and by golly I do believe I let out a whoop like nobody's heard for a long time. The beast started to slow down, kicking less each time. All of those kilos were intimidating, but that mass wore the beast out fast.

Ben lowered his shotgun and stood there slack-jawed. When the longhorn finally dropped from exhaustion, Ben slung his weapon across his back and ran over to help me down before the bull rolled over on me. Once I was far enough away, I sat right down on the soil and laughed.

Ben looked worried.

"Hell of a ride," I said. "Hell of a ride."

Green emerged from his hiding place in the mesquite, rifle raised.

"Put it away, Deputy," I said. "You don't need it."

"Why not?"

"No need to shoot something that's too tired to fight." I nodded at the bull. "The longhorn's too tired too, so you'd best be on your way."

Green kept the rifle pointed at me.

The glint of something metal on the bull's neck caught my eye.

"Ben," I said. "What is that?"

Ben moved to the side of the longhorn. It let out a snort, but otherwise didn't protest. He stroked its flank gently, speaking softly to it. He reached up to the creature's neck and pulled off a slender metal collar. He turned it around in his hand.

I said, "That's like the harness you had back at the ranch."

He nodded.

"So, that's why this one was acting strange." I put my hat back on. "But does that mean Francis was controlling it?"

"Could have been anyone."

"Back yonder I opened a door. I suppose whoever has control of this big fella might not have wanted us seeing what was in there."

"Well, that sounds like a technophobe conspiracy theory, J.D." Ben scratched his head. "Might be right, though."

For a long minute Green did nothing. Then, his gaze fell on Elliot's body and the rifle was all but forgotten. Green walked forward in a daze, felt for a pulse in the ruined neck of his partner, and shook the poor body until he knew for sure it wasn't going to start moving again. He sobbed, burying his face in his hands.

Ben and I took a step away so that he could be in peace.

When Green spoke, his voice was flat. "He had a wife."

With a grunt, I righted Green's cruiser. It was dented badly, but otherwise appeared to be functional. "Son," I said, "it's a hard thing losing a good man. I'm sorry."

He looked at me. His eyes glistened. "They just got married."

"All the more reason to find his murderer."

Green's focus snapped on me. "Murderer?"

"Someone had that thing under control. Through this." I held up the harness. "We aim to figure who."

Green swallowed. "We should handle this," he said. "The sheriff's office, I mean."

"That they should," I said. "But they can't solve this one. Not without trouble from Austin."

"What do you need?"

"Time."

"How much?"

"A day. Take the good deputy to his family. It won't be easy. Come morning, tell the sheriff what happened and bring her over to Ben's ranch to check the facts. By then we might have something y'all can help with."

He nodded.

I turned to leave but paused. "Why were you out here?" I asked Green.

"Report came in of some illegal rustling. Said you might be here too."

"Who called it in?"

Green licked his lips. "Not supposed to say." Then he caught the scowl I was giving him. "A kid. I don't know. There wasn't an ID on the message."

Chapter 26

The smell of burnt plastic flavored with a hint of metal reached us about halfway back to the hideout.

"You smell that?" Ben asked.

"Yep."

"That's not good, is it?"

"Nope."

We rushed through the brush, pushing our way through to the door. The smoky haze got thicker the closer we came. The clearing was a caustic, choking cloud by the time we arrived.

The door was closed. Thick, black smoke seeped out of cracks along the edges and from a vent a short distance away. The post, where I'd attached to the bunker's computer, had been bashed. Ruined. It was twisted and torn apart.

Everything I did to try to make sense of the situation failed. It was a puzzle with a missing piece. Maybe it wasn't a puzzle at all. Maybe I was trying to put together pieces from different puzzles and ending up with a damn mess. Seemed like I'd been doing that my whole life.

"Head on back," I said, trying to keep the resignation from my voice. "Once it's cooled I'll go in and see what there is to see."

Ben scratched his head. "That's it? This is big, J.D. We can't just sit around."

"Nothing for it."

"Are we even going to be able to open the door again?"

"We'll deal with that once we can deal with it."

I moseyed a short distance and sat down against a tree. My knees protested bending and protested again when I straightened them out. Tenderly, I slipped off my boot, getting my first good look at the injured leg since riding the bull. It was ugly. Blood was crusted all over the inside of my boot, sticking to everything. The bandage was torn and bunched up to the side, where it wasn't doing anyone any good.

"Another one?" Ben pulled a new wrap out of his pocket and tossed it on my lap. "Take care of this one, old man. Damn." He sighed and also tossed me his canteen.

I took a swig. It was warm. A person could have passed it off for tea. The sweltering heat of the day had snuck up on us, baked us right in our boots. It wasn't even noon and I could see the waves of heat rising off the tops of the hills. Down in the protected valley the brutal sun was somewhat filtered, but it was made up for with humidity.

"So you're just going to sit there and wait?" Ben asked.

"Might have my luck at those tracks." I pointed to a boot print about a meter from where I sat. "That and the broken twigs just a short distance over there. Take a good look."

He looked, and as far as I could tell took the look seriously.

"That's a fresh track in a dry forest. See the bright wood just under the bark? That gets dull when it's been exposed to air for a day, shorter in this heat. I know I didn't do that and the only animal tracks I see around here are from the kind of animal that stabs its friends in the back for money."

Once he finished peering closely at the tracks, he looked me over. "You sure you're going to make it out here if I leave you?"

"Come back by sundown if you can."

"I will, but that's a long day in this heat."

I shrugged. "Make a few calls for me while you're out there."

He raised an eyebrow.

"No connection down here in this valley." I tapped my ear. "Tried to call earlier."

"Hills don't block the signal."

"Something's doing it."

Ben spent a few moments fiddling with the tech in his head, but came to the same conclusion. There was no connection to the outside world here.

"Get Abi over here, soon as she can manage it. I expect she's mad enough that she wants to help." A wave of exhaustion washed over me, but I shook it off. "Call Court too. We're going to need her people if we end up putting together a posse."

"Court? Really?"

"Really. It's that big. Sometimes an outlaw is your best hope."

"Yeah, I know. I used to roll with Cinco Armas, remember? They're really not a good place to hang your hope."

"No, they're not."

We looked at each other in silence for a moment. "Anyone else?" Ben said finally.

"Yeah, one more thing." I nodded back down the path where we'd come. "That deputy. He's probably going to call the sheriff."

"Probably already has."

"You might as well talk to her too. Tell her she's welcome to join the posse, but if she tries to stop it there's going to be trouble."

He gave me a weak smile. "That's not a very coherent group, you know. There's going to be violence."

"It's a posse, Ben. There damn well better be violence."

"That's not—"

"Go."

Ben left. Half an hour later, I'd finished the water in his canteen and bandaged my leg for a third time. It seemed there was some value staying off of it, so I used my knife to fashion a walking stick from a fallen branch. Mesquite isn't oak, but it would do.

After a failed attempt at following the tracks—the trail simply disappeared—I settled into some shade, pulled my hat down on my head, and waited. Whoever those tracks belonged to either knew how to move without leaving a trace or got picked up in a flying vehicle.

Noon came and went, and the filtered shade failed to keep the sun off my hat and the heat off my head. I sweated like a fat man eating chili peppers. An hour later, I stopped sweating, and that's when I knew I was in trouble.

A man ought never underestimate the hot heat of a Texas summer. Nobody, not the fairest child or the toughest soldier, can survive when the heat comes to visit. All that water that makes up our frail bodies gets baked out, leaving us with dry tongues, burned skin, and death. That heat mummifies our remains and leaves us as warnings for fools who come after. It's a shame nobody heeds warnings.

Large birds with naked heads circled high above. Not a good sign. They were the kind of birds who came to pay their visit once the heat cooked your meat just right. Scavengers would come on land, seeking out the fresh meat. A crow landed just a few branches away and cocked its head as if asking how long I was planning on sitting there.

Thick haze still clung to the hot afternoon air. No breeze bothered to carry it away, so there it stayed. The afternoon passed in heavy silence. It got hotter.

My eyes snapped open. When had they closed? The sun had moved, but it was hard to tell how much time had passed. My hands were red where the sun now beat down on them. With a huge effort, I moved back into the filtered shade. My knees refused to bend, but the strength in my metal arm achingly obeyed.

The crow bit my face.

I snapped up, alert again, and swatted at the bird. It flew away, watching from only a few meters away. My gaze met that of the black bird and it stared back at me. It seemed disappointed. The bird shook its head and stretched its greasy black wings, batting aside green leaves.

How could it be disappointed? It was a bird. Then again, how could it not be disappointed? Here I was about to die from heat in a land where dangerous heat was a daily thing. Sure, this was hotter than the hottest day I'd ever been through, but that didn't excuse my lack of preparation. That didn't excuse stupidity. Now, everyone who depended on me wouldn't get what they needed. My tribe would never get those horses. The people of Dead Oak wouldn't ever know freedom once Quintech took over their implants. Hell, even the outlaws of Cinco Armas would be slaves to that same tech. It was a game changer, and here I was the only man with enough pieces to the puzzle to make a decent shot at a solution.

"What're you looking at?" I muttered through a thick tongue. "I did my best."

The crow didn't seem to care. I touched my cheek where he'd bit me and came back with a thick smear of blood.

"See?" I said. "Still alive."

The crow stared at me from its backdrop of green, lush underbrush. A thought pushed its way into my head like a trout swimming through molasses. There was green here. A lot of it. All this green wouldn't happen without a water source. It might all be underground, but there was a chance there was a spring nearby.

My joints protested the very idea of moving. Dizziness dropped me again once I was up, but I gritted my teeth and forced myself back up. I didn't know which way to go at first, so I just walked. Deeper into the mesquite, where the land seemed to hold some sliver of its life. The air seemed cooler the farther I walked. My skin felt tight. Dry.

It's not hard to follow tracks in soft earth. Animals fall into their routines just like people. They'll walk the same path every day their whole life if nothing stops them. I fell into the trail, spotting at first rabbit tracks, then deer. It might not have been far, maybe less than a kilometer, but it felt like forever. More than once I had to pick myself up off the ground, not remembering falling. My mouth was so dry it hurt. Tongue so swollen it nearly choked me.

The crow followed, and when I first heard the soft murmur of the brook I thought the crow was muttering at me. I refused to let hope get hold of me. It wouldn't be water. It had to be something else. Not only was I going to die, but now that I was deep in the forest they would never find my body.

A splash from up ahead. A splash. My breathing quickened. Still, thirsty as I was, I didn't rush forward. Instead, I crept as quietly as I could, parting the branches so that I could see what had made the noise.

Horses. Three of them. They stood in a brook not more than a meter wide. I must not have been as sneaky as I wanted to be because the trio froze and stared at me.

The largest was the same black I had tried to catch. Her coat was glossy and thick muscles worked as she shifted uncomfortably. Here she was, looking at me like I was walking in on her secret garden. This must have been where the horses found water. This was how they survived.

Cautiously, I walked forward, hands out.

Two of the horses turned and ran. Not the black, though. She stood, the whites of her eyes showing. Her muscles tensed up, but she didn't run.

I tried to talk, to give her a soothing word or two. My dry throat refused to make any sound. Ten meters away from her, I tripped, stumbled forward, and landed in a heap.

When I looked up, she was gone.

Above, the crow cawed.

No. I wouldn't die there. Stubborn only gets a man so far against the forces of nature, but that's pretty damn far. I forced myself up on my knees, leaning heavily on my metal arm. I crawled the last ten meters to the brook.

The water was cool and a little gritty. It was the most delicious thing I had ever tasted. The next couple hours I sipped, then gulped, water. Once my canteen was refilled and I could reliably stand, I started back to the hideout.

It was time to get that damn door open. Again.

Chapter 27

Halfway back to the clearing, the whole forest shook from an explosion.

Someone else got to the door first. Could this day get any shittier?

Slowing, I picked my way carefully closer to the clearing. This forest was old, and the ground off trail was covered in dead material. Every step had to be carefully chosen. Crouching low, I crept up closer until I spotted someone up ahead, messing with the door. It was still closed. The man turned, ran in my direction.

It was Tucker.

He ran, trundled through the forest, and ran right smack into me. By then I had my pistol out, the tracking dot pointed right at his head. His hand twitched toward the sawed-off shotgun strapped to his belt.

"Tuck," I said. My voice was nothing more than a rasp, barely managing to sound like language at all.

Tucker must have heard the threat in my voice because he stopped.

"'Preciate it if you'd hold still," I said.

"What, so you can shoot me?"

"Ought to." I picked up my pistol and pointed it back at him. "For the bank. Mind telling me what you're doing out here?"

"Business as usual." He stuck a thumb back at the door. "Saw the smoke and thought I'd come for a little salvage."

"On private land?"

"Ain't it all private land?"

"All the way out here?"

With a crack, the clearing behind him lit up in a column of light. A concussive force hit the two of us, staggering me a step back and making my ears ring.

Tuck gave me an apologetic look. "This ain't so far from my own place, as a matter of fact." He shifted his weight back and forth. "Put that gun down, Sheriff. You know you're not going to shoot me."

I tried to connect to the console. "Dead," I muttered, keeping an eye on Tucker as I poked around the clearing. His knapsack sat a short distance away, its contents spilled across the ground. The door was still solidly closed.

"No kidding," Tucker said. "Damn door won't open, but you know there's gotta be good stuff in there."

"You think?"

"Sure, door like this isn't the kind of thing you build for some old storm shelter." He licked his lips. "Some of that tech would have survived the fire."

Tucker made a move and I spun, pistol trained on him, so fast that he dropped a tin of snuff. The dirty brown contents scattered into the dirt.

"Fuck it all," said Tucker. "I'm not going to draw on you, J.D. What the hell's gotten into you?"

My shoulders were relaxed and my grip was steady. A long minute passed and I didn't say a thing.

With all the deliberation of a fat worm after a lazy rain, Tucker raised his hands and laced his fingers behind his head. "Been a long day. I don't need none of this," he said. "Hell, it's been a long couple days and you know I got you to blame. I'm not robbing anyone, and you ain't a sheriff. How about you let me go?"

"And what? Let you walk away so you can come back round to finish me off? So you can make sure there aren't any witnesses?"

He snorted. "You're a shit witness. Nobody's going to believe a washed-up old bank robber like yourself. Hell, you're about as reliable a witness as I am, now, aren't you? Tell me what's really on your mind, hoss."

"You were going to kill Trish and that deputy back at the bank."

His eyes went cold.

"You incinerated the place and you stole the tech after we agreed to destroy it."

His eyes narrowed and his voice dropped dead serious. "You agreed to destroy it. I had to do what I had to do. Can't blame a man for doing what he has to do, can you?"

"Then I'm going to owe you."

"For what?"

"This." I took one long step forward and hit him with a metal backhand nearly hard enough to break his jaw. He stumbled back, slammed against the black door, and skidded down it. His flesh blistered where half of his cheek rested against the hot metal.

It was tempting to leave him there to cook, but I just couldn't bear to see an old army buddy go out like that. I dragged his unconscious form into the shade. Judging by the sun, it was getting late and the worst of the heat was over.

I do believe my mood was improving.

That left the problem of the door. My brow furrowed, the dry skin of my face cracking in the hot afternoon. The day had cooked me—seared my skin and cracked my lips. Muscles had been roasted, which seemed appropriate given the couple days of tenderizing they'd suffered. My metal arm still pinged its warning, but a man can only be warned for so long before he learns to ignore it. A warning's nothing, after all. It's like that WRONG WAY sign stuck off kilter in the gritty sands of a long-lost highway.

The door was stuck and the computer that opened it wouldn't wake no matter how much I swore at it. I stood there puzzling over it for a long while, trying my best to pry the door open or dig around the edges. The walls of the compound were shallow under the rich soil and made from stronger stuff. It wasn't black metal, but the smooth concrete looked to have the sheen of something heavily reinforced. The surface reminded me of buildings in Austin or that bank in Swallow Hill.

Tucker grumbled and shifted as I rifled through his pockets, but didn't wake. Finally, I found what I was looking for: the can of foam door that he'd used to dissolve a door in the bank. It felt almost empty. I tossed the can on the ground. Useless.

An hour later, when Zane arrived, the angry sun twinkled through the tips of the trees and I was trying to open the door with cuss words and spit. It wasn't working. He landed his car gently, tipped his hat to the awake and now fully hogtied Tucker, and stood there with one hand on his hip, watching me.

"City boy," I said, noticing him wince at the term, "you got any ways to open this door?"

He studied it close for a minute, eyes flashing in the late-afternoon light. Finally, he straightened up and said, "Just need to hack the computerized system, far as I figure."

I raised an eyebrow at him and stuck a thumb back at the post in the middle of the clearing. "Have at it."

He did. A small panel in the side of the twisted post opened after half an hour of poking and prodding. I was impressed that he'd found it, but I was careful not to let it show. In the end, the access did nearly as much good as my cussing and spitting, but with less of the psychological benefit.

Ben found the two of us staring at the wall scratching our heads. I'd heard his truck rumble up to the edge of the woods, where he must have parked. The rancher didn't make any attempt at being quiet when he came crashing through the forest either. He was out of breath when he broke into the clearing.

"You're okay," he said after a bit, more a statement than a question.

I nodded.

"I wasn't sure, with the heat and all." He tossed me a skin of water and I drank. "I'd have been here sooner, but—"

"Don't worry about it, son," I said.

Ben's brow furrowed when he looked over and saw Tucker. Wheels turned in his head trying to figure out why the ugly man was tied tight to one of the shrubby trees.

"Isn't that Mr. Hale?" Ben whispered.

"Right where he belongs," said Zane.

"What'd he do?"

I nodded at the door. "You got a way to open this?"

He smiled. "I thought they might be tough to open, so I brought my tow package."

"Your what?"

He disappeared back into the woods and returned with the truck. The thing hovered over the clearing with an odd thumping noise. My belly did a flip as he came closer. Once he'd landed, he hopped out, attached a thick cable to the back of the vehicle's frame, and then hopped up into the back and started rummaging around in the tools. He found what he was looking for and attached it to the other end of the cable. It was a half sphere, ringed with a faint green glow.

"Truck's sounding funny," I said.

He nodded. "Some jackass tricked a bull into ramming it."

"Tow package will still work?"

"Yeah, this ought to do it."

Tuck snorted. "Sure it will."

"Shut up, Tuck," Zane and I both said at once.

"Hey," Tuck said in a more placating tone. "Can y'all untie me now? I'm not going to hurt anyone. Hell, I don't even have any weapons."

Ben slammed the sphere against the black door. With a low thunk it stuck, the green glow on its surface intensifying. He hopped into the truck while Zane and I moved a good distance back so we'd be as far away from the cable as possible. Tucker looked worried about his position, but I figured he was safe from any direct danger.

Gravity-manipulation engines were inexpensive and didn't require much power. Utility vehicles like Ben's truck held a powerhouse of a gravity drive that allowed him to haul massive loads. Hell, its biggest limitation was the soft, squishy man behind the controls.

The first tug shook the ground under my feet. Ben's gravity drive was leaking, which meant he was messing with the gravity unevenly around the truck. It was a little worrisome, but probably wouldn't be too dangerous.

Or, maybe it would.

My boots slipped across the loose soil. Trees near the hovering truck were bending and swaying. My stomach made a mad dash to my throat. Zane gripped my elbow and I could see that he was having trouble as well.

The door still didn't budge.

Ben looked ill at the controls. His face was flushed and twisted into a grimace. He loosened up and shook it off. After a deep breath, he looked back at me and gave me a thumbs-up.

"Again?" I hollered over a sudden rush of wind.

"One more time," he said. "I'll give it all."

He gave it all. For a moment, I was weightless. Zane gripped my elbow. His fingers dug in somewhat painfully. I held him back, not wanting to let go of the one thing I was sure I could hold.

Then we were falling sideways, away from the door. Dirt kicked up, branches flew past. Zane gripped a mesquite tree, keeping the two of us from falling fifty meters sideways. Tucker floated in the air, tied securely to a tree.

The door held, but the truck didn't. The rear square of its frame twisted under the pressure, squealing as the truck's multiplied weight pulled it against the door. As it seemed to be just ready to give, the half sphere at the end of the cable flashed green and came loose, sending the truck crashing through the forest and up into the sky.

Zane and I landed hard on our butts and watched the truck fly off into the distance. It slowed, turned, and returned to land on the opposite end of the clearing. Zane and I didn't move.

Ben looked exhausted. He stumbled out of the truck and leaned against it, gasping. After a while, he looked our way, resignation on his face. "Francis really doesn't want us getting into his lab," he said.

"Just makes me want to get in more."

"Yeah." Ben looked up at the sky. "Abi's on her way."

"We had the door open."

Ben nodded.

"It was right there," I said. "Right there open and waiting for me. If I hadn't turned back, we'd be on our way already." I grabbed the hat off my head and twisted it like I wanted to tear it to shreds.

"It was my fault," said Ben. "I shouldn't have needed your help. I should've stayed better hid from those deputies."

"Seems like a hell of a lot of coincidence," I said. "The deputies, the longhorn, the fire. All at the same time. Like someone planned it."

I stroked my stubble and stood there for a few minutes. It still wasn't making much sense, but it seemed more important than ever that we get into the hideout. Maybe the fire would destroy everything, but if there was any chance we could pull information out of there, we needed to try.

Zane rested his hands on our shoulders. "Gentlemen." His hand on my shoulder felt good. Tension eased out of my muscles. "This is nothing to worry about. We'll set up camp here and when Abi arrives she'll know about any tools from the junkyard that might get us through this door."

I shrugged his hand off my shoulder and turned to face him. "Set up camp? Is that your advice or the advice of Goodwin? For all we know, they're behind all this. What's their profit from us waiting when our town might be in danger? Hell, when a whole load of towns might be in danger?"

He stuck a finger right in the middle of my chest. "Settle your damn self down, J.D. I'm my own man."

"Are you?" I peered at him through my modified eye. "And as your own man did you come up with the idea of putting this damn tech in my head? Tech I can't get out without your help? Was that your own damn idea?" My face felt hotter than the oven-hot air around us. I shoved Zane. Not hard, but there was so much rage.

Zane squared off against me and met my gaze. "Do it, J.D." His fists were tight knots at his sides. "Take a swing. You'll see what a city boy does to stand up for himself."

My jaw clenched till my teeth were sore. Zane wasn't my friend; he was a man from the city working for a company that sure as hell didn't have my best interest in mind. They were rotten to the core, and I'd had enough trying to make things work with Zane.

Still, I needed him. For as long as my purposes aligned with Goodwin's, I needed to keep Zane around. His tech skills and understanding of the corporate structure were critical, or so I figured.

And dammit if I didn't want him close just for the sake of having him there. "Get," I said. "Set up camp over there, but make it a small fire. There's enough smoke around here and these trees will be mighty dry after all this heat."

Zane opened a storage compartment in his car and pulled some fancy-looking weaponry off a gun rack. I placed my hand on his shoulder. "Leave them," I said. I didn't think there was any threat in my voice.

He glared at me. "It's for protection."

"Well, I'll feel safer if I hold the guns for now."

Zane opened his mouth like he was going to protest.

"Gravity well," I said.

He blinked. "What?"

"You said Tucker Hale trapped you in a gravity well when you went to visit him. There's no such thing in his place."

"That...That doesn't make him less of an asshole."

"No." My fist was clenched so tight the knuckles turned white. "But it means you were lying about what happened there. Who placed the camera?"

Zane looked at me pleadingly.

"Who put your camera in the butcher's shop?"

"I did," said Tucker. His eyes sparkled with amusement. "That city boy's stars sparkle just like anyone else's."

I stuck a finger in Zane's chest. "And that's why I don't trust you."

Zane shoved my hand away. "I'll carry what I want to carry, J.D." He put the pistol back on the rack and locked the case. "But for now I'll do as you ask."

"We're safe here. Nobody's coming after us right now. If something does, then we've got plenty to hold them back."

Zane nodded and got to work making the fire.

As the sun set over the hilltops, Abi arrived on my skidder. She flew low, skimming the tops of trees and coming in nice and quiet. She landed gently a distance away from the door and walked over to me with slumped shoulders. Her eyes had bags under them, and their redness told of recent tears.

I tipped my hat when she approached.

"Howdy," she said.

There wasn't a thing I could say that would make Josephine's death hurt any less. Hell, it hurt me so bad just seeing Abi's pain. "I'm sorry, Abi."

She shook her head and stared at the dirt.

I placed a hand on her shoulder. "Ben tell you about the door?"

"Yeah. He called me earlier."

"Any ideas on how to get it open again?"

"It's locked?"

"We have to get in there."

She looked at the wall, standing there next to me and staring for a good long time. After a few minutes she said, "I don't know, J.D. I don't think there's going to be any...Hey, what's this?" She picked up Tucker's nearly empty can of foam door. Shaking it, she held it close to her ear and smiled. "There's some left."

"Not enough to make a door, though."

Abi looked at me like I was stupid, which more and more I suspected might be true. Shaking her head, she walked over to the door, which was no longer searing hot, and climbed up so she could reach the top. She shook the can and sprayed a single, sputtering line across the top of the door. Then she put the last bit of foam at the top corner of the door, right where the hinges would be hidden behind layers of concrete.

All I did was stare.

As the foam bubbled, it started oozing out of position, seeping along the front of the door, where it wouldn't do any good. Abi grabbed some leaves, using them to sweep the nanite goo back into place, where it bubbled some more. Along the side of the door, the foam slowly worked its way down the crack between the door and the wall, expanding it as it went. There, it hardly needed any coaxing, but Abi kept a close watch on it, anyway.

Minutes passed. Slowly, the edges of wall around the door eroded away. It wasn't enough to let us see through, but it was enough. Abi ran to Ben's truck and rummaged around in the back, emerging with a meter-long crowbar. With the crowbar slung over her shoulder, she strode confidently up to the door and gave it one long look.

With a smirk, she jammed the crowbar between the door and the wall and applied a little pressure. The door popped off, forcing her to jump back before it slid down and crushed her toes. It landed with a whump, and black smoke lazily rose from hole in the hill.

We were in.

Chapter 28

As the sky grew dark and the sounds of the night life rose in the forest, five of us ventured into the still-smoky depths of Francis William Brown's hideout. Abi pulled out a multi-tool and clicked it so that it emitted a soft, blue light. We wore handkerchiefs over our faces to filter the smoke, so we looked like a band of thieves.

"Just untie my hands," Tucker pleaded. "I'll help y'all out."

Ben gave him a shove. "You'll help our brains out of their damn skulls."

"You can trust me."

"Sure," I said. "I know I can trust you. I'd trust you to do what you think's got profit for you and to hell with anything else."

The hazy room opened up in front of me. It stretched back into the hill a dozen meters, with smaller branches making a large area give the impression of something cramped and small. The far wall was a bank of computers, mostly slagged by the intense heat of a fire. One side seemed mostly untouched, and Zane moved to investigate. I held up a hand to stop him.

"Careful," I said.

He pushed past me without any sign that he'd heard. My handkerchief smelled like tobacco and oil. Abi furrowed her brow at the melted wall, so I pointed to where the scorched metal looked the worst.

"Miss," I said, "see if you can't figure what started that fire."

"You bet." She placed her multi-tool on the table so that its flickering blue light spread through the entire room.

"Ben, keep an eye on Tuck. Bastard's crafty."

Ben nodded. Tucker leaned up against the corner of the wall near the entrance while Ben watched him warily from the stairs. Tucker's gaze followed me through the haze.

Every surface of the room was covered in thick, black soot. Anything that had been wood or paper had long since gone the way of the buffalo. Hell, even most of the plastic was gone and large sections of metal were twisted and sagging. The table in the middle of the room looked surreal. When I poked it with my toe, one corner of it shifted and made one hell of a racket.

Zane pried a cube from the twisted face of a computer bank using a slim knife. Everything around it was slag, but the cube was clean, shining silver.

"Data cube," Zane said, smiling. "Very retro."

Tucker snorted. "You're trusting the city boy with that?"

"Shut up, Tuck," I said. I turned to Zane and raised an eyebrow.

Zane scowled at me and set the cube down on the wobbling, three-legged table. "I don't have the reader for it, anyway." He went back to the computer bank and continued to dig.

"That's how it's done," said Tucker. "Sleight of hand. Boy's probably already copied the data, or switched cubes on you."

Zane crossed the room before I could blink. "Just what are you implying, Mr. Hale?"

Tucker grinned.

"Are you accusing me of being a spy for Goodwin?"

"Aren't you?"

Zane's face was a furious crimson, his fists balled at his sides. After several long seconds, he breathed out and relaxed. He turned back to his work and didn't say another word for quite some time.

One of the walls appeared to be solid steel, but closer inspection revealed flaws brought out by the heat. Tiny, almost imperceptible lines were etched in the otherwise black surface. When I rubbed them with my fingernail I could feel it catch. I traced it around until I could feel the outline of a panel that was about a half meter on each side. Pressing it didn't seem to move it. Pulling it using Ben's odd half sphere didn't yield any results. It seemed stuck.

"It was probably controlled by the computer," Zane said after a while.

"Better just give up," said Tucker. "Takes a clever man to break into something like that."

I tried my best to ignore him.

Tucker kept talking. "That's never really been your thing, has it? You need a veteran salvager on your side."

"Shut it, Tuck." I stared at the wall, as if scowling might force it open.

"I mean, if you couldn't shoot it or punch it, it wasn't a problem you could solve, now, was it?"

"Ben," I said.

"Yeah?"

"If Tucker talks again, shoot him in the leg."

Nobody said a damn word.

"Tuck," I said. "Shooting and punching are good solutions, but you know I have more than that. I've got my charm."

Silence.

"Oh, and this." I turned to the wall and kicked it with every ounce of my strength. The panel dented, making the line of one corner pop out just a little. I pried it back with one of the fingers of my metal hand and tore the entire thing loose. Tucker rolled his eyes but didn't say anything.

The panel had concealed three drawers. The top two were full of food and drink. Bottles of milk had cracked and broken from the heat, and everything in the bottom drawer was coated with a thick sludge of partially cooked dairy.

The bottom drawer was packed with harnesses like those Ben had been modifying, but the shape was different. These weren't designed to control horses or longhorns. They were much smaller, with a rounded top and softer leather.

The harnesses would fit perfectly on humans.

"Aha!" Abi said from across the room. She popped up from behind the wobbly table with a shred of something pinched between her fingertips.

I dropped the harness back in the bin and peered at the piece in Abi's hand. It was thin metal, like a piece of a tin can. When she rubbed away the soot, there was the faint hint of color.

When nobody seemed to understand what they were looking at, she said, "See the orange and blue? With the swirl?"

I nodded. "It's familiar."

"It's from an incendiary grenade. Slow burner, probably." She turned it over in her hands. "Or maybe an old one that didn't burn properly."

"Old," I said. "Like from an old Civil War stash?" I turned to Tucker.

Tuck's hands were free. He lunged at Ben, deflecting the shotgun just before it went off. The thundering shot scoured the wall and left my ears ringing. Tucker shouldered Ben forward, knocking him on his ass. Tuck bolted out the door.

Pulling my gun, I ran after him. When I crested the top of the steps, he was five meters away and moving toward the cover of Ben's truck. I thumbed the pistol active, and aimed it at my old army buddy Tucker.

But I didn't shoot him.

My shot slammed into the head of a coyote, centimeters from Tucker's neck, as it leapt at him from the hood of the mangled truck. Pasted skull splattered Tucker, pulling him up short. He turned back at me, rubbing his eyes.

His voice was high and panicked. "It was just a job!"

Two more coyotes rounded the truck. I shot one, taking off nearly its entire front left leg with one shot. The other got close to Tucker before I could shoot.

Tucker's eyes got wide looking at me. No, not me. He was looking behind me.

I dropped to my knees and covered my head with my metal arm. The coyote flew over the top of me, skittering to a stop just a meter away. I reached out, grabbed its head in my big metal fist, and squeezed. Its head crunched and the coyote went limp.

My ears were still ringing, but I felt Ben move up behind me. He went left, so I turned right. His shotgun roared twice and I picked off another coyote with my pistol.

Tucker screamed.

A coyote had his arm and it shook. Blood sprayed everywhere, plastering the side of the truck and darkening splotches of earth. I couldn't get a clear shot. He was moving too fast. If I shot, I'd hit Tuck—if not in the body, then at least in his arm. I couldn't shoot him. Shit, I just couldn't.

Ben didn't have any such problem. He took two long steps forward, leveled his shotgun, and fired. The shot tore the coyote to shreds, turning most of its head and body into paste. Tuck collapsed, mouth open in a silent scream. His arm below the elbow was a mess of bone shards and bloody meat.

Coyotes screamed and howled, worked into a frenzy. There were more in the woods, surrounding us.

Stepping forward, I scooped up Tucker. He was a heavy man, but with my metal left arm he was like lifting a kid. I slung him over my shoulder and made my way back into the hideout. When I got there, I handed Tucker off to Zane and went once more out into the darkness. I picked up the black metal door and waved Ben in. Once everyone was inside, I pulled the door up as a makeshift blockade. The howl of more coyotes echoed through the valley.

"Tuck!" I roared.

Abi was staunching his blood with her shirt. His face was red and tears rolled tracks through the dirt on his face. His eyes turned to me, whites showing all his fear.

"You're either in here with us or out there on your own," I said through my teeth. "I won't pull the trigger on you, but I'll set you out on your way."

He sobbed. "But—"

"Get your butt out of my face, soldier." I leaned down close. "And quit blubbering. We need you here and now. We need to know what you know and we need it now."

Abi cinched the makeshift bandage hard and Tucker screamed. When he'd had enough screaming, he met my eyes and nodded.

"All right." To Abi, I said, "Fix him up proper."

"I need Auntie's tools for that."

"What can you do with what you have?"

She poked the bandage that made up the stump of Tucker's arm with her finger, causing the soldier to wince. "I've done it."

"It's not enough."

"Well, I've got a kit in the skidder."

"Can you patch him up with that?"

"I can get some neural links patched in before he heals over it. It's the best time to do it. We'll fit him with a false hand later."

"No," said Tucker. The lids of his eyes were wide.

I looked at him questioningly.

"No metal." Tucker's brow was gleaming with sweat and blood. His teeth turned up in a snarl. He was fighting unconsciousness with everything he had.

"Fine." My hands were shaking and my belly was in a knot now that the adrenaline was wearing off. "No metal. Do we still need the kit?"

Abi shook her head.

"Good. We'll stay here till morning, then we move out." To Tucker, I said, "Now, it's time to talk."

He was out cold.

"Dammit." I picked up the remains of the incendiary grenade. "He ran when we found this. Any bets that this was his? Someone paid him to burn this place earlier."

"Why'd he come back, then?"

"Regret, probably. Indecisive bastard. He regretted leaving behind anything that might be of value." I tossed the piece of grenade to the floor. It was starting to look like the whole trip was a waste. "So, what else do we know?"

His voice laced with anger, Zane said, "Depends on who you trust."

"What's that supposed to mean?"

"I could have backed you up out there, J.D. If you'd let me carry my guns, I'd have been some help. Maybe your ugly friend wouldn't have lost a hand."

I wanted to fight. I wanted to yell and holler and let loose on the city boy, but the energy just wasn't there. All I said was, "Trust's a hard thing to come by."

"It sure is." Zane nodded at the data cube on the table. "So do you trust me to see what's on that?"

The data cube reflected the dim light. It was the only shiny thing in a field of soot and ash. It had answers, but as far as I knew, there was no way to get at them. Was Zane asking to leave with it? I couldn't let that happen. He'd fly off to Goodwin and the corporation would have every bit of technology Francis had been working on. If that included mind control that worked on humans, it'd only be a matter of time before those who worked the ranches and farms were replaced with slaves. As bad as people's lives were, that would be worse.

Now that Zane knew such a technology existed, how long would it be before Goodwin had its own version? It seemed each new wave of technology made people's lives worse and worse, but nobody ever thought of stopping it. Nobody ever stopped researching the worst of the worst. Technology just kept marching forward, ruining the land, the water, and the people as it went. In the old days it would take time to start turning bad. Technology would make people's lives better for a while before proving to be harmful. As technology progressed, so did the speed of its betrayal. This technology would maybe improve the lives of those rich city folk for only a year or two before they found it being used against them. The smart move would be to never let Zane get this tech back to his people.

Had he already done so? Communication in the valley was obstructed, but maybe Zane had some tricks that weren't available to regular folks. He could be betraying us instantaneously. That was the benefit of instant communications.

"I know you have a glow cube," Zane said. His voice had an accusatory tone to it.

"Sure."

He held out his hand.

I dug it out and placed it in his hand. He didn't move for a second, staring at the scuffed piece of hardware.

Zane set the glow cube down and activated it. When the display hologram flashed to life above the cube, he squinted at it and cocked his head to one side. "How do you even..." He must have spotted something, because he smiled, poked a few times at the display, and stepped back. The cube went dark and popped in half.

"What the hell?" I said. "You have it for ten seconds and you broke—"

"Shh."

My jaw kept working like there were words, but I just didn't have any.

He smiled an impish grin at me. "It's supposed to do that."

"Huh." I wasn't convinced.

The city boy pulled the two halves of the cube open, revealing a smaller cube inside made of a shiny metal like the one he'd found in the console. It looked like an exact duplicate, as a matter of fact. Zane switched the two bits and powered my glow cube back up.

Zane scoured the data on the cube for hours with me watching the whole time. Every few minutes he would mutter a curse unbefitting of his civilized nature. Abi went back to searching the place for more clues, and Ben went back to staring distrustfully at Tucker.

"I'm on your side," Zane said. "It's not like I'm going to run off, you know." He flipped through a few images. They were hazy but clear enough to see that they were nothing more than landscape photos.

"You're on your own side. Just like everyone else out here."

"Fair enough. But they don't have to be opposite sides. We can be allies."

"Sure."

Zane looked up from the display. "That didn't sound convincing."

"Wasn't meant to be."

"It's not like we're going to get anything off of this." He cycled quickly through some images. "It's barely compatible, so much of the data is unreadable."

"There's got to be something."

He sighed. "I'll keep looking."

"Wait." I grabbed Zane's shoulder. "Go back."

"What?"

"Back. Go back two pictures."

He waved his hand, swearing when it didn't respond on a first couple tries. Finally, he got the image to cycle back.

"That's it. See that building there?"

"The tower with the glass dome?"

"You think that's Quintech?"

"Could be, but there's no location information on these images. It tells us there's a building, but not where the building is."

"Take a closer look."

He squinted at the flickering image for a full minute before giving up.

"Those hills in the background. See how one has that broken look to it?"

"That's near Swallow Hill."

"We figured that already. But since we can't fly there, it's going to take too long to search those hills. We need an exact location."

"I have the exact center," Abi said. "I calculated it while you were visiting the bank."

I pondered that. "Those blue lines."

"Yeah."

Ben and Abi were peering at the image now, somber looks on their faces. We all knew what it meant. We'd need to go into the most dangerous place in the Texas outland and take apart whatever was projecting that field. Until that happened, there wouldn't be any way to get enough firepower close enough to take Francis down.

"Zane," I said, "can you pull up any other information related to that picture?"

He furrowed his brow. "There's a lot," he said. "Blueprints, diagrams." His eyes widened. "Even some partial research notes. Everything but location."

"But we know that already from Abi's calculations." I rubbed the bridge of my nose. "We might just have enough here to put together a decent attack."

Ben spoke first, "You'll have to walk there."

"Why?"

"You're the only one besides Tucker without full headgear. You can't fly because of the field, and I'm guessing they'll have tightened ground security after the bank."

"Walking's too slow." I tapped my leg. "Plus, doc says to stay off this if I can. Can we use that six-wheeler that Tuck rode off with?"

"I doubt it," said Zane. "They'll be looking for something like that. These people aren't stupid, you know. Those things are noisy. Easy to target and track."

My head pounded. "So, we need a way to cover ground fast that isn't flying and isn't noisy."

Zane shook his head. "Then what can you do?"

"Get some rest." I pulled my pistol and took over his position watching the exit. "Tomorrow's going to be a hot one."

Chapter 29

The horses thundered across the plain, racing from nowhere to nowhere. Why were they galloping so hard? They didn't seem to be running to anything or from anything. They were just running for the pure joy. For freedom.

High above, I banked forward and down, sliding in gently behind the herd.

Zane rode to the right, standing in his red convertible like a showman whooping up a crowd. The wind swept the tight curls of his hair back and his black duster billowed out behind him like a cape. He was clearly enjoying himself, not bothered at all by the sweltering heat of the early morning.

And it was hot. The night had been one where you can't sleep for fear of waking up roasted like a pig. When morning came and the sun kissed the earth with its new day, the temperature did nothing but rise.

To my left was Ben. He rode his damaged truck with a fierce look that mixed frustration, anger, and determination. The leaky gravity drive on the thing still washed over me from time to time, a sensation I felt in my belly like I was falling. He'd tinkered with it for an hour after the sun came up just to get it in good enough shape. After Zane had come back from dropping Tucker and Abi off at the junkyard, Ben had tossed out a few choice cuss words and declared the truck good enough.

I waved Ben off farther to the left and lowered my skidder so that I was only a few meters above the soil. We were moving fast, not anywhere near as fast as the skidder would go, but fast enough to resemble the last time I'd tried to corral this feral herd.

If I ran up to the horses fast, I'd have to slow down when I got to them. My only way of doing that was to fire the thrusters forward, and that'd be a lot like firing cannons at a horse and then asking it to stand still.

Zane and Ben dropped to the same level. Ahead, and a little to the right, was our destination. The valley that held Francis's hideout was also going to be where we corralled the horses. Once they were stopped, we'd approach them on foot and collect the ones that still had enough training to make them workable.

The lead horse—that same black I'd tried to rope before—banked hard right, pulling ahead of the rest and looping hard around Zane's side. Zane swooped out to try to bring it back in, but it stopped hard, turned, and ran in the opposite direction. Several dozen other horses followed suit.

"Keep at 'em!" I shouted, waving Ben and Zane forward.

There were enough horses left in the herd. Hell, for my plan we only really needed one. There was no reason to catch all of them or even the best of them. There was no reason to go after that towering black.

Yet, she was the one I wanted.

I waved the others forward and banked my skidder hard right. Waves of dry heat baked my body as the sun made hell out of earth. My lips were cracked and dry, my face red from the blistering heat of the previous day. None of it mattered. All I wanted was that horse.

Rushing wouldn't get it. With my metal hand seated firmly in the control console, I had to negotiate my lasso one-handed. It wasn't hard since I'd set things up just right ahead of time. I looped the rope around the hook, just so. The loop dropped free and with a whoop I started it spinning.

The horse ran hard, outpacing the other that had followed it. She was a beautiful creature, all black and shining in the morning sun. The rhythm of her thundering hooves beat like a primal drum in a music that played across the landscape for anyone willing to listen. As I drew slowly closer, her cadence quickened into a new pattern. She was running.

I threw the lasso hard as I could, but the wind took it and pulled it off course. The thing fell useless far off target. Without missing a beat, I looped it back up and set it spinning again.

The second throw was closer. It touched the horse on the flank, bouncing harmlessly off her side. The touch of it seemed to startle the creature and she started a long arc to the left. I ground my teeth and kept my pace, slowly gaining ground. Still, I didn't dare let myself get too close.

The third throw of the lasso looped nicely around her neck. I let out a whoop of joy just as she turned hard.

The rope ran under the skidder and the pull rolled me ninety degrees. Rocks whipped by, nearly close enough to knock off my hat. Using the neural controls, I immediately compensated for the change and flipped back up. I eased up and applied a little pressure.

She applied more. My skidder lurched forward, and the tension tuned the rope like a guitar string. I let out a little more rope, increasing our distance little by little. She pulled, and she gained ground, but she wasn't getting away. Once I had some distance, I eased the thrusters and flexed a bit of solid-fueled muscle to slow us down.

The horse slowed from a run down to a stop in about the span of five paces. I matched her movement. She snorted. I snorted back.

Then I landed and stepped off my skidder.

She eyed me and skittered back a few steps. I eyed her back, stepping slowly closer. When I saw the whites of her eyes, I stopped. Her whole body moved with deep breaths. We stood facing each other for a good long time. Her breaths slowed, but her eyes still showed fear.

Her eyes weren't focused on me. She was looking at my metal arm.

"I know, girl," I said in my most soothing voice. It came out more as gruff, but it was the best I could do. "I don't like it either." My metal arm wasn't going to do me much good, so I pulled it into my poncho and hid it as best I could.

One thing I learned living among the ranches of Texas is that horses aren't stupid. Well, they are, but they're never stupid when you want them to be. Just because she couldn't see my metal arm didn't make her forget about it. This old lady had been living away from people for a long time, surviving just fine in a sweltering heat that should have scoured the land clean a long time ago. She didn't have any need of me and she sure as hell didn't need to have anything to do with my tech.

I reeled the rope in and took a step forward.

She took a step back.

"It's all right, girl. No need to worry."

Another step forward.

Another step back.

"My apologies," I said. "I wish I could let you run free, but I need your help."

She snorted.

"There's a bad man. Maybe more than one. I need a way to travel fast without warning them that I'm coming." Reaching down to my belt, I touched Ben's harness. If I could just get a few steps closer, I'd be able to attach it to the horse and she'd settle without any problems.

She looked at me with those big brown eyes. The whites had disappeared and her expression now seemed to be one of calm understanding. It seemed to be one of acceptance. Whatever it was, it drove a big stab of guilt right into my belly. How could I use this technology on her?

There wasn't time to mess around. It might already be too late, but if it wasn't, there definitely wasn't time to get to know a horse and to let the horse get to know me. There wasn't an option other than the tech, was there? This was the whole reason we went way the hell out there. My thumb fingered the back of the harness, where a nodule held the most offensive tech I'd ever had the pleasure to run across.

Stepping forward, shoulders relaxed, I unclipped the harness from my belt—

Her hoof snapped out so fast I hardly had time to blink. She kicked the hat right off of my head and made a noise like a neigh and a scream mixed in one. I stumbled backward, tripped, and ended sprawled on my back with hooves still above me. The whites of her eyes were showing again, and her pupils were tiny pinpricks.

Hooves slammed down on each side of me, missing my legs by mere centimeters. The ground shook with their crushing force and the horse skittered backward.

After a minute, I sat up. The offending harness was still in my hand, so I tossed it away so that the big girl could see what I'd done.

"That's fine, we don't need any of that."

But I wasn't so sure. There hadn't been much trust, but it was gone now. Rebuilding trust was harder than earning it in the first place. Her eyes darted to where I'm sure she remembered I'd hidden my metal arm. What made her distrust technology like this? It didn't matter. That distrust was there and it was going to be tough to get past.

Meanwhile, the sun was making its long walk across the sky. The hot early morning was turning into a scorching late morning. Noon would be brutal if we were still out here in it. There was plenty of water packed on my skidder, but this couldn't take all day.

Standing, I held my hand palm forward and took a few steps forward.

She let me. I don't know why, but she did. The rope was still around her neck, though I wasn't holding it anymore. I pulled the lasso off over her head and let it drop to the ground.

She was so beautiful. Her hide was rough and smooth at the same time, her coarse hair shining in the morning light like black gold. She leaned into me when I touched her cheek, seeming as happy to get the attention as I was to give it. Long minutes passed with her nuzzling my chest and me scratching her ears.

This was the next step in my plan, but it felt like so much more. A tear nearly came to my dry eye as I stroked her hide. I felt like this was how it should be. Standing next to that great beast seemed natural. It seemed right.

I felt complete.

Chapter 30

The walk back was long, and the sun was as angry as it gets, but I walked it with a horse at my side and a head held high. It was too soon to ride the horse. She was still too skittish and it was too hot. She wouldn't do me much good exhausted. I couldn't ride the skidder, since the horse would bolt as soon as the first rocket fired.

So I walked, leading a horse with one hand and a drifting skidder in the other.

My leg was somehow able to deal with the journey. It was stiff and a little painful, but the hurt of it was completely eclipsed by the pain of my ribs and the now rhythmic shooting pain from my arm. I vowed to do something about that at the next opportunity. It seemed whenever I rode my skidder, the arm drew a little bit of power, so the thrumming ache disappeared. That didn't charge it much, though, and now that it was disconnected it hurt like hell.

It was noon when we reached the place where the rolling plains narrowed into hills and the protected valley made an oasis for mesquite and grass. Francis's hideout was empty, but we stopped to rest. The area was trampled recently, indicating that Zane and Ben had managed to get the horses at least this far.

We stopped by the brook on our way through for a rest and a drink.

"You'd best keep this place your secret," I said to the horse. "Lot of folks would take it from you if they knew where it was."

She drank, cautiously at first and then with a great thirst. I got my own canteen out and filled it up, stomach grumbling. I was hungry. It was hot.

I was at peace.

Was there a reason to ever leave this valley? I had been searching for peace all these long years and now here it was. Horse at my side and hat on my head. A man could live out his days like this. The world could go to hell and never find its way into this little protected piece of land. I'd be safe. Dare say, I'd be happy. The hint of a smile crossed my cracked lips.

The horse was looking at me.

"You're right," I said. "Too much to do out there. Too many people depending on us."

Zane's voice came from the edge of the clearing. "We thought we'd really lost you this time."

"So much for keeping this place a secret."

"Oh, I wouldn't say that." He stepped forward. His duster hung pulled neatly back to reveal his rifle at his side. He had a satchel hanging loosely from his side. There was expectation in his eyes, begging almost. "We need you, J.D. They've gathered at Ben's ranch."

"You got the horses?"

"You left us to handle it ourselves. I don't know anything about horses, and Ben—well, I don't think Ben likes me very much."

I looked at Zane for a good long while.

"Yes," he said finally. "We got the horses. Couple dozen of them. Fine ones, far as I can tell."

I stroked the horse's mane.

"People are scared. I'm scared." Zane put his hand on my shoulder. "Why have you always hated me?"

For a moment, I forgot to breathe. My heart was running full speed, but my body was relaxed. I didn't hate Zane. In fact, as much as I disliked city boys in general, my instincts had always told me to get closer to Zane. Trust him. I turned to face him, but no words came to me.

Zane broke the silence. "When you didn't come back, I didn't know what I was going to do. Ever since I saw you that day after chasing the horses, my loyalty's been with you. They always said men like you didn't exist anymore, that men of noble strength and solid values had gone the way of the rhino." Zane looked me in the eyes. "But here you are."

There I was. I wasn't noble. I wasn't a man of solid values. I hardly knew what that meant. A man of tradition like myself might appear noble, but did that make it so? "I'm not—"

He kissed me with a heat that rivaled the noonday sun. It shocked me at first, but memories stirred and the feel of human contact shook me until my body woke up and I kissed him back. It felt right, being together. We fit. Our fingers interlocked and we pulled apart, only to find an irresistible magnetism pull us back together. We stayed locked together, releasing everything that had built up inside us. Passion and frustration worked into a kiss alternately soft and rough.

We stopped only when the horse nuzzled us apart.

Zane pulled away, laughing. "Muffin," he said.

"What?"

"Her name. It's Muffin."

"That's a terrible name."

"It's a wonderful name." Zane stroked her chin and gave her a little kiss on the nose. "And it's her name."

"Tell me something," I said. "Why did you hit me that time outside of Court's hideout?"

He smiled. "You had it coming."

I gave him a flat look. "You were already working with Tucker."

"Trust, J.D." Zane bit his lip. "You can't trust anyone, can you?"

"Near as I figure it was a distraction. You wanted me thinking of something else so I wouldn't figure out what you were tricking me into doing."

"Tucker had just scouted the town. He figured, same as you did, that there was something going on and that the bank was the center of it." Zane took a step back. "He decided he needed help. He thought it'd work best to place cameras and see if we could find some way to motivate you. Didn't think it would happen so fast."

"And you figured I'd be more likely to help if I didn't think you two were working together?"

"He figured that." He smiled. "I only went along because I didn't have any better ideas."

"Seems there have been a lot of distractions."

Zane had a sad look in his eyes. He shook his head. "I was trying to do the right thing." He took a step back and looked at me, eyes narrowed. He waved a hand, indicating my whole self. "This won't do, you know."

"Trying to change me?"

"No," he said, reaching into his satchel to pull out a bundle of leather. "Just trying to change some of your clothes. I meant to give you this last night, but we couldn't get to my car most of the night and I was too damn angry with you in the morning."

Words failed me, so I took the bundle and unfolded it. It was a dark leather duster, nearly black. On the back was an embroidered crow made with dark metal thread. On closer inspection, the material seemed lighter than real leather and the lining was a sleek mustard yellow that shined like silk. It was smoother than silk. I shrugged off my ridiculous leather poncho and slipped the duster on. The left sleeve was cut to work with my long, metal arm. The elbow was farther down and the sleeve billowed out more to allow for the larger hand.

"Bulletproof," Zane said.

"Of course."

"Really bulletproof. You can get hit point-blank with a .357 Magnum and walk away with hardly a limp. It'll stop most knives, and it'll shield you from a flamethrower in a pinch. The lining will keep you ten to twenty degrees cooler than the outside air, or warmer if you need to keep warm at night."

I scowled. "See? This is the problem. You use tech to solve every damn thing, like it's going to make life better."

"You have a better way to stop bullets?"

"I don't want to *need* to stop bullets."

"You're going into something dangerous. You can't expect to not get shot. Hell, you depend on tech to heal you. Why not depend on it to stop from poking you full of holes in the first place?"

My jaw clenched, working back and forth. I didn't have a good argument for him. "Slippery slope," I muttered.

He squeezed my hand and nudged closer. "And getting slipperier."

"And here," he said. "I got you this." He dropped a small cylinder into my palm.

"What is it?"

He stared at me for what seemed like several minutes with his jaw hanging low. "You...You don't know?"

I shook my head.

"It's a battery, J.D. It goes in your arm, right there." He poked a finger at a spot just under the armpit of my metal arm. "I noticed you were flinching every time you moved that thing, so I figured your battery was low. When

I saw one in the junk drawer of Francis's hideout I swiped it."

"Huh." I dropped the battery into the pocket of the duster.

"How long have you had that?" Zane asked. "Twenty years without a new battery?"

"Twenty-four. And it recharges."

"Still..." He gave a disgusted sound and shook his head.

I clicked my tongue and Muffin stepped up beside me. Zane gave her an apple from his satchel and I admit to feeling a twinge of jealousy at her affection. We led her and my skidder the few kilometers back to the ranch. Having him there with me felt good, like that moment of peace before a war. For once, could I let myself sink into someone, to become a part of another person? Could I be more than the lone gunman or the man who walks the desert?

Not yet. After it was all over. Then I'd try. Once I knew we were safe from this threat, if Zane still stuck around, then I would know it was something. I watched him as we made our way back to Ben's ranch. His jaw worked as he talked and the twinkle never left his eye. It only convinced me that he was a distraction. But he was a hell of a good one.

We crested the last hill on the way to Ben's ranch, and I stopped.

A small army had formed, and they were preparing for war.

Chapter 31

"Howdy," I said to Mina on the front porch of Ben's house.

She didn't say a word, but continued to assemble her rifle. Wavy hair was pulled back in a long braid and her face was painted in what must have been an approximation of war paint.

I sat next to her and waited while she worked. The yard was a bustle of activity—all manner of men and women working like a beehive of activity. Legs and Rosa were there with a whole pack of shiny-headed fools. My tribe was nearby, working on cleaning weaponry and readying makeshift armor. A group of Navajo worked with them, outfitting some of Ben's old farm equipment with armor and weapons. Near the barn, Trish worked with a few deputies, readying a dozen horses for a ride. The way she handled herself around the creatures made me think she really knew what she was doing.

"They're all getting along," I said.

"There was some trouble," Mina said without looking up. "But nothing a few strong words could not handle."

"Thanks."

"Troublemaker." Mina stopped working and looked at me.

I raised an eyebrow.

"You're a troublemaker. I can see it, but nobody else does."

Patting the pockets of my new duster, I found a tin case of cigarettes and tapped it until one came out. It made an odd sweet smell when I lit it, but it was pleasant enough. I'd have to remember to thank Zane.

"Why am I here, you ask?" Mina continued. "Well, I'm here because the children are here. You know, the ones you were teaching about the glory of war? They were the first to volunteer for your little posse. Why are they here? Well, they're here because Broadfeather said we needed to be here."

"You should have stopped them. None of you should be here."

"Talk to Broadfeather about it. He says there is a threat to our way of life and so we must fight."

"But you have no chance. You won't even get close."

Her jaw set hard. "The horses can get us close. We will be like shadows striking in the night."

I shook my head, but she was right. Quintech might not even see them coming if enough tribesmen rode a night mission. If they could get in and strike fast, they'd be able to cripple any big defenses set up around Swallow Hill. Once enough tech was disabled, the flyers could swoop in with heavy weaponry. The plan made sense. It could work.

"Where are the kids?"

"'Round that hill," she said. "They're working on the big gun."

I shook my head. "Mina, we gotta get them out of here. This isn't a place for kids."

"Really?" Her voice was laced with sarcasm. She reached into a pack at her feet and brought out my Smith & Wesson Model 500 and a box of ammo. "Here, I brought you these. Thought you might like to have them."

The gun felt heavy in my hand. Awkward. The Model 500 was a huge gun, almost obscenely so. Toting this thing around was asking for trouble. Thing is, trouble didn't seem to stay away if I didn't ask for it. Maybe it was finally time to own up to that trouble and give a little trouble back.

"It'd be better if the Navajo stayed out of it."

"Well, they're in it, so just forget about that. Maybe you should visit more often."

"Dibe seemed to be a peaceful sort."

"Well, she left for home, but she seemed moved enough to leave some of her people to help." She threaded a cleaning patch and rod through the barrel. "They won't fight this battle, but they'll help us prepare."

There was silence while Mina finished lubricating all of the moving parts of her rifle. She took good care of the thing. I looked over my weapon, reacquainting myself with it. It was heavy, but it was the kind of heavy that meant something. When I holstered it, it was like saying hello to a long-lost cousin.

"Been a busy few days," I said.

"Sounds like it." She snapped her rifle closed and worked the action, smiling at the sound of it.

Ben stepped out of the house wearing his old black leathers and hair so spiky it looked like it might be a weapon. It probably was. "Sounds like what?" he asked.

"We need a posse, Ben," I said. "Looks like we got an army."

"Great, right?"

I shook my head.

"It's not great," said Mina. "Armies invite army-sized resistance. We're the smallest army in Texas. What we're doing here is suicide."

"Not if we're smart," I said. "Not if we keep our strike small. Disable their tech, get Francis, and get out. Nothing more."

Mina and Ben exchanged nervous looks.

"Walk with me," said Ben. Without waiting for a response, he started out toward the barn. I followed, marveling at the sights as I went. The armored vehicles were some serious business. Plates of black metal were being attached to the vital points of flying cars, tractors, and even Ben's broken-down truck.

"What is this all about, Ben?"

"That data cube," he said. "There was a lot more on it than we thought."

"Like what?"

"What do you know about the Civil War?"

Marcus, Gertie, and Haley, the kids from my tribe, were assembling a Civil War–era long-range missile launcher. They weren't having much luck, but the grins on their faces were enough to make it obvious that they did not understand the gravity of their situation.

"I fought in the war," I said, my voice low. "You know what that war cost me."

"But what did you know about it? Why was it fought?"

"We fought for the right to live," I said. "We fought for freedom."

We walked for a minute in silence, watching the heat mirages in the distance make the windmills sway in hypnotic dance. We passed Legs and a few of his thugs taking target practice at an old rusted barrel. He wasn't a bad shot, but his buddies could hardly hit the thing. Rosa outdid them all with her thick-barreled rifle. Not only did she always hit the bullseye, but the caliber of the rifle was such that the entire bullseye was obliterated in the process.

I sighed. "This isn't an army, Ben. Armies have discipline."

"What if I told you Quintech was behind it?" Ben said. "And Goodwin was the other side. What if the Civil War was just a front for a war of corporations?"

"Bullshit."

Ben stopped, but I kept walking. My first thought was to ignore his stupid fool theories. Hell, my gut had always told me to ignore that kid. He'd always done his best to be the kind of person I ignored. That didn't make it right, but I still did it.

I turned around but kept moving backwards, hands raised in the air in a show of surrender. "You got it, Ben. All my talk was nothing. I'm just a corporate stooge working for a blood-stained buck."

"I didn't think you'd listen."

"You're damn right I won't listen." Rage was bubbling up in my belly, hotter than the sunbaked stones under my feet. "You're telling me everything I fought for was for shit. You're telling me it was lies or that I'm a liar. How the hell do you think I'm going to react?" With that, I turned and walked the rest of the way to the barn in silence.

Trish tipped her hat to me as I approached, and I tipped back. She was geared up in her duster and sheriff's star, like she was here for official business. Her pistols hung at her side and her rifle hugged her back; she was ready for that official business to get ugly. She brushed down a knobby-kneed gelding and talked pretty to it. Zane emerged from the dark confines of the barn as I approached, having brought Muffin down after we had arrived. I tipped my hat to him as well, and he gave me a grim smile that didn't touch the worry in his eyes.

When she'd finished brushing the gelding, Trish turned to me and eyed me up and down. "Nice getup."

Before I could respond, Zane said, "Thank you," and placed an arm around my waist. "Makes him look dashing, doesn't it?"

"He's always had a rugged charm, if you ask me." Trish touched the sleeve of my new duster. "This seems a little soft for his usual image."

"I'm right here, you know," I said.

"Wait till he breaks it in," Zane said. "He'll have it roughed up in no time." With that, Zane disappeared back into the barn to chat up some of the deputies within.

Trish broke into a big grin. "You've done well, J.D."

I scowled. "No arrest warrant for me?"

"Just the one."

I raised an eyebrow.

"I'll hold off until after all of this."

"Now you're going to hold off?"

"I have been holding off, old man. Why do you think I sent my rookies after you?"

"It got one of them killed."

"No. *You* got one of them killed. You turned the other one into a much better deputy." Trish stole a glance at Green, who was working on getting a saddle onto another horse. "You showed him what it's like out there. He knows that next time his quarry isn't going to play so soft with him."

"You didn't have to send anyone. You knew I wasn't up to anything bad."

"I couldn't just let it be. You know how this works. You used to be in my position. There's pressure from folks around the area and from bosses up the food chain.

Someone breaks into a company stronghold and you sure as hell better get a man on it or you're out the door."

She was right, of course. Still, thinking of that deputy gored right in front of me left a sour taste in my mouth. He didn't need to die. It was my fault he'd met that fate, and the guilt was going to suffocate me if I let it. When guilt does that, sometimes it's only anger that keeps you afloat.

"When this is done, I'm bringing you in, J.D." Trish poked my chest with her sharp pointer finger. "You can come quiet or you can come kicking, but you'll see a judge. Plea your case and you know he'll let you walk."

"He won't." I brushed her hand back and looked her right in the eyes. "I've seen it done a hundred times where someone did what's right and paid with hard labor.

"But you're a hero out here." She gestured at all of the people working on the ranch. "When word got out that you were putting together a posse, people came. All them who heard it. Even Cinco Armas comes when you call. Never thought you'd fall in with that crowd."

"No choice," I kicked at the dirt, sending plumes of dust into the air. "This whole time I feel like I've been moving one thing to the next with no options. If we don't take their help, then we're not getting anywhere. I hate it, Trish. It rankles me, and if there was something else I could do then I'd do it."

Trish looked me over for a long minute. "We know you'll do the right thing, J.D. You're the one person we trust to put things right. That means something. There's nobody here who wouldn't stand up for you."

"I don't want them to stand up for me. I broke the law knowing damn well what the consequences were. A deputy got killed and I'm responsible for that death. Hell, if I were still the sheriff I'd send me up the river for good."

"You would, wouldn't you?" She sighed. "Just be there so there's no trouble. Last thing I need is more trouble from you."

Sticking my thumb out at the barn, I said, "How are the horses coming?"

She bit her lip. "Good? I mean, good."

"What's wrong?"

"Nothing that will affect what we're doing. More of them need harnesses than we hoped, but Ben's supplies are good. Most of them are doing fine."

It hurt thinking of all those horses controlled by that tech. We were turning willful creatures into mindless machines for no other reason than the fact that they were willful. What other choice was there? There wasn't time to properly break and train the horses. Only the oldest had any training and those had gone years without a saddle or a rider.

"Chips away at a person's soul, doesn't it?" I said.

"We'll make it right once this is over. Ben said he'd trash the harnesses and start training the horses proper."

"Sure."

"Like you said." Trish poked my chest. "Sometimes there's no choice. You just do what you need to do."

I didn't respond other than to tip my hat again and walk back up the hill to where Ben had joined the gangsters in their target practice. The rancher seemed to fit well with his old crowd. He gave shit as well as he took it. He lined up his shot, but set down his weapon when he saw me. He fell into step next to me. Legs and Rosa followed.

Once we were back at the house, I turned and faced the groups working in the expansive yard. Putting my fingers in my mouth, I blew a long, loud whistle. One by one people started looking, then approaching. After a minute, the majority of the posse had gathered and was looking expectantly at me. In all, it was nearly a hundred folks geared up for war and another dozen kids and peaceful folk.

"Folks," I said, projecting my voice. "This is a mighty fine posse you've gathered up here. Lot of you are here to help and that exactly what's needed."

Dozens of blank stares pointed up in my direction.

"We don't know everything about what we're up against." I took one last drag on my cigarette, dropped it to the ground, and stepped it out. "We know we can't fly in because the tech doesn't work in a circle around the town. We also know that anyone with eye or ear augments needs to stay back until we can disable the, um, the..."

"Sub-quantum net," Zane said.

"The kid can make you see and hear whatever he wants," I said.

Rosa asked, "What kid?"

"Francis Brown." I took off my hat. "Boy got into some kind of ugly a while back. Seems he's been pulling up info from Quintech. Reviving some of its more dangerous projects." A few of the older posse members nodded their heads in recognition. "He's just a kid, though. We need to get Francis back here. We'll figure out his role in all of this once it's all settled down."

"The source of the bad signal was in the bank, but that's been taken care of. I hear tell there's a backup and a tower. Our goal is to take down the tower and get out."

Legs took a step forward. "Heading for it? Safer to hit the tower from way downtown, don't you think?" He stuck a thumb out at the cannon the kids had been assembling.

"No," said Zane. "We can't do that."

I raised an eyebrow at him.

"Goodwin runs the sub-quantum net out of Austin. Picture the two fields like soap bubbles sitting up next to each other. You pop one, the other might go as well."

I shook my head. "Too many innocents around, anyway. The tower is close to town and we don't know how many townsfolk are working there. Last I was in Swallow Hill, the town seemed mighty empty, so its likely people are working at the Quintech facility. Swallow Hill was a company town and still is."

"When do we loot Quintech?" Legs asked. "When do we blow it up?" There was a murmur of approval from the crowd.

"No," I said. "We don't blow it up. We don't leave any trace that we were around, and we sure as hell don't let anyone know that we've formed a small army. We move in small groups of no more than ten. We move fast. Get in. Disable them. Get out."

They rumbled with discontent.

"Now I know you're concerned with the tech that's in that place." I nodded to Trish, who had finally come up to the back of the crowd. "The sheriff will handle it, all legal and nice. None of us needs to get overly destructive. Just trust that it's being handled."

Legs looked like he was about to say something, but Rosa elbowed him and he kept his fool mouth shut. Others seemed to take his lead and the mood was generally one of uneasy anticipation.

"You'll all get your orders," I said. "Keep up what you're doing and we'll move out in an hour. Hopefully we'll get some letup from this heat."

With that, the group dispersed and folks returned to their tasks. Ben hung around next to me, fidgeting.

"Spit it out," I said after several long minutes of silence.

"There's not going to be any letup in this heat." The hesitation in his voice told me it wasn't really what was on his mind.

"Probably not the only thing that won't go according to plan."

He nodded.

"One of the things a person learns on the field is that the fella whose plan changes as fast as the situation is the fella who wins, but all else equal, the fella with the biggest gun walks away."

"What the hell is that supposed to mean?"

"It means everyone here's going to need to know their part and not just follow orders." I stopped talking for a moment while the kids of my tribe test fired the cannon. "They're also going to need to know how to come up with their own plans on their own."

"We're fucked, aren't we?"

"Just make sure no one drops from the heat."

Ben gave me a sloppy salute and disappeared into the house. I strolled aimlessly for a time and ended up back down at the barn. The horses were nearly ready. The ones that would take a saddle had been saddled. Those that wouldn't were corralled in the barn. Trish was in the barn, but I couldn't bring myself to enter. Instead, I circled around back of the barn and sat in the shade for a spell.

My ear pinged and a message in my right eye told me that it was a call from Francis.

"Say what you need to say, then," I said.

One moment the trampled cow path was empty, the next Francis was standing in his white suit and slicked-back hair.

"Our plan's almost finished," said Francis in his deliberate voice. He enunciated each word with a diamond cutter's precision. "There'll be peace and no more need for justice."

"There's always a need for justice, son." I took care to breathe very slowly. His presence riled me up, and it wouldn't do to lose my cool and take a swing at him. It'd be more embarrassing than anything, since he was only a projected image.

"Not if we're clever. Not if we put reasonable limits on people and set them to doing what they're supposed to do."

"And what's that? Work? Kill each other for food?" Well, there I was riled up already. I kicked dirt in frustration.

"The killing was just a test to see how far we could go. When we're done there's not going to be any need for killing."

"What happens until then?"

Francis shrugged.

"What happens? What are you planning?"

"It's a secret."

I slammed a fist against the wall of the barn. "We don't need any damn secrets. Secrets is what got us here. They ain't getting us out."

A long moment passed, and Francis did nothing but stare at me with his emotionless eyes. The still air carried so much weight I could hardly breathe, but I waited. I calmed myself. If there was only something I could say to the boy to get him to back down. If only there was something I could say to get some more information on what he was planning. Mind control was clearly part of the plan. Changing perception through eyes and ears was a good start, but the tools Quintech had been on the verge of completing would give an even higher level of control. He'd have a slave army if he got it working, but did he have it working? It seemed he was still missing part of it, or he'd be using it against us already.

Unless he already was. A shudder ran up my spine.

"It'll be done soon, Sheriff," said Francis. The corners of his mouth twisted up slightly, but his eyes stayed dull and unfocused. "It's a pity your little army is going to get broken up."

I scowled at the boy's fading image. "What makes you think it'll be anything like that, boy?"

"Because," he said as the last hint of his image stepped into the sunlight and faded from view. "You're not the only one with long-range weapons."

Chapter 32

I rounded the corner of the barn at full sprint, lungs tearing at the scorched air. My boot slipped in the dust and the bandages on my leg tore. The pain in my ribs made every breath a dagger in my side, but I ran hard as I could.

"Run!" I hollered, waving my arms frantically.

The first shot hit. It wasn't a bomb so much as a solid, fiery punch from the sky. It thunked into the ground in the middle of the yard, shaking the earth enough to nearly throw me off balance. Then it blossomed in a silent bloom of heat enveloping half a dozen gangsters and leaving nothing but standing skeletons of metal and machine. Legs made a leap straight for his skidder, trailing smoke the whole way. He landed next to it in a smoldering heap.

Then there was chaos.

Broadfeather shouted, fierce energy whipping the old man into action. He called for the tribe to run, but there was no direction to it. Hopi and Navajo scattered.

But not Marcus.

Marcus was frozen with a look of absolute terror right on top of the only viable military target on the entire ranch: the long-range artillery. Wrench in hand, Marcus turned his pale face up to the sky. When would the next strike hit?

Trish and Deputy Green disappeared into the barn. There was noise inside, like screaming. It was screaming.

The horses.

I ran to Marcus. "Run!" I hollered as I yanked him from the artillery. His eyes stayed glued to the sky until I yanked his head down to look at me. "Marcus, I'm counting on you."

His expression turned from confusion to fear.

"We're being sniped at from a thousand meters."

Marcus's eyes got wider. "What do we do?"

"Run. You're in charge. Find the rest of the kids and head for the windmills." I gripped his shoulders. "I'm counting on you."

Fear disappeared from his face, replaced by something like determination. He nodded, looked around, and ran.

The icy grip of plans gone wrong stopped me for a second. There were a million ways this ended badly, and it hadn't even started. I could stand right there in the yard, accept my fate. It was my doing, bringing this down on those who followed me. It would get worse before it got better.

But it would get better. I thought of Zane. Maybe he would stick around. Maybe the judge would let me walk. Maybe there was still a life of peace for me somewhere up ahead. I blinked out of my stunned silence and ran into the barn.

The ground shook twice more as I dashed across the barn. Green rushed past the other direction, leading two horses as fast as they'd go. Trish wrenched at the gray gelding's rope, but was having no luck because the horse was on the verge of panic.

Most of the horses weren't. They were an eerie calm, like there was nothing wrong and no reason to flee. They were saddled, ready to go, but they were tied to a long, solid steel railing that ran the length of the wall. Muffin, on the other hand, snorted and pawed the ground, looking at me like she knew it was all my fault, like she somehow knew that I was the one who had caused all this pain.

The far corner of the barn exploded inward, bursting in a shower of flame and metal. The sunlight that stabbed the smoke blinded me momentarily. The sound of screaming metal pierced the air as the roof started to collapse in slow motion.

I ran forward, pressed my way between two docile horses, and grabbed the steel bar in my metal hand. I twisted hard as I could. Crushing, twisting, pulling, the bar finally wrenched free from its place on the wall. It was attached in two other places, one on either side.

"You get that one," I shouted at Trish. She ran to it and I ran to the one near Muffin.

Another explosion outside shook the whole barn. Air smelled of ash.

The barn continued to collapse. The roof was getting closer to the horses and all of the walls seemed to lean under its shifting pressure. It could go at any second.

I grabbed the bolt where the bar attached to the wall and crushed it hard as I could. It nearly split from the pressure, and it only took one good pull to yank it free. On her side, Trish got hers loose and was freeing horses from her end.

But I couldn't let go of the bar. My arm went dead, like the lifeless metal that it was. The pinging pain stopped and in its absence I finally understood how bad it had been.

268

How could I have ignored it all this time? How was I even thinking clearly through all that pain?

Muffin looked down at me, down at my tech. Her hooves danced back and forth, fidgeting with the will to leave, to just run. She must have felt as confused and frightened as I did. I pulled at the fingers as hard as I could, trying to pry them open, but they wouldn't budge. The heat of the burning roof was baking me.

"J.D. I can't get them to move!" Trish pulled at the reins of a couple horses. Those two moved when led, but none of the others followed. Those horses that still had free will fled as soon as they were loose, but those with the harnesses stood there as if nothing was wrong. It was just another normal day in the giant black barn-oven.

"Just go," I said. "Get those two out."

The wall exploded in a fury of fire and force. Two horses were thrown back, burning and dying as they flew. The bar that I still held followed, twisting my arm back and yanking me meters back. Muffin reared up. Her kicking hooves narrowly missed my hat.

I couldn't calm her, couldn't control her. Ducking low and pulling away was about as good as I could do to try to survive the next few seconds. She pulled hard, ripping at her rope like it was strangling her. I was dragged up and over and back, but she couldn't get free. The horses next to her did nothing. Their eyes were a picture of calm focus while Muffin showed me all whites and screamed. Horses nearby were half-burned and torn apart.

Out of the corner of my eye I saw Trish ride a horse out of the barn, leading another. Walls crashed around me, but nothing fell on Muffin and me. Another horse was crushed by a section of roof. The wall twisted and collapsed, the flaming roof blocking our escape. Flaming heat seared my face, nearly blinding me. Still, the duster protected my body. I wondered how long it would keep me alive in the fire. It felt needlessly cruel.

It could have been the heat shifting the metal, or it might have been the last dregs of power responding to my relaxation, but the rod slipped free from my metal grip. As it moved, all of the ropes attached to it came free.

Muffin stared at me, having worked off most of her panic. She fidgeted and took a step back.

I ran down the row, yanking harnesses off as many horses as I could reach. Each, in turn, panicked. Attacked. Ran. There was still room for them to flee through the door.

"Let's get out of here, girl," I rasped in the most soothing voice I could manage. I reached out slowly, touched the side of her face. She leaned into it.

When I stuck my foot in the stirrup, Muffin didn't shy away. She knew the routine and when I grabbed the reins she responded perfectly.

Another explosion. Muffin staggered back. The wall with the door caved inward, buckling.

But there was a gap a meter up in the broken wall. I led Muffin away from it, as far as we could, given the space that was still safe.

Another shot slammed into the barn, crushing then exploding the wall where the horses had been tied.

"Hyah!"

Muffin galloped at the wall, from nothing to full speed quick as could be. She leapt through the hole, passing the flames. We burst out just as the entire wall folded inward and a wave of heat chased us as we went.

We peeled out at full gallop, shouting and guiding the horse with my good hand. My metal arm hung limp at my side, useless until I got power to it. The scene before me was a horror show.

Trish and Green were loading several tribesmen into her cruiser, which had somehow remained unscathed among a series of craters. Ben's truck was missing, along with my skidder inside it. Where were the rest of the tribesmen? Where was Broadfeather?

Where were the kids?

The artillery was ruined, hit hard by more than one bomb. The yard was a mess, though the house still stood.

Legs was on the ground, struggling to mount his skidder. He pulled himself up on one remaining arm, the flesh of his torso exposed and burned.

He collapsed to the ground.

Rosa dropped from the sky on her skidder, not waiting to properly land before jumping off. She landed by Legs and cradled his head in her arms.

Waves of force and heat hit, shattering the earth with tremendous force. Muffin reared up, eyes rolling in panic. She staggered sideways and nearly fell.

When she finally stopped fighting, Legs and Rosa were gone. Where they had been nothing was left. No grass, no earth... No skidder.

They were in the sky, so far already that they were hard to see.

So many others had failed to escape. There were too many dead to worry about. I forced it into the back of my brain.

There was movement at the edge of the field of windmills. Muffin turned to follow in flight, when Chief Broadfeather rose, dazed, from the ground. He had a gash in his forehead and his bloodied fingers still gripped his walking stick.

I reined Muffin in and swung around next to Broadfeather. Letting go of the reins, I reached down and hefted him up onto the saddle in front of me. He swayed a bit, threatening to fall, but after a bit of work I was able to steady him on the horse.

Two more shots hit in rapid succession. One crushed the house into splinters; the other was just close enough to send a shower of earth raining down on Broadfeather and me.

"No," I choked. The weight of death was too much. I needed to move to save myself and to save Broadfeather, but I couldn't. A pressure on my chest felt like it was crushing me.

A fat bomb thunked hard into the ground at Muffin's feet.

But it didn't explode.

There it sat, rust red and smoking hot. It had a black tip and stubby little wings for guidance. On its side was stenciled the label: "GOODWIN."

Muffin wasn't in the mood for my stupid, stunned silence. Without any direction, she took it upon herself to get Broadfeather and myself the hell out of there. She ran hard and didn't slow down until we hit the windmills.

Mina was there, along with several others from my tribe and the Navajo. They were few, far too few. Mina helped Broadfeather down from my horse, pulling him close to steady him.

"How bad?" I asked, not really wanting to know the answer.

Mina's look told me everything I needed to know. "Too many," she said. "A dozen or so aren't accounted for. Better than I'd hoped, but…"

Broadfeather coughed, crimson spatters going everywhere. With one hand, he motioned us close.

"Chief," I said. His eyes were unfocused. Skin was so pale and cold.

"Keep the Hopi Way." Broadfeather's voice was faint. "Lead the people."

"I can't be chief," I said. "And I'm no spiritual leader. I'm not who you want me to be."

Broadfeather's breath was a wet rattle. Maybe a laugh? "Not you, Crow." He squeezed Mina's hand. "A chief must be wise."

Mina nodded. A single tear ran down her face.

"Crow," Broadfeather said after a time. "Your spirit leads with strength. I wanted you there to show that we had both wisdom and strength." He swallowed and his lips quivered on the edge of speaking for a long time before the words came out. "It takes both."

His eyes closed forever.

Every breath shook as my lungs spasmed. I closed my eyes. Wept. Every second that passed, I expected more shots to rain down from the sky, but they didn't come. The chief was gone. So many others. Not a damn one of them would have been there if not for me. "Those goons with Legs. Some of the horses..." There was a familiar sound behind me. It was the low hum of a flying car. I turned.

Marcus ran up, Gertie and Dustin in tow. They looked like they'd been pan-seared and dipped in shit, but they were alive. Dustin's right arm hung limp at her side.

"You done good," I said.

He looked at the ground. "Haley," he said.

She wasn't there.

"I couldn't find her. We had to run."

I put a hand on his shoulder. "You made the right choice, son. You saved people out there."

Mina rushed up to help Dustin with a makeshift bandage. Gertie stared straight ahead, not seeming to react to anything. It was the long-off look of someone who'd first experienced death.

She was just a kid. They all were, even Marcus. How could I even pretend to involve them in this? Their pain was all my fault. Every bit of it. I taught them that fighting was an option. It was lucky they were even alive. So many others weren't.

They were part of it because I refused to do this alone. I'd tried to gather a posse and ended up with an army, but what happens to armies? Death. Destruction. The soil gets watered with the tears of mothers. Husbands. Wives.

Marcus looked at me, his eyes dry. Angry.

"You did your best, son," I said. "Now you need to help look over these folks."

His lower lip quivered. He opened his mouth as if to say something, but instead turned and ran.

It was time to survey the damage, take account of who we'd lost and how to move on. I couldn't do it. My knees hit the hard earth and I buried my face in my hands. First Jo and now this. I wasn't sure if I could take it. Haley. She was just a kid. I'd always moved through my life taking one step forward after another. Now I didn't know which way was forward anymore.

A whistle from behind broke me out of it.

Zane stood in his convertible black car, rifle in one hand and a coiled rope in the other. He grinned down at me like none of this was affecting him, like he didn't feel the weight of war crushing him like a boulder on his chest. Maybe he'd never been in war. Maybe my memories were wrecking me more than they should. Or maybe he didn't care as much about these people.

Maybe he did.

As the car lowered I saw who was in it: Ben, bloodied, but alive.

And Haley. She hopped out of the car and ran up to hug Gertie and Dustin. They hugged right back and the three stayed there for a long time.

"You got them," I said. Relief washed through me.

"Just in time." Ben grinned a quirky grin at me. "And it looks like you rescued the plan." He nodded at Muffin.

It took me a moment to figure out what he was talking about. "But we—"

"Absolutely have to do it now," said Zane.

I nodded. He was right, of course. "I'll ride in alone," I said. "You all come when the field drops." My heart pumped hard again. Too many had died, but until there was no one left, someone needed to fight. I needed to fight.

"Mina," I said. "Wait a spell, then get back onto the yard and see if there's anyone left. Tend to any wounded. Find shelter for the night."

"We will." She whistled and gathered up the remaining people, giving them orders and sending them out to scout the edges of the yard.

"And, Mina?"

She raised an eyebrow.

"There'll be coyotes. Mean ones. Keep an eye out and shoot them as soon as they show up."

She nodded, grim determination on her face.

With that, I mounted Muffin and rode off. There was one more stop I needed to make before heading to Swallow Hill.

Chapter 33

Josephine's junkyard was as quiet as the end of the world. The door at the gate had been propped up to be some semblance of a barrier, but the place didn't feel safe anymore. Heaps of metal no longer brimmed with potential. They were nothing but piles of junk. Jo's humble sanctuary—her defended castle—was nothing without her. Blood still darkened the earth around the door to her shack.

"C'mon in," Abi said.

"It's your place now?"

"As good as."

Keith waved from atop a pile of junk, rifle in hand. He had a crazed look in his eyes. Tucker sat next to him, his arm a bloody stump. He held a beer in his one good hand.

Abi waved back and smiled. "Keith didn't feel safe after the last time he tried to leave. I don't think he's entirely right in the head, you know?"

"That might be partially my fault."

"Is there anyone you haven't driven crazy, J.D.?"

"Where is she?" I asked.

Abi pointed to the shack.

"Find water for the horse, if you could," I said. "I need to pay some respects before we go."

She led Muffin away without a word.

Hat in hand, I made my way to the shack. Each step was harder than the last. The pain of knowing—of seeing—waited for me inside. She had been so full of life. Nobody ever got away with anything around Josephine. She kept her place so well that nobody ever even tried to argue her right to it. She was a force to hold back the storm, but she was more than that too. She had been so caring. So peaceful. Now she was at peace.

Josephine's body lay on the table in the center of the shack. Her hands were folded neatly across her belly, and the damage done by coyotes had been closed up and covered. The wrinkles on her face, which had once shown her ferocity, now only showed her age. They'd softened into an expression of serenity that seemed at once beautiful and unfitting. She was never serene. Her eyes had blazed with fire and now they were cold forever.

A tear came to my eye, but I didn't brush it back. If anyone deserved to have tears shed for her it was Josephine.

"I'm sorry, Jo," I said. "If I hadn't come here they wouldn't have been after you."

Something didn't figure about that. If Francis had sent the coyotes as a way to torment me, then how did he know that she was the one to go after? Why wouldn't he have gone after my tribe instead? They were much closer to me than family. A flutter of worry hit me before I remembered that Mina was capable of taking care of herself. The coyotes might come after her, but she'd be ready for them. No, something else didn't make sense. There must have been another reason that Francis went after Josephine.

The safe seemed like a good place to look. In the corner, where the blood had been hastily cleaned up, the safe was still wide open. Peering into it, I was able to see the blood-soaked contents at the bottom. Once they were out, I spread them across one of the shelves. There were bonds, some from a modern Republic of Texas and some issued by the United States of America. She'd never be able to cash those ancient bonds, but a collector might pay good stars for them had they not been soaked with blood. The Texas bonds looked to be a small fortune.

There was tech too. None of it made much sense to me, and my heart fell when I didn't see any kind of data cube.

"You won't find much there." Abi was leaning against the doorframe.

"When I first told Jo I was going to Swallow Hill, she tried to stop me."

Abi rested a hand on Josephine's elbow. The young woman's face was hard to read, but her lip quivered and she bit it. Her eyes were dry, but maybe all of her tears had already been cried.

"Abi, did she have dealings with Quintech? Did she know about the town?"

She refused to look at me, instead studying the contours of Josephine's face, as if Jo would give her some advice on what to say. Finally, in a voice so quiet I could barely hear, she said, "It wasn't Jo who was tied up in Quintech."

The implication of her words slowly sank into my skull. "You?" I asked.

"Jo said never to tell anyone. Ever."

We were both silent for a time.

Abi spoke first. "She said I was little more than a baby when she found me. She was visiting her sister in a town—she never told me what town it was—and she figured out that I was going to be taken for a program. My mama wasn't happy to send me, but it was going to be for a good cause. Folks made some mighty sacrifices during the Civil War and the years after. This was going to make everything better. It was going to give them an advantage."

"It didn't, did it?"

"Does it matter?" Her eyes met mine and there was anger in them. "Auntie Jo figured out that they weren't just experimenting on kids. They were performing experiments that had no chance of leaving the kid human. Mama didn't know what to do. Auntie did. She took me away and hid. She stayed off grid until she could get some fake creds. She ran from her sister and her husband. Her husband wanted to sell me back to Quintech."

"There was a bounty?" I scratched my head and looked out the door. "Why?"

She licked her lips. "They'd already done something to me. I was already part of their system, their collective mind."

"You're a wiki?" Wiki's were a kind of human hive mind that depended on ultimate information sharing.

"No, something else." She pulled her hair up and showed me a tiny metal port at the base of her skull. "It was new tech back then. Now, it's rare, but only the wealthiest can afford it. That's how I'm able to drive your skidder. I just plug in and it's under control."

"They'd rather have killed a little girl than risk a leak."

"Something like that. Or maybe they were afraid I'd return and mess up their system."

Her words were spoken with flat determination. She wasn't telling me what she could do; she was telling me what she was going to do.

"I didn't just come here to pay my last respects. I came looking for a key." I placed a hand on Abi's shoulder. "Jo wasn't with Quintech, so she doesn't have a key," I said slowly. "But you were with Quintech..."

"And I *am* the key."

Chapter 34

The twin hills behind Swallow Hill rose up in the glow of the setting sun, and the streets were empty. My metal arm hung limp at my side and my headgear was switched off. The spare battery sat heavy in my pocket, ready for whenever I needed the strength my artificial arm could give me, but I didn't want it yet. The horse had allowed me to move quickly to town, and staying low-tech allowed me to do it undetected. That was the hope, anyway.

I hopped off Muffin and tied her up in front of the tavern. She needed water and probably food, but she wasn't going to get it for a while. Stroking her cheek, I apologized for the inconvenience and genuinely felt sorry for dragging her into this mess.

There was a backup for the tech that we had destroyed in the bank. That and a tower. With an army just outside the barrier, all I needed to do was drop that field and they could fly in and disable the Quintech tower. Granted, the army was smaller and scattered. Who knew if they would be able to organize in time to do any good. I couldn't bother with that. All I needed was to know where the backup was so I could take it down. The long ride to town had given me some time to think of strategies for gathering that information.

I was done with strategy.

Kicking the door open, I strode into the tavern like the reaper with a job to do. Four men sat playing poker. Three were in grungy, old clothes. One was dressed all fancy.

They all looked at me with jaws wide open.

Before they could react, I grabbed a handful of Fancy's hair, slammed his head into the table, and dragged him away.

"Any of you follow," I said, "you'll get a bullet in your foot."

I pulled the man outside and tossed him to the ground. He rolled and tried to stand up. I kicked him hard in the face, bloodying his nose. He scrambled backward, so I drew my revolver and stomped on his ankle. Bones crunched under my boot and the man screamed.

The door to the tavern opened.

I shot a man in the shin, and he stumbled back inside.

"Where is it?" I asked.

He just stared at me, the whites of his eyes showing.

I pressed my revolver up against his knee. "There was something in the bank. Where's the second one? The backup?"

"I-I don't know."

My gunshot echoed off the hills and the man's knee splattered all over the dirt road. His screams died fast when I put a boot on his chest and pressed the hot gun to his neck.

"Where is it? I know you work for them. Just tell me where it is and we'll be done for the night."

"The hill." His voice was a quiet rasp, like it hurt to say it. "The one on the left. Right at the top there's a bunker."

Without thanking him properly, I cracked him across the head and sent him to an early slumber. Untying Muffin, I mounted up and made for the hills. Time was running short, so I spurred her into a hard gallop, despite the approaching dark.

The hill was deceptively far, but Muffin closed the distance quickly. How much longer could she take this? She smelled distinctly like horse and sweat. A path that wove its way up the slope led directly to a grassy patch at the top. The light was nearly gone by the time we got there.

Two turrets sprang from the ground. I drew and fired on them both before they could swivel around to gun me down. Edgy nerves saved my life. The first exploded in a shower of sparks and the second took two shots and went dark.

I took a moment to reload the revolver.

There, right between the turrets, was the entrance to the bunker. It wasn't much to look at. Nestled in the grass and made to look like rocky soil, it would have been hard to spot if not for those turrets.

Beyond this hill, were others: knobby things, cramped and bulbous. The land got rockier back this way, and a network of canyons seemed to stretch for kilometers.

The door to the bunker opened with a howl. A ladder disappeared into the black pit and was more than a little intimidating. I holstered my revolver and lowered myself in with one arm. My augmented eye would have been able to see perfectly, but the dim light was insufficient for my natural senses. I felt my way forward, touching the walls as I went.

It would be so much easier to roll a grenade down here and be done with it. Tucker would have been the perfect ally for this job. He'd always had my back. Why had he ditched me at the bank? What would have made a loyal man like Tucker Hale betray the only man who'd shown him any kind of companionship? It must have been money.

I shook my head. Focus.

The dry ozone of electricity filled the room with its static charge, but underneath it was something foul. There was the dry scent of sweat and piss.

Something moved in the darkness. A hiss of movement, like paper moving across stone. I held my breath.

It came again, this time quieter. The sound was like a rasping breath in the darkness.

Brushing my hand against the wall to my right, I stepped forward. The surface was cool and smooth, like steel. Two steps farther and I felt something running from ceiling to floor. It felt like a cord or a tube.

Should I cut it? I rolled it in my hands and was surprised to find that it pulsed slightly, like it had fluid pumping through it. There was another one right next to it.

The sound came again, louder this time.

My eyes still hadn't adjusted. Outside was twilight, but a dim light suffused the room from above. Behind me, faint shapes came into focus, but forward was still a mystery.

Another step. Here, thin wires protruded from the wall in bundles. Curious, I followed one of them away from the wall. As soon as I let my fingers slip from the solid safety of the steel wall, my heart raced. I was disconnected from the whole world. There I was in darkness, trusting senses that weren't sight.

The bundle of wires ran along the floor, and I followed it for several steps. The smell was stronger there, and the steady rasp of dry breathing was right in front of me. Someone was there. No natural sense told me for sure, but I knew it in my heart. Something alive was right in front of me. It knew I was there.

It was scared.

The sense of fear filled the room, its infectious nature swelling right into my belly and causing cold sweat to bead on my forehead. It smelled sour and wet. I ran my hand up the bundle, finding where it touched the thing in the middle of the room.

The tubes sunk into flesh. The soft smoothness of human skin ran under my fingers in the darkness. My heart raced. What was down here? Who was it? It must have been another Kiva, like in the bank. The image of that grisly scene flashed before my eyes.

"Who are you?" I asked.

There was no response but a long, dry breath in the darkness.

That's when I cracked. Blindness was suffocating me, making the bunker feel like it was constantly crashing down around me. There was only so much a man could take.

I switched my headgear on.

The child before me drew in a sharp gasp.

Wires plunged into red, raw skin at the base of his skull. Leads had been attached to irritated skin all along his spine and across his limbs. Tubes ran into his belly, pumping fluids in and out like he was nothing more than part of the plumbing. He stank.

Somehow I knew that he wasn't quite awake and he wasn't quite alive, but that he was aware of himself through me. My vision was part of his system.

Then he was gone.

My natural eye still saw darkness, but the augmented eye erased the boy. Maybe he preferred not to exist at all. His soft skin still felt slick underneath my fingertips, but he was completely invisible.

Francis appeared from nowhere.

He was upset, showing emotion in a way I'd never seen on the boy. He pulled at his hair. "What are you doing here, J.D.? How did you get here?"

"This," I said, indicating the place where I knew the boy was. "What is this, Francis? What the hell is happening to this boy?" I could barely form the words I was so spitting mad.

"It's the price we pay for a world where justice isn't needed. It's the one thing." He cocked his head to one side and the emotion drained from his face. "The human brain has wonderful computing power. It has the ability to construct whole worlds from nothing."

"This is a child."

"Of course it is." His eyes regarded me coolly. "Children are small and require little maintenance. Their capacity for imagination is not quite so bounded. Tests were far more successful."

I roared in frustration and drew my revolver. I pointed it at Francis.

"You can't shoot me," Francis said. "I'm not here."

"I'm coming for you, Francis. I'm coming for you and I'm going to kill you."

I took a deep breath and felt my way to where the invisible boy was. Finding his head, I pressed the gun tightly against his temple.

"I'm sorry, kid."

I pulled the trigger. The vision in my right eye flashed white and changed. Francis disappeared. That would disable his tech for a while, anyway. How long we had, I could only guess. We needed to hurry.

When I climbed out of the bunker, my ears were still ringing and a little bit of me was dead.

Also, I was surrounded.

Chapter 35

Doing the right thing might not be easy, but it definitely doesn't make a man popular. There I felt like a monster after shooting that kid, and being surrounded by villagers with pitchforks was not helping.

They had guns too. The boys from the poker game looked like they were leading the group. One had a shotgun trained on me and the other had a pistol and a flashlight.

"You get your hands up, fella." Sheriff Flores pointed a rifle at my chest. "You shot Theo back there, and we're going to have some words about it."

"Listen, fellas," I said. "I'll raise my arm, but I need a battery first." I shrugged my shoulder and showed that my arm wasn't moving.

Flores shifted uncomfortably. "Just hold on, now. You'd best walk as you are down to the jail. We'll figure what to do with you down there."

I figured it had something to do with a noose at dawn.

The hot night air was stiff with tension. Glancing around, I saw half a dozen fingers on triggers and I'd bet not a single safety was on. It'd get ugly fast if one of them was itchy.

"Gentlemen." I blew smoke out the side of my mouth. "I'm not the one who done you wrong."

"The hell you ain't," said Theo, the man I'd shot for walking out of the tavern. He'd rigged a crutch out of a spare board and was leaning against it heavily. In his other hand was a sawed-off shotgun. "You're comin' with us as a prisoner or a corpse." He lowered a shotgun at me. "I got my preference."

"I'm not going to kill any of you," I said. The image of the kid I'd just killed flashed in front of my eyes. "A man's got to have morals."

Theo twitched.

Far away, a sound like thunder filled the skies. The darkening sky lit up like the midday sun. Townsfolk turned, shouted, swore. A second later, the force hit us, knocking us back. They had taken out the perimeter towers. Cavalry was on the way.

It was also a perfect distraction.

I stepped forward, to the side. Flores's rifle barked, but missed. My fist hit his jaw, staggered him back.

The roar of gunfire erupted behind me. A shot thumped into my back, not penetrating but feeling quite a bit like being slugged with a brick. I staggered, stumbled forward. Dropped to a knee and stopped.

The sky darkened. I didn't move. Long seconds passed and under my duster I thumbed my tiny BB pistol.

Theo asked, "Did I get him?"

I came up shooting. The zip of that ridiculous pistol fired again and again. Half a dozen shots went out and half a dozen villagers dropped with leg wounds. There were more people than I could see. They were back in the shadow of the night. The guy holding the flashlight dropped it, more concerned with the blood gushing from his shattered shin.

Turning sideways to the shooters in the dark, I deflected a couple bullets from my duster and metal arm. The targeting laser on my pistol flashed, guiding one tiny bullet after another.

A shotgun roared behind me and the impact stole my lungs and dropped me to my knees.

Flores used the opportunity to level his rifle at my face.

Another low sound, like a far-off rumble of thunder, tickled the edges of my hearing. Closer, closer. The flyers wouldn't be close yet. Not for another minute or two. What was that sound?

"Well, shit," he said, shaking his head. "I suppose putting you in a hole's a lot less trouble than putting you in a jail."

I looked down the barrel of that gun.

Then it struck, like a whisper on the wind. From the gray dusk, a single boomerang swooped through the air and cracked Flores on the skull.

"Hyah!"

Marcus rode in, then. The sound was the thundering hoof beats of that gray gelding. He hunched down low on the steed, hardly slowing as he approached.

As he passed, I grabbed hard and pulled myself up, barely holding onto the saddle. It was a rough ride. Painful. Bruising in ways I didn't know possible. Soon we were far enough away that the villagers faded into the distance.

"Much appreciated," I said.

Marcus tipped his hat. "You said to look after those who needed it."

"That I did." I took the battery out of my pocket and loaded it into my arm. Power came back on immediately, though the new battery had a low whine as it worked. It didn't ache at all, so I figured that was a good sign. "Now you'd best head back, kid."

He scowled.

"They need you, Marcus. They need you now and they're going to keep needing a man like you."

Marcus nodded, tipped his hat, and walked away. He wanted to help, but where I was going would be too dangerous.

"Zane," I called him on my headgear. I was getting used to that kind of thing. It almost came natural.

Zane's voice came in clear. "Headed right for you."

A few minutes later he was there, with Abi and Tucker in the backseat. I hopped in to ride shotgun and Zane rested a hand on mine.

"You did it," he said.

I pulled my hand away, irritated. "It don't add up," I said.

"What doesn't?"

"Quintech is dropping Goodwin bombs. I thought they were rivals." We rose high above the Quintech complex. The air up high was cooler and thinner. It was a relief breathing something that didn't scorch on its way down.

"It's complex," said Zane. "I'm not a history professor."

"No, of course not. They wouldn't send a history professor."

He cocked his head to the side. "Why would you say that?"

"Goodwin keeps other corporations close by having dealings with them. Closer they can get, the more power they have over them, near as I can figure."

Zane's expression got grim.

"Same works for people."

"Oh, this again."

I stood up. The car shifted under my weight. "Would you tell me if they sent you to fall for me? Would you even know?"

Long minutes passed in silence. Tucker chuckled to himself in the backseat.

"You're being paranoid, J.D.," Abi said.

She was probably right. "Why's Tucker here?"

"Look, Crow." Tucker cleared his throat. "I'm sorry about how that all went down last few days. I can't leave you on your own. We go way back and it wouldn't be right."

"Zane's paying you?"

"Yup."

"What are we waiting for?" I asked.

"Sheriff's getting in position," said Zane. "Turns out the tower has some ground-to-air batteries and we can't get close enough yet."

I sat back down in one of the cushy seats and reloaded my revolver. I checked my BB gun and made sure it was also fully operational. The compartment containing ammo seemed to have plenty left. My knife was sharp. My duster and hat were both in good shape, no worse for wear after the gunfight.

"Let's go," I growled.

Zane didn't blink for several seconds. "What happened to you down there, J.D.?"

The memory of it threatened to stop me right there. The feeling in my gut swelled, but this wasn't the time for regret. Not yet. "There's only one kind of person who kills kids, Zane."

We drifted over the last rise, and the entire Quintech complex stretched out before us. Grim, gray buildings dotted the landscape like warts on skin. A thin road broke free from the broken tangle of hills, arcing to and passing under an enormous black gate in the fence that surrounded the scattered buildings. Some structures had fallen, whether to war or age or something else, it was hard to say. There was, however, one building that stood tall. The top of that great, black building was a glass dome, shining with a flickering glow in the night. Just behind the dome stood a tower, which stretched almost as tall as the surrounding hills. Two turrets the size of longhorns jutted from the base of the dome.

"Head for the gate," I said, pointing to the open gate along the ground route. "We'll go in low and walk the last half-kilometer."

He did as I said, and soon we were a few meters up passing through the enormous black gate. There was tech around that might have once been security. Bots lined the road, dormant or destroyed. On closer inspection, the gate itself was more than just open; it had been wrenched open by some incredible force. Likewise, the doors to the building directly in front of us were torn from their hinges. The way was open for us.

The first workers we saw were unloading a truck on the other side of the gate. There were two of them. Their eyes glowed a constant eerie green as they moved about their task. Their movements were fluid and smooth, like humans, but when they turned their gazes our way, they seemed to stare past us like robots. When Zane flashed his lights their direction they stopped and stared at us while we stared at them.

They used to be people. Their slack jaws and waxy skin made them look like walking corpses, but they were breathing. The taller of the two blinked once, tilted his head to one side, and then went about his business. The other one stared at us and didn't move.

"Kivas," Zane said. "Like the one you saw at the bank."

"And in that bunker." I swallowed. "You're sure they can't be helped?"

"They've been hollowed out. There's nothing left of what they used to be."

"How do you know that?"

Zane looked at me and said in a hard voice, "Goodwin ain't exactly innocent."

That's when the husks attacked. One second they were slack-jawed workers, the next they were bloodthirsty killers. One lunged at the car, leaping several meters and latching onto the bumper. The other threw the heavy box he was holding, narrowly missing my head.

I drew, aimed, and shot the husk on the ground through the skull. The other one scrambled up on top of the hood. Zane grabbed it, broke its neck, and tossed it over the side. A part of me died that I thought was already dead from shooting the kid in the bunker. It was a part that seemed to become emptier and emptier but was always empty. Somehow it kept hurting and it kept right on dying.

Zane put a hand on my shoulder and this time I didn't force him away.

"Let's go," I said.

The wide open was making me nervous, so I nodded down at the broken door and Zane guided us in that direction. When we were close I hopped out of the car.

Three buildings away, the tower loomed in the dark, backlit by the glow of moonlight in the darkened sky. At the base of the tower was a shining glass dome surrounded by weapons. Two massive rods—energy weapons of some sort—jutted up into the sky. They would need to be disabled before the remains of our army could attack the tower. That tower was the key to everything, but all of the buildings were connected. Entering a few buildings away would give us cover on our approach, but it would slow us down.

As I used my metal hand to grip the side of the car, a twitch of power crushed the metal under my grip.

"Sorry," I said, grinning sheepishly at Zane.

"Do you wreck every tech that you touch?"

"Yes." I pulled Zane close and kissed him hard. "Yes, I do."

Chapter 36

The smell of dry piss hit like a flash flood. It filled the entryway and the air practically thickened with its presence.

Abi stepped tentatively into the building, her eyes like cold steel. She clutched her rifle so hard her knuckles were white. Tucker followed, the narrowed slits of his eyes seeming to expertly scan everything all at once. Zane's expression was one of barely concealed mirth.

"Last chance to turn back," I said. "Nobody will think less of you for it. Likely not all of us are coming out, if any at all."

Abi said, "I need to get to the central control for this place. Best odds of that are that tower, but it's possible we'll get what we need in the underground labs."

"Underground labs?" I asked.

"You studied the blueprints, right?"

"Um, yeah, of course."

She shook her head. "I give up on you, J.D."

Tucker grinned. "Me too."

Something moved deep inside the building. A sound, somewhere between animal and human, echoed through the halls.

I sniffed. "You see a coyote, shoot it. You see a person, shoot them. We're not here to mess around." I drew my revolver. "And if you see Francis, hit him as hard and as fast as you can."

"J.D.?" Zane asked.

"What?"

"Does everything look the way it's supposed to look?"

My right eye seemed to be giving me the same image as the left. If the system came back online they'd likely be different, but no, that hadn't happened. There was no way to know if another backup would come online to start making things hard for Zane and Abi.

"Looks good so far. Our best shot is to hope real hard that he doesn't have another backup."

Zane had another idea. "If you start seeing funny, you let us know before it gets bad. It wouldn't be hard for them to trick us into friendly fire."

"If he starts overriding your tech, then you won't be able to hear my warning."

He held my hand and folded it into a fist. "Not if you warn hard enough."

The lobby was a monument to a battle raged long ago. Bullet holes did more than pock the marble walls. Someone had come in here and reshaped the walls with a hail of gunfire. It was as extreme a redecorating as a person might get, including even a skylight that opened up to offices above. Layers of dust covered burn marks and cracked, caked filth that might have once been blood. One corner was a nest of cleaned, cracked bones.

The far wall writhed as we moved through the room. A brown mass covered a several-meter radius and hissed as it slowly spread.

Tucker pointed to the mass and put a finger to his lips.

Something moved above. The clack of claws on stone echoed from somewhere unseen. Each noise caused the brown mass to react in a wave, and each wave expanded the mass a little more.

"What is it?" I whispered to Zane.

He peered at the mass for a minute, then shrugged. "Let's not find out."

The short hallway that connected the next building was visible across the rubble-strewn lobby. Someone had put up a barricade, but whatever it was meant to stop hadn't stopped. Half of the barrier was swept away and gaping open. Pushing through, I crept as quietly as my boots would let me. It wasn't very quiet. Not quiet enough. The mass on the wall crept closer to our exit.

Bugs. Millions of bugs spread in a mass across the wall. More spots along the wall sprouted their own smaller masses. A few started flying.

"Seed bugs," I whispered. "They'll bite, but it's not bad. Just keep quiet and move quickly."

Tucker and Abi crept past me while I stood in the entryway. Zane met my gaze as he passed and nodded assurance. The mass of bugs crept closer and closer with each light footfall. When I moved forward, a few of the bugs flew from the wall, flitting around my face. I flinched, and my elbow hit an ammo box that was balancing on the barricade.

The metal box fell. Noise pierced the dead silence like a nightmare car crash. All at once the seed bugs burst from the wall, filling the room and hallway in a great moving shadow. They pulsed as one mass. Everywhere, they clouded my sight and crawled on my skin. Each breath threatened to take in bugs.

"Go!" I said and shoved the others forward. Bugs swarmed into my mouth. There were so many. I choked.

Abi and Tucker scrambled through the door before the wave hit. The bugs bit. Each bite stung like hell.

A hundred bites burned like a hot brand.

I lurched through the door at the end of the hallway and Tucker slammed it shut behind me. Bugs crawled on his skin too. He swore and swatted.

Abi shouted a cry of pain, rubbing the back of her neck. I looked to see, but the bugs got in my eyes.

Somewhere in the darkness something growled.

Zane cried out in pain.

Gunshots.

"What?" I asked, swatting the bugs away as best I could. "What is it?"

On my arm, where the first bugs had bit me, a piercing white-hot pain shot straight down the nerves. To the bone. My knees weakened. Another pierced my neck like a hot iron.

Somehow through the red haze of pain I saw Tucker pick up Abi.

"Move," he said. His voice sounded more annoyed than anything.

It was impossible for me to figure any other plan, so I grabbed Zane and ran. Tuck pulled us down a dark hallway with glossy, slick floors. The bugs followed, biting, swarming into eyes and mouths. Zane swatted at them furiously. There were so many.

Molten lead traveled the length of my legs and settled at the base of my spine. Every inch of my skin felt rubbed raw and screamed at my clothing. The spot where my metal arm met flesh was the worst, with grating inflammation flaring with every movement. The sight of my own hand shocked me; it was puffy and red, with fierce yellow pustules forming on the surface.

Breathing hurt.

"In here," said Tuck. He held open a door and shoved us through. He managed to close the door without letting the bulk of the swarm in and even managed to toss something out before the door sealed shut.

"What was that?" Zane asked through gasps.

"Bug spray."

A whoosh sounded from outside and soon the steel door was so hot that wisps of smoke started coming off of it as the paint ignited.

My breath wheezed and the thundering of my heart was the only thing I could hear. I collapsed against the wall, next to Abi. My eyes were swollen shut. Breathing got harder; each breath rasped painfully. In. Out. In. Out.

Out.

Out.

I clutched my neck. Breath wouldn't come in, hard as I tried. Something brushed against my hand. Agony. More air eked out of my lungs.

My eyes opened. Tucker was on top of me, a knife pressed against my neck. There was rage in his eyes, but there was pain there too. A tear beaded at the corner of his eye.

A long moment passed. Tuck locked gazes with me. One of his hands held mine down, while the other pressed the knife up against my neck.

A high-pitched noise, like a whistle, sounded. It was several long seconds before I figured out that it was my own breath. The whistle started high, but got deeper and wheezier. Soon my breath was coming in great rasping gulps. Tucker let go of my hand and stepped back.

The others were gasping too. Their bodies—or more likely their nannies—were fighting off whatever venom came with the bug bites. Pain slowly eased and with a great effort I forced myself into a sitting position.

"Almost had to give you a tracheotomy," Tucker said.

"Thought you were going to murder me." My voice came out in a gravelly whisper.

"I thought you were dying."

"Would have been a damn shame for me to die without you having the pleasure of murdering me."

Tucker slapped me on the knee, sending icy hot waves of agony through my whole leg. "I'd never murder you, J.D. I've got too many good war stories with you in them and it'd be a damn shame to stop telling them."

"Why didn't you get it?"

"Nanny-venom," Zane said. His voice sounded worse than mine. He winced. Angry red welts covered his face. "Targets the nanomachines in your blood. It kills them and gives you a hell of an allergic reaction at the same time."

Tucker smiled. His face was covered in tiny red spots, but to him they were nothing more than an annoyance. Smug son of a bitch.

The attack left me weak, but Abi was worse. She didn't get the swelling like I did, but nasty hives and sections of her skin had a worrisome blackened look, like it'd been kissed by flames.

Flames. The steel door was hot to the touch. We wouldn't be going out that way. Tucker had led us to a stairwell, and it appeared as if up and down were both viable options. Options. Options were good. The floor and stairs were smooth concrete, and the walls were undecorated cinderblock. This hadn't been a public area of the facility, by the look of it. I struggled to remember the layout of the buildings from the diagrams on the glow cube. Would we be able to cross to the next building if we went up a level?

"Down," Zane said between gasping breaths. "The buildings are connected below, so we should be able to get where we need to go."

"Up," Tucker said. "We don't know the buildings are still connected down there, but I saw the skyway with my own eyes on the way in."

"We're sitting ducks up there," said Zane.

"We're trapped if it goes bad down there."

I got an arm under Abi's shoulder and helped her up. She gasped when I touched her and gritted her teeth against the pain.

"We do both," I said to Tucker. "Take Zane and I'll take Abi. You two should be able to punch through defenses below and take out those cannons. They'll tear the flyers to shreds if they stay up."

Tucker narrowed his eyes at Zane. "I go alone."

I didn't have it in me to argue. "Fine."

Tucker said, "I can slip past their defenses."

He was right. As the only unmodified person around, he had the best shot at sneaking around undetected.

"You remember what to do if the situation goes bad, don't you?"

"Blow it up?"

"Yup."

The stairwell was concrete and steel, crumbling from some unknown trauma. With my augmented eye, the glow of my cigarette was enough to see the dark outline of the way ahead, even once Tucker's light was out of view. Abi moaned. Her head lolled to one side before snapping back upright again. Zane's brow knit with worry.

The light from the cigarette was only enough when I puffed hard, so I kept a steady pull on the tobacco as best I could. As we ventured farther down, the air grew sickly and dry. It had a mummified taste of death on it, and I was glad for the spice of my smoke. At the bottom of the stairs the landing opened up into an undecorated space a few meters on a side. I helped Abi sit down on the last step and squatted down to look her in the eyes.

She met my gaze, held it for a few seconds, then blinked, unfocused. Zane handed her a flask and she took little sips from it.

Zane pulled me to the side. "She needs rest."

"How long can we wait?"

"We have some time. Tucker will draw most of the attention. If we wait here, we can sneak through."

It made sense. "Except that's setting Tuck out to dry. He'll take all of the focus if we're not in position when he strikes."

"The goal is to get Abi to the main building where she can link. Tuck knows his place in this."

"He'd be killing himself as a distraction."

I glanced to Abi, but she wasn't sitting anymore. She had a look of cold determination on her face and she stood with fists balled at her sides. She took smooth, controlled breaths through her nose.

"We're going," she said, leaving no room for argument.

The steel door at the bottom of the steps opened onto another hallway. A short distance in, the hallway opened up into a larger room, the extent of which wasn't lit by my dim cigarette. The place had a musty feel—air heavy with silence. The darkness seemed to press in, tempting me to use the tech in my eye even more to see into it.

The figure stood at the edge of blackness, staring at us with two pinpoints of blue light.

Zane drew.

Then it was gone, melted into the dark as soundlessly as if it were a shadow.

There were only a few paces between the door and the larger room. We crossed them quickly, peering cautiously around the corner as we got there. The figure was gone, disappeared somewhere into the unknowingly large room. Despite the stuffy air, the surrounding area was polished and clean. A chemical hint of recent cleaning still lingered in the air behind the musty scent of unmoved air. Shrugging, I moved into the room, headed roughly through the middle in the direction that the main building must be.

The room was huge, seeming to stretch on forever into the dark. The way footsteps echoed in the giant chamber made the effect sharper. After a distance, it was clear that the single underground room stretched below several, if not all, of the buildings in the Quintech complex. The structures above were tiny compared to the vastness of this room. Columns supported the roof, some crumbling but all still standing. The room seemed to be an open lab, littered with tables, computer equipment, and strange tech I couldn't identify.

And some that I could.

"That's your arm," said Zane, standing over a duplicate of my very own prosthetic.

From the thing's shoulders snaked the half-dozen tendrils that I knew were identical to those rooted in my own body. They were like the tendrils on the earpiece Zane had given me. The strength from the arm needed to be supported throughout my entire body; otherwise lifting something might tear me apart. All of that was the reason my nannies had to work overtime to repair the damage that the machine constantly did to my body. They had told me that when I woke. They had told me again when it was clear that I didn't understand. Still, looking at the arm made my stomach drop. How much of me was left?

Hair at the back of my neck stood up. Puffing the cigarette, I expanded slightly the ring of light around us. Abi gasped.

Dark forms surrounded us. They were human—or human shaped, anyway. Their dull eyes stared at us with a faint blue glow. There were dozens of them.

"We need to get out of here," whispered Zane. He gripped my hand and we moved together, though I don't know who was supporting whom.

We passed tables that held consoles like the one Abi had attached to my skidder. There were diagrams of how the tech attached to a person's brain and nervous system. It made me sick to my stomach. There were other pieces that I couldn't identify. Guns too. Heavy ones. Fancy ones. My prosthetic hand was a universal component that fit an enormous array of weaponry. They'd made me into a tool of war. Everything was polished and clean. Every table was arranged in perfect order, like pieces were being laid out on a buffet. Every so often we passed a work in progress, with parts of a device arranged in orderly rows along a table. More often the devices were fully intact.

"Wait," I said.

Zane let go and glanced back nervously. Abi leaned against a table, breathing hard. Behind us, the figures were following.

"What do they want?" Abi whispered.

"They're husks," said Zane. "Kivas hollowed out and used for manual labor. They're probably running a default program and keeping an eye on us."

"Why, though? Why aren't they attacking us? It's not like there aren't enough weapons."

"I don't know," said Zane.

Puffing the cigarette, I got a little closer to something that had caught my eye. It was big and heavy, but seemed useful. It was a weapon. Of course, it was a weapon. The expansion had thin plates of black metal flaring out around it in an apparently defensive shield. I slotted my arm in, feeling my power slide into its dormant form. My awareness expanded, sliding out into the black metal form. It felt good. It felt right.

I could feel the finely articulated plates moving at the slightest effort of my will. It was like my arm had grown into a brilliantly complicated piece of machinery and instinct told me how to use it. The plates slid closed at my command, and my new arm's attachment condensed into a manageable size.

One of the husks stepped forward. It was a middle-aged man in a lab coat. He said, "The tech doesn't make you bad, Sheriff. It makes you more efficient."

"I'm not the sheriff anymore."

The man's eyes were blue embers in his skull. His face remained completely expressionless. "You'll always be the sheriff to me."

The phrase seemed oddly familiar. It was clear who was talking through this husk. "Francis?"

The man nodded stiffly. "You are getting better, Sheriff. Every piece of technology you incorporate into yourself makes you more like me. Stronger. Faster."

"Like you?" It was odd having this conversation with an emptied-out husk of a man, but my hackles were raised. "The way you reject what happened to your mama and wreck other people's lives? That's not better, that's just insane."

Zane put a hand on my shoulder. "We have to go," he whispered.

But I wasn't done. I jammed a finger in the husk's chest. "Tech doesn't make anything better, boy. It didn't make me better and it doesn't make you better. It sure as hell doesn't make Texas better."

"No," the man said. "No, it doesn't, does it?" His eyes focused on my metal arm with its new attachment. "But we still upgrade."

Far above, something exploded. The earth shook with a shock and dust rained down from the ceiling. Tucker.

"Time to go," said Zane.

The door to the next stairwell was only a short distance away, just at the range of my ember light. I shoved the husk aside and covered the distance in a few steps, kicked open the door, and vaulted up the stairs. Zane and Abi were close at my heels.

The air was easier to breathe as soon as the door opened. Higher up, the heat hit again. There maybe wasn't much oxygen down there, but up above, breathing seemed to cook the lungs. I tossed my cigarette aside. The stairwell continued upward, and by the artificial glow coming from the hallway I knew we must be in the right building. This was the building with the tower, and likely the one where Francis had holed up. This was the building heavily defended, with gun turrets and shielding. We had made it.

Now all we had to do was go up.

Chapter 37

At first we sprinted up the stairs. This lasted most of a single flight. Almost. The outside wall was glass, and in many places the night air rushed in, mocking us with a dry wind that didn't cool. Then, we jogged. Half a dozen stories passed at a decent pace. Once Zane started falling behind, Abi got an arm under him and helped him forward.

"This is the toughest thing I've done all week," I said.

Zane gave a weak smile. His skin was pale and still pocked with angry sores from the bugs. "Once we get up there, it's going to be a fight," he said between gasping breaths. "Francis will have hell of an automated system."

"Should we wait for Tuck?" Abi asked.

"No," I said. "He's taken out that battery. He'll move to the next target rather than join up with us."

Abi checked her rifle, then checked it again. "No matter what happens, keep them off of me and get me to the console."

"You got it," I said.

Then we were there. I flexed my shield, and articulated plating spread out into a diamond shape. The steel door might have been unlocked, but for the sake of simplicity, I gave it a quick bash with the shield.

The door flew ten meters before hitting a wall at the end of the corridor.

A hail of gunfire ricocheted off of my shield, jerking it around and forcing me to brace it. Zane shot twice, and the incoming fire eased a bit but didn't stop.

Stepping forward, I pushed closer to the last turret and gave Zane the shot he needed.

"Seems he doesn't want us here," Zane said. He stepped into the slot, fired again with his rifle, reducing the turret to junk parts. "Or he's even worse at social niceties than you thought."

We were at the middle of a T intersection. Ahead was a short hallway at the end of which was the mangled door and another intersection. To the left and right, the corridor curved along the outer edge of the building. Windows lined the outer walls.

The floor shook in the thump-thump rhythm of heavy fire. Outside the window, the sky lit up in blaze of activity. Energy weapons and explosions alternated in the air. The flyers had arrived.

By the flashes of violence in the sky, I could see dozens of vehicles darting, attacking, and fleeing. It was a chaos that must have been Cinco Armas and maybe more.

The first Kiva rounded the corner at a jog. He wore a stark white full-length lab coat, and a pair of thick goggles adorned his forehead. He was an older man, with stringy gray hair falling to his shoulders. His blue eyes flashed as he saw us, his face expressionless as he raised a battered shotgun.

Zane dropped him with a punishing shot to his chest. Before that Kiva hit the floor, another rounded the corner.

Shield up, I distracted the new one—a young woman with chestnut hair and a vacant expression. She held a long black knife in one hand and a small one-shot pistol in the other. She fired her shot wide and charged with the knife raised.

She used to be a person. She used to be beautiful. Her neck was still adorned with a pearl necklace, and her wrists held matching bracelets. Her dress was old, threadbare, and obviously once quite extravagant. It's all I could think of as she threw her body on the shield. The black-bladed knife whistled past my ear as I lifted her and tossed her backward. She used to be a person.

But she wasn't anymore.

My Model 500 revolver slipped into my hand like it was meant to be. Three shots thundered in righteous mercy: one to her heart, one to her neck, and one to her head.

Zane had two more Kivas pinned behind a door. They were big ones, armed with shotguns. These were protecting themselves, showing significantly more self-preservation than the others. Zane moved forward to try to root them out.

"Look out!" Abi shouted.

Too late.

The air ionized. Crisp ozone.

Blue light—blinding—pierced the wall next to Zane and sliced through his chest. He fell back, screaming. Smoke filled the room.

I dove forward, hoping to guess where Zane had landed. The shield covered the two. Light where the beam hit my shield sent flickering shadows dancing along the darkened window. The glass glowed where the beam had hit, highlighting edges where it had cut clean through.

"You all right?" I asked.

He nodded but spit dust and blood. His skin, pale before, had gone white as clean sheets. I grabbed him with one hand and pulled him forward. The beam stopped.

I pounced up and fired two shots through the wooden door, dropping the two Kivas cowering behind it. A hulking husk stepped through the gap in the wall. He hefted an arm just like mine, slotted into an enormous cannon. He aimed and the cannon started to whir.

Abi fired two shots and the huge man dropped, his head a ruined mess. Holstering my revolver, I held out a hand to Zane.

Zane was in a bad way. He coughed up blood and favored one of his arms. He was able to get to his feet, but there was something wrong with his ankle. It was twisted at an odd angle and there was no way he'd be standing on it if not for the tech in his body. When he moved, he had to grasp the side of his torso with one hand. He must have been suppressing his pain. The welts on his skin seemed worse.

The hallway opened up into the room with the domed ceiling. Outside, a battle still raged. The makeshift army had taken down one of two huge energy cannons, but the other was still firing. It swiveled and fired in a rhythmic thump-thump that resonated in my chest. It didn't hit often, but when it did, it hit hard. Smaller turrets were hitting more often, bullets piercing even the heavily armed vehicles.

Francis stood near a half-circle console in the center of the room. Wires were strewn everywhere, snaking across the floor and up to the antenna at the back of the building. The walls were lined with flickering displays. The effect reminded me of Court's hideout, only bigger and in worse condition. There was even an Umbilical snaking from the console to something behind the back wall.

Francis looked up when I entered, his face an emotionless mask. He was a wreck. This was not the crisply dressed boy projected for communications. This was a kid ruined by neglect. His clothes hung from his bony body in rags, the white of his suit long since worn down to a rusty brown. His sunken eyes were set in a face sallow with hunger and aged by the elements. The boy's white hair fell in long wisps of ghostly blond. His fingers frantically worked across a console.

"Stop," I said. "This has gone far enough."

He didn't seem to hear, continuing his feverish activity. He was up to something, up to something bad, I'd bet. I pulled out the BB gun and pointed it at the boy.

A car crashed through the glass dome, bringing with it a shower of glass and the rush of clean night air. The deafening cacophony of combat roared through the room as her car skidded across the marble floor.

I raised my shield against the glass, and Abi ducked under its protection. Trish crouched in her crashing car, battered but still holding her twin pistols. She jumped and rolled as the car slammed into the console, and before I could recover, she stood up and trained both of her pistols at the boy.

"Sneak over there and plug in," I whispered to Abi. "You have a shot at this. You can do it."

She nodded and started making her way around behind Francis.

Then Francis jammed a bundle of cables into the back of his head and the world changed.

Trish fired as he moved, but he was too fast. She kept squeezing bullets, but the boy ran. At least, that's how she probably saw it. In my modified eye, I could see the same thing. He was now the Francis I'd seen before. Healthy, clean, smug. He smiled a handsome smile and his eyes twinkled. In my other eye he ducked down behind the console and hid like the coward he was.

"Trish," I shouted. "He's still right in front of you!"

Trish blinked with confusion, turned to me, fired.

She didn't hit me.

She wasn't aiming at me.

Zane, behind me, staggered. A well of blood erupted from his shoulder. I raised my shield, protecting as much of his body as I could.

"Stop the weapons, Francis," Trish said as she walked forward. "Call them off. It's done."

"That's not Francis, Trish." I stood up and walked forward to meet her.

The guns outside stopped. What was Francis playing at? A distraction?

"Quit protecting him, J.D." Trish looked at me with her jaw set hard. I knew the look and no smart man wanted to be on the other end of it. "I'm going to bring him in." Her cruiser drifted behind her, presumably following her mental commands. "I'll bring you in too, if I need to."

There was no use talking. The words would come out wrong, anyway.

"I'll go," said Zane. "I can distract her and you go for Francis."

"No." There was no way to know if he could hear me. "Too dangerous." If Zane gave himself over to Trish, then Francis would have the upper hand.

I leapt at Trish and bashed hard, ramming her with all my strength. She was heavier than she looked, but I was damn strong. My legs pumped and kept pushing until the two of us toppled over right into her cruiser. I grabbed one of her pistols and tossed it aside.

Trish kicked me back, drawing her other pistol. As she raised it to fire, the cruiser began to drift upward.

Zane jumped into the fray, knocking Trish's pistol away. Blood sprayed as he moved. The cruiser lurched under his weight and started to spin. The pistol clattered onto the hood.

"Go!" Zane said.

I didn't go. I lunged forward, dipping out of the way.

Trish grabbed Zane's leg and heaved, toppling him backward so he smashed his head against the plastic edge of the vehicle. With one leg, she swept my shield aside and kicked me hard in the face.

I staggered backward, nearly falling over the edge. She followed up with a punch to my gut that left me reeling. "Stay out of this," she snarled.

She turned to Zane, who had managed to rise to one knee. She reached to draw her pistol and found it wasn't there. The cruiser spun faster.

"Go," Zane rasped. He was on his knees and didn't look like he had the power to get up.

I put a hand on his shoulder. "I won't leave you with her."

Trish hopped onto the hood of the cruiser. The car dipped to one side and the gun slid closer to the edge.

"It's too late for me," said Zane. "My nannies are gone. The bugs got me."

"No."

"She'll just take me away. She doesn't see what's real."

"I'll tell her." I clenched my fist. "Hard."

Trish grabbed the weapon, but I had my shield up between her and Zane.

"Don't move," she said.

I moved. Shield first, I rammed into Trish. She was ready. She took my momentum and sent me stumbling over the edge. My metal hand grabbed out and for a second I was dangling a few meters over the marble floor.

But it was too long.

"Don't move." Trish had her gun pressed against Zane's forehead.

There's no way he could move. Nobody was fast enough to get out of that. It would be suicide to twitch in that situation. It would be suicide to think about twitching. There was no way—absolutely no way—that Zane would move with that gun at his head.

The cruiser spun faster and faster, drifting out the window into the open sky. Skidders hung all around, their riders watching in a silent agony. What were they seeing?

Zane didn't move. The fight was over. I pulled myself up onto the cruiser, careful not to make any quick movements.

"I'm sorry, J.D.," Zane said. "You need to stop that boy."

So long as Trish had her gun pressed against Zane's head, Francis had the upper hand. All Francis needed to do was make her see something that would cause her to pull the trigger. A gun in his hand, or a knife. A look in his eyes. I couldn't go after Francis without the risk that Francis would make her pull the trigger. Zane was a hostage.

"I love you, J.D." Zane said. He flicked his wrist and a pistol snapped out of his sleeve. He met Trish's eyes, raised the weapon, and—

Trish pulled the trigger.

The loss hit me harder than the gut punch. Rage boiled up in me as Trish turned my way. She'd killed him. Zane was dead.

She'd killed Zane.

I roared in fury and charged. With a backhand I sent her pistol flying off into the darkness. I punched with my right hand, not caring that it was a mistake, not caring that it hurt so bad as my fist slammed against her reinforced skeleton. Rage was all I had.

Trish was tougher than me. She took my punches, whether they came from the natural fist or the metal one. She rolled with the strong hits and stood against the weak ones.

Trish was stronger than me. I threw a sloppy haymaker with my metal fist and she caught it in her hands. I shoved hard and she shoved harder. She twisted against the joint and despite my strength I had no choice but to drop to one knee.

Trish was smarter than me. Hell, she'd always been smarter.

But I was bigger.

I reversed my effort and pulled, lifting her straight into the air. My reach was long enough that she couldn't hit back. She couldn't kick. My breath came in hard rasps. Rage was easy. I held Trish over the edge of the car. We spun fast now, high above the Quintech building.

Bracing myself against the spin, I prepared to throw her far as I could. But I didn't. I couldn't. I slammed her down hard on the floor of the cruiser, hoping it was enough to stun her.

It wasn't.

She was up in a crouch as fast as I could blink. A couple quick jabs sent me reeling. She grabbed a handful of my hair, rage in her eyes. She pulled back for a punch that I knew would knock me out if it didn't kill me.

A gunshot sounded. Trish clutched her shoulder and dropped me.

Below, Abi stood with her rifle aimed in our direction. The gunshot gave away her hiding spot. Kivas leapt up to surround her. The console was still too far away.

Abi backed away, firing her rifle at one Kiva after another. There were too many.

It was all happening so fast. The cruiser spun around and around. Trish stood up, recovering from the shot. She lunged at me.

I jumped.

The plan was to hit the edge of the broken dome, use it to slow my fall, and then deal with Francis and the remaining Kivas. It almost worked.

I missed the dome, clipping it as I passed and spinning out of control in my fall. I struck the floor hard, my fall softened only by the wires on the ground and the snapping of bones in both of my legs.

Waves of molten pain surged through my body. My breath came in labored gasps. I was too far back to shoot Francis. The angle was wrong to help Abi.

Abi screamed. Gunshots.

"Do it, J.D.," she shouted.

Grabbing the floor with the metal arm, I inched myself forward. If I could only round the end of the console, maybe I could get the shot I wanted. It was too far. Already, the edges of my vision darkened. Pain threatened to overwhelm me. It was too much. Too much. Despite my effort to be at peace, here violence had snatched my life away again. Zane. Zane was gone. Maybe Abi too. Everything I fought for was ruined. Every time. My shoulders slumped and I fought back sobs.

There would never be peace for me. At the end it was easy to look back and see the mistakes of a hard-fought life. Of course, there couldn't be peace. The world would never allow it. Anyone resembling a righteous man would never see peace in a world like this. Not for one minute of one day. The world was full of such violence and hatred and pain that any second spent at peace was complacency.

Every idle moment, a guilty pleasure. There would never be peace in Texas. Not in my lifetime.

That didn't mean it wasn't worth fighting for.

I calmed myself and looked down at the floor. Right there, under my hand, was the Umbilical, just like the one Court had talked about. It ran from the console back into the main computing center, but there was another branch on this one. It ran straight down into the floor. With an agonizing effort, I pulled my way forward with my metal arm. When I got there I ripped open the floor and saw what must have been a maintenance slot. It was a connector much like the one on my skidder.

Francis stood next to me with a revolver inches from my head.

"Don't mess with my shit, old man."

"Who did you meet? Who told you this was the right thing to do?"

His eyes narrowed. The gun in his outstretched hand stayed steady.

"The way I see it, you had your ideas, but you didn't act until you met someone smarter than you." Outside, lightning flashed across the sky.

"He is not smarter than me. Nobody's smarter than me."

"Maybe. But there are things you don't understand and he helped you get your head around it. Helped you cope."

"So what if he did? He let me cope with all the wrong you did. You killed Ma. You're the one who needs justice and the whole world is going to get the peace it deserves." His gun didn't waver. He kept it steady in his outstretched hand, and even when I shifted to the side it stayed trained right at my face.

"Ben got worried when you left. He's the one who told you that the world needed peace, wasn't he? He's the one who said I needed justice."

Francis didn't move.

"He was right," I said. "But the world doesn't deserve the peace you're giving it, and there's no way to make me suffer enough to make up for what I did to your family."

"What makes you think I won't shoot you down right now?"

A long moment passed. Lightning lit up the sky again, flashing up above in the dark clouds. The cannon fired again. "You're not armed," I said.

"I'd be a fool to walk around without a weapon, wouldn't I?"

"A fool or a child."

"I'm not a child." His muscles twitched and he seemed to grow taller. "I grew up the moment you killed my Ma. I grew up when I looked around and saw Texas was broken. *Your* Texas was broken."

"It's the best we could make it."

"But not the best *I* could make it. I'm bringing peace and an end to all that shit you people have felt the need to deal with all along."

"Like freedom?" I propped myself up against the console.

"Freedom? You call that freedom? People will feel free when I have this working. People will feel loved."

"What about the kids you hook up to the machines? Will they feel free?"

He twitched. "That's a prototype. It won't always be like that."

"Now you're hooked up to that same machine. You're driving it, aren't you? It's using your brain to drive its alternate reality."

He winced. "It needs imagination."

"I bet."

In my good eye I could see that he wasn't next to me at all. He wasn't holding a gun. The starved, sickly boy was cowering against the other side of the console. His face was glistening with sweat and his hair was plastered against his head. He'd gone pale. The bundle of cables ran from the back of his head to the console.

The blackness almost took me. I slipped, put too much pressure on a broken leg, but recovered.

I let the shield drop from my arm and jammed my hand into the console on the floor.

My awareness burst with information. I was the building and every bit of tech in it. The weapons outside felt like the bristling hairs on the back of my neck. The Kivas wandering the halls were like crawling bugs on my skin, but I could also see through their eyes and control their bodies. The antenna was a sense all its own. Through it, I reached the world. The eyes of everyone around became like my own senses. Their ears became my whole world.

In a split second, my focus moved to the cluster of Kivas nearby. Four of them dragged a kicking Abi down a curved hallway. I could see through her eyes and I could feel the adrenaline coursing through her veins. The sights of the Kivas were there for me too, but I had more control over them. With a mere thought, their hearts stopped and what was left of their brains shut down. Relief washed through Abi as she freed herself from their grip.

There was no time to linger. Another presence exerted its control. It was a stony presence, an unmovable will that stood like a tower in a field during the chaos of battle. It was Francis. He was still connected and now via the machine his mind was working against mine.

He was frightening.

The battle raged outside. The sense of it nearly overwhelmed me. A few seconds were all I would need, but if I dropped the building's defenses I might not get that. Cold, calculating logic told me to leave those defenses up. Solid logic told me to let the army suffer a little longer for the greater good. It was undeniable.

But that logic didn't come from me. It came from Francis. His mind was closer to mine than I thought possible. His thoughts echoed in my head, and for a brief second I felt what it was to be Francis. It was frightening. He didn't have the logic and reason I'd always assumed. His mind crawled with pain and fear. His life was an inability to cope with the raw emotion of being alive. Whenever something hurt him, he killed the part of himself that was hurt. Over and over again he crushed himself until the only thing left was a monster, and then he moved on to do the same to the world. His mind was strong and his logic was sound. He almost convinced me to step back.

But stubbornness beats logic any day. I shut down the turrets.

Far below, Tuck fought back a wave of coyotes. He was injured and bleeding, but the look on his face showed both rage and satisfaction. It was his moment of revenge. Tuck cut down one coyote after another, wading through the makeshift defense of something on the ground floor. Something nearby...

He was headed for a power generator. If he took it out, power would drop in the entire facility. That would take everything down hard. Francis's cold logic told me that the hard collapse of the field might snap Goodwin's tower all the way over in Austin. It would also cause a dangerous crash of my own hardware, possibly killing me.

I denied logic again. The coyotes that had hardware in their heads dropped dead. The rest fled like the scavengers they were. Tuck pulled the pins on a couple grenades and tossed them into a hole he'd already punched in the side of the generator building.

Seconds remained.

Far away, I could sense another force. Instinct told me to fight it, keep it at bay. This must be Goodwin's tower. Goodwin's field encompassed all of Texas. Zane had told me this, but now it made sense on an instinctual level. My smaller field existed as a thorn in Goodwin's side, constantly drawing power and constantly posing a threat.

What a threat too. An increase in power, even a slight one, could set off a resonance that would bring both fields down. Both towers would be slag in the aftermath. The sub-quantum net would cease to be. Technology as we knew it would be done. Person-to-person communication would stop. It would be impossible to mentally control cars or machinery. Prosthetics like my own might cease to work. The nanomachines would stop.

Tech would be set back hundreds of years.

If I powered it down, the tower would likely never be active again. It was unstable. I could feel it at the edges of my fingertips. The field would collapse soon, even if I did nothing. Getting it started again was not something that could be done through this facility. Not anymore.

An age seemed to pass in a single second. Outside, Cinco Armas poured into the console room. They swarmed the surrounding buildings and obliterated what remained of their enemies. The deputies still alive rode side by side with brutal outlaws in the assault on Quintech. They'd destroy everything soon.

A world without tech would be better. There was no doubt in my mind about that fact. How much pain came from the horrors of technology?

The iron logic that Francis poured into my mind told me that people would die when that field dropped. Cars would fall from the sky. Society would collapse. People who had modified themselves with technology would be ruined. I would be crippled, maybe killed. Logic told me what I knew already in my gut.

He was right. The cost was too much.

With my last second connected to the machine, I lowered the field gently. With as much ease as I could muster, shutting everything down.

All I needed to do then was disconnect from the machine.

The explosion took out the generators, dropping the whole place into darkness. Like a jarring kick to the head, I was booted from the system. It felt like a large hunk of my own brain was cut out of my head with a rusty knife.

When my eyes opened, the room was dark. Somehow, disconnecting had sent me flying across the room, though I didn't remember much of the flight. Francis shifted on the floor just before the blackness came. Dully, I realized that I should do something about the boy before I slipped away into unconsciousness.

The last thing I was aware of before I slipped away was fat, warm raindrops falling from the sky.

Chapter 38

The cemetery outside of Dead Oak was a quiet place on a hill surrounded by wrought-iron fence and shrubs that had died ages ago. Too many of the graves were fresh. Too many were my fault.

Josephine's headstone was a simple slab of steel etched with her name. Abi had arranged it after she took over the junkyard. After the attack on Quintech, she'd returned to help Ben handle the longhorns. She had a talent for it, but it would be a long time before Ben's ranch was fully operational again. She'd done well handling Ben's stubborn streak. Now they had each other and maybe there was hope.

Zane's grave sat apart from the others. It was a simple plaque, reflecting the red of the setting sun. It had his name and the day of his death. An inscription read, "A hero of all men." He'd certainly been a hero to me. He had been hope to me. My love for him had proven that life in the wastes could be something more than gunfights and starvation. His love for me had shown me that there was something worthwhile left in myself. He was gone, but I'd carry that love with me for the rest of my life.

Not all of my failures rested in that cemetery. Broadfeather had been buried with my people, near Overpass. Mina led them now, and they were better for it. Broadfeather was a wise man, but a damn fool for thinking I could lead the Hopi. Others of the tribe had been buried near him, all of them gone too early.

The Navajo returned to their nation in the north. They'd proven themselves to us and we had proven ourselves to them. No, they wouldn't poke bears, but they wouldn't feed them either. Maybe one day Mina would move the Hopi up to join with the Navajo Nation, but not yet. Not until it was the last option.

A month had passed since the fight at Quintech. My legs were nearly ready to shed the braces that allowed me to walk. I'd stood trial for the bank robbery and the attack on Quintech. Even though every damn soul at the hearing knew I was doing what was right, the judge ruled me guilty. After Cinco Armas looted Quintech—their goal all along— and Francis escaped punishment, the judge said he had no choice but to send me up the river. Hell, I almost agreed. The rule of law needed some support from time to time, though I suspect the judge was taking a good portion of his pay from Chester Goodwin himself.

"What'll it be?" Sheriff Trish said from the base of the hill. I hadn't heard her approach.

Zane's grave hurt the most. The thought of it still made rage boil in my gut, but I knew she wasn't to blame. She couldn't have known.

Why hadn't I trusted him? No, that wasn't it. Why hadn't I trusted myself? It had always felt right, being with Zane. When we were together we'd always worked. Why had I doubted it so much?

Goodwin. It was Goodwin I didn't trust and I'd eliminated the one thing that really posed the corporation any real threat. With the tower gone and Quintech destroyed, Goodwin would be free to exact whatever cruelty he wanted on the people of the outlands.

It was time for my prison sentence to start. That morning was my last hour of freedom, granted to me so that I might set my affairs in order. It was a special compensation, granted to me out of respect for my time at war and my service as a sheriff. It was given to me out of trust, since they knew I was a man of honor.

I turned to Trish. She waited patiently for my answer. On one side of her was her cruiser, the honorable path to a life of hard labor in the Iowa wastes. The other side was my skidder, the path of dishonor. The life of an outlaw waited there for me.

She stepped up to me, looked me in the eyes, then hugged me. She hugged hard, and sobs welled up in my chest.

"I'm sorry, J.D." She squeezed me tight. "I should have known it wasn't Francis in that car. I didn't notice the change."

"You couldn't have. He was subtle. Quick."

"A person can't put a gun against someone's head if they're not willing to fire. It's just..."

"I know." Of course, I understood. She had pulled the trigger of the gun that had killed Zane, but it wasn't her fault. It was Francis. The boy was broken inside. He wasn't a sad boy to be pitied anymore. He was a ruthless killer.

"Zane was special, wasn't he?"

"We were going to make something of it." I swallowed back a sob. "After."

She stepped away from me and looked me over. "There's never an after, is there?"

"Nope."

"I won't come after you. Someone else might come, but I don't think so. Not right away, anyway."

"Be careful," I said. "There weren't long-range launchers anywhere around Quintech. When I was in the machine, I would have felt them. There was nothing that would have dropped those bombs on Ben's ranch."

"You think it was Goodwin?"

"Or another player entirely."

"You think there's a war coming, don't you?"

"Not if bombs fall on us every time we gather and talk about war. If Quintech could listen to us through our headgear then Goodwin can do it too. All they need to do is track where we are and what we're talking about. It wouldn't be hard for their computers to do that without even making people listen in."

"That's either sobering brilliance or conspiratorial nonsense."

"Oh, and one more thing to get you thinking." I smiled. "I owe Court a favor."

"What does that mean?"

"It means that I owe her a favor. Whatever she wants." I basked for a moment in the setting sun. "Thing is, though, she needs to ask first. If I keep moving, I'll be fine."

Trish turned, hopped in her cruiser, and started pulling away.

"You're needed out there."

"I know."

My skidder sat there, ready for me to leave. I powered it up, programmed a destination, and set it on its way. If there was any law out there, it would track the skidder. Farther downhill, Muffin stood tied to a tree. She whinnied when I approached and I smiled a sad smile and rubbed her nose.

Once we were on our way, I turned her north and gave her the lead. We'd go to where the hills became mountains. The law wouldn't bother us north, in the Yellowstone wastes. It'd be harsh, but I'd make my life there as a free man and for a time the heavy weight of the world wouldn't rest on my shoulders. It was worth it for the freedom. I'd given up everything for my honor, and now it was honor itself that I was tossing aside in favor of freedom. One day I'd return to rebuild that honor.

Until then, freedom would do.

Acknowledgements

A special thanks to my wife Carol and my two boys Isaac and Gabe. Without their support and understanding this book would not have been possible. Also, a great thanks goes out to Scott Alexander Jones, my editor. He not only has helped make this a better book with exceptional copyediting, but also by helping the Texas of this book be more Texas. As it should.

The Rochester Writers Group gets an extra pile of gratitude. The various skills represented in that group have helped me grow as a serious writer.

About the Author

Anthony W. Eichenlaub's stories appear in Little Blue Marble, the anthologies Fell Beasts and Fair and A Punk Rock Future. When the ground isn't frozen solid, he enjoys gardening, woodworking, and long walks with a lazy dog. When it is frozen, he stays indoors where it's safe. He can be found at anthonyeichenlaub.com and on Twitter as @AWEichenlaub.

Other Books by Anthony W. Eichenlaub

<u>Justice in an Age of Metal and Men</u>
Metal and Men Book 1

<u>Grit and Grace</u>
A Metal and Men novella